Frostbitten

A novel by

Heather Beck

Enchanted Publishing

Frostbitten
Copyright © 2014 Heather Beck
Cover Photos: Girl, Siiri Kumari; Wolf, Quapaw; Forest, Alfred Borchard

Library and Archives Canada Cataloguing in Publication

Beck, Heather, 1985-, author
    Frostbitten : a novel / by Heather Beck.

Issued in print and electronic formats.
ISBN 978-1-926990-19-4 (pbk.).--ISBN 978-1-926990-20-0 (pdf)

    I. Title.

PS8603.E423F76 2014   C813'.6   C2014-904310-4
                                         C2014-904311-2

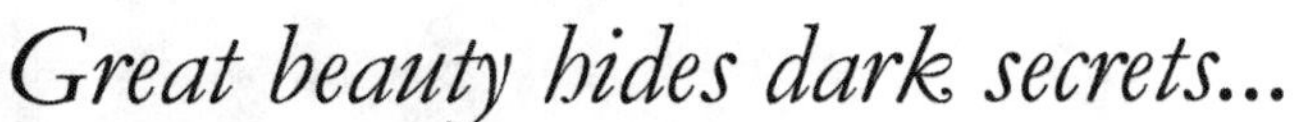

Great beauty hides dark secrets...

Frostbitten

Contents

Part One

Bad Girls

Snow fell gently upon the still woods, leaving everything white and sparkling. The ground, which now resembled a silky smooth frosting, was immaculate in appearance, as if no human dared to tread there. Even the trees were magnificent. Row after row, the cedars reached high into the sky, their identical formation creating the illusion of a never-ending horizon. These trees were like an impassable gate, forever concealing the secrets which lay within the woods.

The scenery was undeniably beautiful, but all seventeen-year-old Anastasia Lockhart could think was, *only bad girls get sent away*.

At exactly 12:45 p.m. on that very day, Anastasia had boarded the northbound train from Toronto, Ontario to the small town of Cedar Falls. She was going to stay with her grandparents, even though she hadn't seen them in four years. Several hours had now passed, and Anastasia was still on the train, watching as the serene setting of Cedar Falls Woods had finally come into view. It was the first time she'd traveled such a distance by herself, and it was certainly not by choice.

Anastasia's mother, Ms. Kendall Lockhart, had sent her to Cedar Falls for two reasons. First, she said it was for her own good. Anastasia was becoming too wild and unpredictable — tell-tale signs that great trouble would soon befall her unless drastic and immediate action was taken. Second, she claimed that she was at her wits end. As a young, single mother with a full-time job, dealing with Anastasia's unruly behavior on top of it all was too much for her to handle.

Believing that the latter reason was the real cause for her departure pained Anastasia in a way she could never express out loud. It had always been just her and her mother, so if she didn't want Anastasia, surely no one else ever would. Instead of expressing her fears, she began to loathe her mother. The tension heightened as she began to prepare for her indefinite trip to Cedar Falls. This resulted in daily yelling matches set off by the simplest of disagreements and ended with the worst fight they'd ever had, right before Anastasia left for the train station.

As ironic as it seemed, Anastasia was once the epitome of a good girl. She'd been studious and somewhat shy, and although she had a couple of friends, she preferred to spend her weekends at the library, reading everything from classic novels to serious non-fiction titles. The library was also a place where she could be alone. She liked it that way, or maybe she was just used to it. Either way, the silence comforted her, and it allowed time for her two favorite activities – thinking and studying people from afar. This was time well-spent since she could now read someone's true character almost instantly upon meeting them. Certain traits and mannerisms spoke volumes about a person, and she'd learned to recognize these signs.

Anastasia's quiet, intellectual demeanor made her favorable in the eyes of her teachers. This was fine in elementary school, but when she entered junior high and it became uncool to be the teacher's pet, she found herself being constantly teased and even abandoned by the girls she used to consider her friends. In a school where being accepted meant everything, unpopularity was a disease easily caught by association, and she was most definitely the carrier.

Sad and alone, it was almost inevitable that Anastasia would gravitate toward other outcasts – the type of teens who skipped school to drink and smoke at the local park. She could read these classmates like an open book, but she didn't care since bad friends were better than no friends at all. It was at that time, upon turning thirteen, when everything went downhill fast. She began getting into trouble for reasons she previously couldn't have fathomed: unfinished homework, poor attendance and talking back to teachers. She was trapped in a vicious cycle, and regardless of her attempts to re-emerge as a good student, she'd already been labeled as bad.

This reputation followed Anastasia to high school, where she began to get into trouble more frequently. However, it wasn't until one month ago, on a cold January night, that she hit rock bottom. She'd been drinking at a house party with her boyfriend, Derek, and when he got into a fight with another guy, they were kicked out and left to walk aimlessly and unsteadily down the street. Eventually, they were approached by a police officer and arrested for underage drinking and public intoxication. After the most frightening and shameful few hours of her life, they were released with only a fine and a very strict warning. At least Anastasia had the common sense to dump Derek, but tragically, she'd already fallen victim to a negative self-fulfilling prophecy. She was now truly a bad girl.

The mere thought of her disgraceful past made Anastasia cringe. Although she was hurt and angry because of her mother's decision to send her away, she was also secretly grateful. She knew that her life was going in the wrong direction. Perhaps spending some time away from Toronto would be a positive change. After all, her reputation couldn't possibly follow her to Cedar Falls.

The train began to slow down as they neared their destination, causing Anastasia's heart to beat faster in anticipation. A large and somewhat worn sign welcoming visitors to downtown Cedar Falls came into view, and then a few moments later, the train finally stopped. Passengers began filing out, and Anastasia was soon forced to follow them. Taking a deep breath, she emerged from the train and looked around at the town she had once known and loved.

Cedar Falls remained unchanged, as if time had never passed. As always, the old downtown core featured vintage stores, a fire hall, library, and a large municipal building. However, it was the train station, which was built in 1905, that was the main attraction. The stores and their owners hadn't changed either. Dale's Diner, which doubled as his apartment, stood tall and proud. After four years, the blackboard sitting outside the diner still advertised his lunch special for only five dollars. There were also clothing boutiques, other eateries, and a couple of small grocery and convenience stores. Everything was familiar with the exception of a medium-sized store which used to be Hazel's Books and Gifts. It was now Stone's Hardware, and with several people coming in and out, it appeared to be doing a great business.

Returning her attention to the train, Anastasia waited patiently to retrieve her luggage. A few minutes later, and with her bag in tow, she searched the area for her grandfather. Unfortunately, she had no luck finding him. Looking at her watch, she realized that he should have met her half an hour ago. Her mother had made the arrangements, so where was he?

Anastasia shivered as the late afternoon sun began to

descend behind the tall cedars that lined the whole town. Everything was darkening fast, and she didn't want to spend any more time at the train station. The train had made its last stop in Cedar Falls for the day, and without people hurrying by or even the ticket collector in his booth, the station was kind of spooky.

Confused and a little hurt, Anastasia reached into her coat pocket for her cell phone. She'd just begun dialing her grandparents' number when someone called out to her.

"Anastasia, is that you?"

Anastasia spun around to see her grandfather, Mr. Fredrick Lockhart, standing outside his car, which was making a slight clunking noise as it idled. Any negative emotion she'd felt mere moments ago melted away as she looked at his bright blue eyes, rosy cheeks and wide, toothy smile. He was a tall, burly man who looked much younger than his actual age.

"Grandpa!" Anastasia cried. Despite her age, she ran toward him and hugged him tightly. "It's so great to see you!" For a few precious seconds, as they stayed in that embrace, nothing had changed. She was still his little angel who could do no wrong. Anastasia felt something that she hadn't experienced for several years now; she felt loved.

"I'm glad you're here, too," Mr. Lockhart said. "It's been a long time."

"Too long," Anastasia agreed. "I can't wait to see Grandma."

Anastasia hurried to her luggage, which had been forgotten in the moment of excitement. When she turned around, her grandfather was looking at her in a strange manner. He appeared to be studying her, and he even wore a startled expression.

"Is everything okay, Grandpa?" Anastasia asked with a

racing heart, fearing that he may be falling ill.

"Of course," he said, quickly regaining his composure. "I haven't seen you in so long, and you've really grown up."

"I hear that's how it works," Anastasia quipped, trying to lighten the mood despite the seriousness of the matter.

Throughout the chaos which was her life for the past four years, she'd always felt guilty about not seeing her grandparents. It wasn't exactly her fault, though. Her grandfather used to pick her up and take her to Cedar Falls for the summer. However, after Anastasia turned thirteen, her mother wouldn't risk letting her out of her sight for such a long period of time. Subsequently, neither of them saw Anastasia's grandparents because of her mother's refusal to return to Cedar Falls after leaving when she was only sixteen. At first, her grandparents had offered to visit them in Toronto, but Anastasia's mother always had an excuse: she was too busy, she couldn't take time off work and the house was too small for company. For a while, the phone was Anastasia's only connection to her grandparents, but they soon lost regular contact, calling only at birthdays and holidays.

"You look so much like your mother," Mr. Lockhart said suddenly, almost as if he hadn't meant to say it at all.

Anastasia's face fell. Coming from him, that observation wasn't a compliment. She quickly realized that she was standing under a safety light, which had probably been switched on seconds ago. She was exposed, and her grandfather was now looking at her like everyone else usually did. Her heart broke more than just a little.

There was an awkward silence as Mr. Lockhart put Anastasia's luggage in the trunk and then entered the car. Letting herself in, she sank into the passenger seat, almost wishing that she could disappear. Never before had she felt this uncomfortable being in his presence.

"I was starting to wonder where you were," Anastasia began to say, desperate to make any sort of conversation.

"I'm sorry for keeping you waiting," Mr. Lockhart said at the exact same moment.

They both laughed, causing the tension to ease slightly.

"My meeting at work ran later than expected," he finally continued.

"How's everything at the store?" Anastasia asked, truly interested.

Mr. Lockhart was the manager of Rural Mart, the only department store in Cedar Falls. Anastasia used to love visiting him at work and was so proud of the fact that he was respected and well-liked by his employees that she would go from department to department, telling everyone that he was *her* grandfather. Even outside of work, he'd always been held in high esteem.

"Not so good, I'm afraid," he answered with a deep frown. "Sales are down after a competitor opened up shop nine months ago. I think I'll even have to lay off a few employees."

"Who could possibly rival Rural Mart in this area?"

"Stone's Hardware," Mr. Lockhart spat out, almost as if he had a bitter taste in his mouth. "Herb's been undercutting Rural Mart by selling the same merchandise below market value. It's absurd, especially for a small store like his. He's probably stocking it with hot goods, though. After all, he did come to Cedar Falls straight out of jail. Once a thief, always a thief, is what I say."

Anastasia raised her eyebrows. She'd never heard her grandfather talk so harshly about anyone, making her realize that the situation at Rural Mart must be very bad. "Your job is secure, right?" she asked carefully.

"As long as I do something about it."

"I mean, one hardware store can hardly compete with all of Rural Mart's departments," Anastasia continued calmly, sensing that her grandfather was becoming greatly agitated.

"People move to Cedar Falls to build on cheap land. The hardware department has always been our biggest source of revenue." Mr. Lockhart suddenly brought his car to a stop outside Rural Mart. "Speak of the devil," he muttered angrily.

Following her grandfather's gaze, Anastasia saw a man emerging from Rural Mart with a stack of papers in his hands. He proceeded to stand under a lamppost, where he began attaching what appeared to be a flyer.

Anastasia recalled hearing about the infamous Mr. Herb Stone when she was young. However, her knowledge of him was very limited. Gossip made him out to be a hermit who lived deep in the woods. She'd only seen him a few times in town, and whenever she did, her grandparents would swiftly take her in the opposite direction. She'd thought this was odd, but as a young girl, she had much more exciting things to occupy her time. Looking at Mr. Stone now, she realized that he still had the same blonde hair and pale complexion that she so vaguely remembered.

"I'm sorry, Anastasia, but this can't wait," Mr. Lockhart said, while releasing his seatbelt.

When Anastasia opened her mouth to protest, it was already too late. Her grandfather was out of the car and marching toward Mr. Stone. She quickly turned off the car's engine and rolled down the window. She wanted to make sure her grandfather was okay, but at the same time, she had a feeling that she shouldn't interfere.

"Hey, you!" Mr. Lockhart called out to Mr. Stone.

Mr. Stone turned around and greeted him with a tight smile. "Fredrick, how are you?"

"Cut the bullshit, Herb. I want to know what you're playing at. There's no way you can be making a profit at your store." Mr. Lockhart suddenly turned his attention toward the flyer Mr. Stone had attached to the lamppost. "You can't be serious!" he yelled, while ripping the flyer off the post. "You're cutting and selling your own lumber now?"

Mr. Stone tore the flyer out of his hand. "It's a free country. A man can make a living any way he wants, especially on his own land."

"I'm surprised you know what freedom is!" Mr. Lockhart continued to bellow. "Didn't you spend half your life locked up in some jail cell?"

Anastasia knew that her grandfather was being irrational, and it looked as if the situation would soon get out-of-control. In an attempt to prevent the impending fight, she hurried out of the car. Then suddenly, she stopped dead in her tracks.

The most gorgeous boy Anastasia had ever seen was coming out of Rural Mart, carrying a bulging bag of groceries. He was tall – at least six feet – and very well-built with broad shoulders and a straight posture. His striking, chiseled features and unruly dark brown hair gave him a unique appearance that was rugged and manly. Nonetheless, Anastasia sensed that he wasn't that much older than her, and with heightened curiosity, she watched as an expression of concern washed over his face as he hurried to Mr. Stone's side.

"My past is none of your business," Mr. Stone snapped, finally getting as angry as Mr. Lockhart.

"Maybe not, but your shady business practices concern me and Rural Mart," Mr. Lockhart shot back.

The two men stepped closer to each other, but before anyone could throw a punch, the boy placed his hand on Mr.

Stone's shoulder and urged him back. The boy said nothing; instead, he gave Mr. Stone a serious look.

Mr. Stone stared silently at the boy for a few seconds and then returned his attention to Mr. Lockhart. "Get out of my way, Fredrick," he seethed, before taking leave of the situation.

The boy followed Mr. Stone, but before entering a truck marked *Stone's Hardware*, he stopped to look at Anastasia, as if noticing her for the first time. His gaze was intense and unwavering, like he was savoring everything about her, from her eyes to her lips and even her very soul.

With a quickening pulse, Anastasia stared back at him. He was so undeniably sexy, but it was his eyes which made her breath catch in her throat. Shining a light shade of blue, they instantly drew her in and refused to let go. The sudden urge to get closer to him was so strong that she unconsciously took a step forward.

"Anastasia!"

Anastasia turned around to see that her grandfather was already in the car, and from his expression, she easily guessed that he wasn't happy with her.

"Stay away from that boy," Mr. Lockhart ordered Anastasia as she entered the car.

"Grandpa," she began, wanting to ask if he was alright after his encounter with Mr. Stone.

In response, Mr. Lockhart turned on the car radio and increased the volume.

Anastasia took the hint.

As they drove through the newer part of downtown, Anastasia stared out the window, watching as the hospital, police station, bank, and a few franchises blurred by. She wasn't concentrating on her surroundings, though. Her mind was too preoccupied with thoughts of that mysterious and alluring boy. She assumed that he was Mr. Stone's son, but if that was truly the case, why hadn't she seen him before or even heard a whisper about his existence?

They arrived at the Lockhart residence ten minutes later, but to Anastasia, the car ride felt much longer. Although her grandfather had calmed down, he still wasn't his usual happy self. He seemed distant, as if he had a lot on his mind, perhaps more than just his recent run-in with Mr. Stone. Either way, as Anastasia stood before her grandparents' house, she was relieved to be out of the car.

The area was set aglow by all-season solar lights which lined the path to a charming two-story house. It was a lovely, secluded property situated on three acres of land, with the nearest neighbor being a ten minute walk away. An abundance of tall trees surrounded the house, adding extra privacy and making it appear as if it belonged in its own little world.

"Everything looks so magical at this time of year," Anastasia commented, realizing that she'd never been to Cedar Falls in the winter. "I see Grandma's still collecting those lawn ornaments," she added in amusement, while looking upon the numerous gnomes which were covered in snow. Their red pointy hats, which poked out from the snow, were the only sign of their presence.

"You know how your grandmother acts around gnomes," Mr. Lockhart said, shaking his head.

"Ohhh, they're just darling!" Anastasia and Mr. Lockhart said in unison, mocking Mrs. Lockhart in a joking manner.

As if on cue, Anastasia's grandmother, Mrs. Rose Lockhart, opened the door, the interior lights illuminating her as she stood upon the threshold. She was of medium height, somewhat plump and had short red hair which was only starting to turn gray. Just like her husband, she hadn't changed at all.

"Anastasia!" Mrs. Lockhart cried, before hurrying out into the snow with slippers as her only means of footwear.

"Hi, Grandma," Anastasia greeted with a smile, noting how her hug felt warm and loving, just like it always had.

"What took you two so long? I was starting to get concerned."

"Let us get inside, Rose," Mr. Lockhart complained, obviously avoiding her question.

Anastasia looked at her grandfather, wondering if he was keeping secrets from his wife. After all, almost getting into a fight was a big deal; she certainly knew that much.

"Silly me," Mrs. Lockhart said with a laugh as she guided Anastasia inside.

The house was comfortably warm, inviting and had a pleasant aroma, like pie had recently come out of the oven and apple cider was brewing. Everything about the house was perfect, from the carefully matched country-inspired décor, to the immaculate upkeep of it all. It was clear that Mrs. Lockhart still took great pride in her home.

"It's so wonderful to have you here," Mrs. Lockhart said as she took Anastasia's coat and hung it up.

"Thank you for having me," Anastasia replied in a slightly rehearsed tone. "It means a lot to me and my mother."

Looking sad for a moment, Mrs. Lockhart opened her mouth to speak but was interrupted as Mr. Lockhart came in with Anastasia's luggage.

"It's going to be a cold night," he said. "I hope you brought suitable clothing."

"She'll be fine," Mrs. Lockhart answered for Anastasia. "I have enough warm garments to clothe an army."

Anastasia forced herself to smile. Although she loved her grandmother dearly, she wasn't quite ready to adopt her high-waist denim and gingham blouse type of style. "I should probably start unpacking," she said, while taking the luggage from her grandfather.

"Dinner will be ready in half an hour," Mrs. Lockhart stated, "and after that, I have a special dessert."

Anastasia looked at her grandparents. "Thanks," she said sincerely.

"My darling, you already said that," Mrs. Lockhart commented with an amused smile. "You know you're always welcome here."

As Anastasia walked toward the bedroom on the main floor, she thought about her grandmother's words. For a very long time, she hadn't felt welcomed anywhere. It was amazing how much could change with a few kind words and gestures.

When Anastasia entered the bedroom, it was like she'd traveled back in time. This room, which once belonged to her mother, had been Anastasia's during her summer visits. It was eerie to see everything exactly how she'd left it so many years ago – three teddy bears sat on the floral bedspread, staring at her with glassy eyes; CDs featuring long-forgotten artists were piled next to an over-sized boom box; even the rocking chair was still in the corner, seating a collection of fashion dolls.

Anastasia's attention was particularly drawn to the white dresser, where several framed photographs were carefully arranged. She smiled as she looked at a photo of herself and Chloe Fairbanks – her former best friend in Cedar Falls. They were at the carnival, and Chloe had a painted butterfly on her cheek, while Anastasia wore a clump of bright pink cotton candy in her hair – unintentionally, of course. Next, she looked at a photo of herself and her grandparents in Cedar Falls Lake. They'd been fishing for minnows, and by the proud smile on her face, she knew that she'd caught some in her small net. Finally, she laid her eyes on a much older photo. It was of her mother and grandparents in happier times.

Unable to look at that photograph any longer, Anastasia turned around and was met with a reflection of herself. She stood before a mirror, and as she looked at her green eyes, long reddish brown hair and tall, slender build, she saw what her grandfather had seen earlier today – she was the spitting image of her mother when she was a teenager.

The last time I looked into that mirror, I'd seen an innocent twelve-year-old girl, Anastasia thought with tears in her eyes. *Now, look at me. Look at what I've become.* Not wanting to accept that she'd lost such a wonderful part of herself, she hastily turned away from the mirror, wiping her tears on the sleeve of her black hooded sweatshirt.

That night, dinner tasted as delicious as it smelled. Hungrily, Anastasia ate the lasagna, savoring the sweet spices which made her grandmother's meals so special. Although everyone was obviously enjoying the food, not much was said. It was almost as if her grandparents didn't know what to say. Of course they made light conversation, but no real questions had been asked. Not that Anastasia was complaining. She was the last person who wanted to talk about the last few years of her life. However, her grandparents' blatant avoidance of the subject made it just as awkward.

After finishing the main course, Mrs. Lockhart brought out dessert. "I remember how much you enjoyed my cranberry pie," she said, while cutting Anastasia a slice. "You used to beg me to make it every night." After a moment's pause, she added, "Cranberry pie was your mother's favorite, too."

As impossible as it seemed, the atmosphere became even more uncomfortable. Mr. Lockhart cleared his throat loudly, as if warning his wife to be quiet, but she refused to take the hint.

"You should call your mother to let her know you've arrived safely," she advised Anastasia.

"I've already sent her a text message," Anastasia said, annoyed that the conversation was starting to revolve around her mother, "but I doubt she'd care either way."

"That's not true," Mrs. Lockhart commented with a small frown. "Your mother loves you very much."

Anastasia couldn't help but snort. "If she was a true mother, she wouldn't have abandoned me. Everyone goes through rough times, but a mother isn't supposed to send her daughter away for someone else to handle."

"You're tired, Anastasia," Mrs. Lockhart said softly. "You don't know what you're saying."

"No," Anastasia snapped, "you're the one who doesn't know what she's saying. You have no clue what my mother is like, and how could you? You haven't seen her in seventeen years!" As soon as the words had escaped from her mouth, Anastasia regretted them. She looked at her grandmother, who was forcing back tears.

"Your...your mother has done the best she can, especially considering her circumstances."

"Grandma, I'm so sorry," Anastasia apologized in a hurry. "I always say the wrong things."

"It's alright," Mrs. Lockhart reassured her, even though she was obviously not okay. "I should start cleaning up," she added quietly, taking her dish into the kitchen despite the fact that her slice of pie had gone untouched.

Silence followed her grandmother's departure, and although her grandfather continued to eat his dessert as if nothing had happened, Anastasia's head was lowered in shame. For the second time that night, she felt her heart break. Of all the stupid things she'd done in her life, making her grandmother cry was her worst crime. How could she be so cruel to someone who had always loved and supported her?

Anastasia forced herself to eat the pie, now unable to enjoy its sweet tartness. She'd already ruined dinner, and she didn't want to hurt her grandmother even more by not finishing the dessert which was made especially for her. It was a small gesture, but it was the best that she could do.

"You don't have to end up like your mother," Mr. Lockhart finally spoke in a tone too matter-of-fact for such a delicate topic. "That's why you're here."

Not wanting to respond to her grandfather's insensitive words, Anastasia stood up hastily and said, "I need to finish unpacking, and I should get organized for school tomorrow." She then hurried out of the dining room, unable to bear being in there for a second longer.

Her grandfather's words haunted Anastasia as she lay in bed that night. From the stories her grandmother used to tell her, to the numerous photographs showcasing a happy family, Anastasia knew that her grandparents once had a close relationship with her mother. Now, Mr. Lockhart spoke about Kendall as if she was dead, and Mrs. Lockhart looked broken-hearted every time her name was mentioned. Worst of all, Anastasia knew that it was her fault.

Kendall was only sixteen when she became pregnant with Anastasia. It all started with some guy who was passing through Cedar Falls. After meeting Kendall, he decided to stay for a while, and their relationship soon turned serious. Her parents disapproved of the relationship, but she refused to acknowledge their concerns; she was too much in love. Unfortunately, when her prince charming found out that she was pregnant, he fled Cedar Falls. No amount of searching could find him.

Kendall's scandalous story spread throughout the town like a wildfire. She was an outcast and couldn't leave her house without people staring and talking about her. Even worse was how her parents behaved. Mr. Lockhart was ashamed of her, and he made his feelings perfectly clear. Privately, Mrs. Lockhart supported her, but she couldn't bring herself to do so in public.

Heartbroken and betrayed, Kendall knew that she had to get out of Cedar Falls. She was seven months pregnant when she packed her belongings and moved to Toronto. She lived off her savings and then social assistance. Once in a while, Mr. and Mrs. Lockhart would send her money, although she demanded that they stop. She eventually found a job for herself and a daycare for Anastasia, and somehow, they managed.

This was everything Anastasia knew about her parents' relationship and the pregnancy. She didn't even know her father's name. She'd inquired once, but after being told it was merely The Asshole, she never asked again. Anastasia highly doubted that she'd ever discover what else happened during that time, but one thing was for certain, she'd never have a relationship with her father.

Sighing deeply, Anastasia tossed in bed for what felt like the hundredth time. Being in Cedar Falls brought back so many memories and, against her will, made her reflect on her present life. As if that wasn't enough, she couldn't get that blue-eyed boy out of her mind. When he'd looked at her, she'd felt a spark, making her believe that he was very passionate. Yet, from the way he behaved with her grandfather and Mr. Stone, she also knew that he was gentle and caring. Despite the obvious attraction, she decided to stay away from him. Developing romantic feelings for some guy was the last thing she needed. Besides, he'd probably end up bringing more trouble into her life, exactly like all the other guys she'd dated.

The minutes passed slowly as Anastasia continued to lie there, listening to the sounds of Cedar Falls. An owl hooted loudly right outside her window, most likely in protest to the strong winds which blew through the trees, rattling their branches in the process. As these sounds persisted, they overpowered Anastasia's thoughts and soon became white noise. She began to relax, and as her eyelids became heavy, she finally gave into the sweet temptation of sleep.

Howl...

Startled by the unexpected noise, Anastasia's eyes flew open and she sat straight up in bed. That had sounded like a wolf's howl, but maybe she was just dreaming. Anastasia quickly wondered if she'd even fallen asleep, and if she had, why she was dreaming about wolves.

Howl...

Now realizing that the wolf wasn't a figment of her imagination, Anastasia's body stiffened with fear. That howl had been near – too near. She'd never heard wolves in Cedar Falls before, far less right outside her grandparents' house.

Remaining still for several moments, Anastasia listened, hearing only the sound of her quick, shallow breath. It seemed as if the wolf had moved on, but she had to be sure. She pulled her duvet aside and then stepped out of bed. As her bare feet touched the cool wooden floor, a shiver went through her body. Quietly, she crept toward the window and then drew the curtains.

The moon and solar lights illuminated the night, making it easy to see that the woods were in great disarray. Pinecones and twigs rolled wildly on the ground, and her grandmother's birdfeeders looked like they'd soon take flight. Even the tall, sturdy trees swayed dangerously in the increasing winds, as if foretelling that the worst was still to come. Yet, amongst the chaos there was no wolf.

Seriously, Anastasia, get a grip, she scolded herself.

Anastasia was about to step away from the window when something suddenly caught her attention. A shadowy figure was racing in between the trees at such a speed that she wasn't sure if her eyes were playing tricks on her. Then, as quickly as it had appeared, it was gone. With a pounding heart, she scanned the area, waiting to see if the figure would re-appear – it didn't. She shivered while thinking about what she'd just seen. Although it was difficult to be certain, the figure had looked somewhat human-like.

Confused and a little scared, Anastasia wanted to tell her grandparents what had happened, but she knew that wasn't a good idea. What if they thought she was making up stories? In fact, maybe she was. Combined, the moon, solar lights and trees could create odd shadows, so perhaps there really was no one outside. She began to relax, even though she was only slightly convinced by her reasoning.

As Anastasia climbed into bed for the second time that night, the events of the day replayed in her mind. She'd expected Cedar Falls to be the same small town she remembered from her childhood. In many ways, that's what she found. However, not everything was familiar. She could've never predicted the odd change in her grandfather's behavior, meeting a mesmerizing boy who lingered in her thoughts and finally, discovering a potential mystery right outside her bedroom window. It didn't take Anastasia long to realize that Cedar Falls was anything but a sleepy town.

❋ ❋ ❋

Part Two

Leader of the Pack

The air inside Anastasia's bedroom was frigid, causing her to subconsciously retreat further under the duvet in an attempt to keep warm. Wind whipped at her hair and exposed skin, chilling her to the bone, and as her eyes slowly fluttered open, she realized that something was wrong. Sitting up, she wrapped the duvet tightly around herself. That's when she heard an odd noise, like a succession of small clinks every time she moved. Carefully, she swept her hand over the duvet, cringing as several shards of glass scraped her skin.

A gust of wind blew through the bedroom, directing Anastasia's attention toward the window. Wildly, the curtains blew back and forth, revealing the shattered pane. It looked like something large had smashed through the window, and as the moon's glow intensified and streamed into her bedroom, she saw dark red blood dripping from the broken glass, pitter-pattering as it fell upon the ledge.

Suddenly, the floorboards creaked and then she heard a low, angry growl. Anastasia's heart raced as she spun around to see a wolf standing at the foot of her bed. She wanted to yell for help but quickly realized that any loud noise may provoke an attack. Instead, she tried to stop herself from shaking as she stared at the wolf. He was large and black, with piercing yellow eyes that seemed to burn into her soul. Her stare aggravated the wolf as he let out another growl and hunched his back.

Knowing that she had to get out of the bedroom, Anastasia slowly began to step out of bed. In response, the wolf snarled, revealing razor-sharp fangs that were covered in saliva. With her first plan unsuccessful, she decided to find a large or, better yet, sharp object. If she acted fast enough, maybe she could protect herself. She looked around, examining everything in her bedroom, but unfortunately, she found nothing that would be even slightly helpful. A cold realization swept over her; she was trapped, and the wolf was anything but friendly.

Aggressively, the wolf pounced onto Anastasia's bed and then crept forward, forcing her backwards until she hit the headboard. As the wolf brought his face close to hers, his breath momentarily lingering like a cloud, she caught a whiff of raw meat. Immediately, she felt like being sick.

"Easy, boy," Anastasia said in a soft, shaky tone.

In a bloodthirsty rage, the wolf leapt on top of Anastasia and ripped his fangs into her left shoulder. She screamed as an intense pain shot throughout her body, immobilizing her in the process. As the wolf's fangs dug deeper into her flesh, the agony worsened and soon became unbearable. Then everything went black.

Anastasia awoke with a start, her heart pounding as she sat up and looked around with wide eyes, only to find her bedroom in perfect order and sunlight shining through the unbroken window. Although she could still feel the terror and even the pain in her shoulder, it had all been a dream.

A shrill, sudden noise made Anastasia jump with fright. It only took her a second to realize that the sound was coming from the alarm clock she'd set-up yesterday. Nevertheless, after the unsettling night she'd just experienced, she didn't need anything else frazzling her nerves. She quickly leaned over and turned off the alarm, all the while hoping that her day would soon start improving.

By the time Anastasia got dressed, breakfast was already on the kitchen table. She didn't often eat breakfast, but when she did, it consisted solely of sugary cereal. However, her grandmother's homemade waffles and a variety of colorful fruits were too tempting to resist, and she was soon sitting at the table with her grandfather, who was reading the newspaper.

"Good morning," he greeted, finally noticing her presence. "How did you sleep last night?"

"With both eyes shut," Anastasia replied, before popping a juicy strawberry into her mouth.

Mr. Lockhart stifled his laughter, causing Anastasia to wonder why he felt the need to be so formal. It was like he didn't know how to behave around her. She thought it was ridiculous, and she hoped that he would soon realize that, too.

"Where's Grandma?" Anastasia asked carefully, still embarrassed by the way she'd acted during last night's dinner.

"She had to work an early shift at the library," Mr. Lockhart replied. After a few moments had passed, he added, "Rose forgot to mention that the library's looking for part-time help. Would you be interested?"

Anastasia merely snorted in response. Spending time in a small, musty library was no longer her idea of a fun time. Besides, she couldn't imagine how cranky the old ladies would be with such a limited supply of romance novels.

"You used to love that library," he commented.

"And now I don't."

Mr. Lockhart sighed as he stood up. "You tidy up here, and I'll get the car ready so I can drive you to school. I don't know if you've noticed, but we had quite the snowstorm."

Jumping up from the table, Anastasia hurried to the window. She was upset to find that at least four inches of snow had fallen, most likely in the early morning hours. Anastasia had momentarily forgotten that she'd wanted to search the backyard for wolf or even human prints, but that would be impossible now.

I guess I'll never know what was out there last night, Anastasia thought with disappointment. *That is, if anything was ever there at all.*

Located five minutes south of the downtown core, on a large, beautifully maintained property was Cedar Falls High – a tall, two-story building that appeared too big for the town's limited student population. Made from gray bricks of varying shades and covered in ivy that was dusted with snow, the school looked classic and very elegant. Playing fields and, of course, trees surrounded the area, with Cedar Falls Elementary and a church also nearby.

"Thanks for the ride," Anastasia said as her grandfather brought the car to a stop outside the school. "You don't need to pick me up, though. I can walk home."

"I'd prefer if you didn't," he replied hesitantly. "Just because Cedar Falls is a small town doesn't make it safe, especially now. I don't want to scare you, Anastasia, but there may be a dangerous animal on the loose."

"What kind of animal?" Anastasia hurried to ask, instantly thinking about the wolf cry she'd heard last night.

"The police haven't released many details, but there have been multiple reports of missing pets and mauled deer."

"Could it be a rogue bear?" Anastasia asked with some uncertainty, still reluctant to mention the events of last night. If she told him about what she'd heard and quite possibly seen, he'd either worry or think she was crazy. She couldn't help but feel that it was in everyone's best interest to just keep quiet.

"It's a rogue something," Mr. Lockhart answered. "I highly doubt it's a bear, though. They're hibernating at this time of year."

"Well, whatever it is, I'll take my chances," Anastasia said, while noticing a small group of students who were walking past. As they looked directly at her, whispering and laughing, she knew that she was being talked about in a negative manner. More than anything, she wanted to fit in, but she wouldn't achieve that by having her grandfather drive her to and from school, especially when the other students were either walking or driving themselves.

"Anastasia, it's really not a problem," he began, "I can meet you..."

"I said I'll walk," Anastasia interrupted as she exited the car. Quickly realizing that she was being too harsh, she added in a gentler tone, "You didn't sign up to be my chauffeur. I know the way home."

"I'm just asking you to be careful."

"I will," Anastasia promised as she closed the car door.

As her grandfather drove away, Anastasia studied the people who surrounded her. She was frustrated but not surprised to see that the school was segregated into cliques. Apparently, even small towns weren't immune to the clichés of high school.

There were the geeks, who wore scarves, mittens, snow pants, and puffy, downy-filled coats despite the sunny and somewhat mild winter morning. Excitedly, they huddled together, while talking about the latest episode of some science fiction TV series. They were the only other students being dropped off by their seemingly over-protective and worrisome parents.

Then there were the cool girls, led by a queen bee who'd just driven her expensive-looking car into the best parking spot. With long, loosely curled blonde hair, perfect make-up, fashionable clothes, and a saunter worthy of the catwalk, she looked exactly like a model. Her obvious efforts to be flawless didn't go unnoticed by her friends, who immediately greeted her with great enthusiasm.

Sighing, Anastasia began walking toward the school's entrance. That's when she noticed *him* – the boy she'd seen yesterday with Mr. Stone and had affectionately nicknamed Gorgeous – standing near the door, unaffected by the noisy students who filed into the school. He appeared to be waiting for someone and was looking straight at her; however, his stare wasn't judgmental, like the other students from moments ago. Instead, he looked at her with interest and perhaps even desire. Despite Anastasia's attempt not to be seduced, she felt her heart flutter.

"Oh my gosh! Is that Anastasia Lockhart?" someone suddenly called.

Anastasia looked at the girl who was hurrying toward her and then broke out into a big smile. "Chloe!" she exclaimed as they hugged. "It's so great to see you!"

Parting from their embrace, Anastasia stepped back to look at her childhood friend. It appeared that Chloe had grown into a mature, confident young woman. Her brown hair, which she used to wear in two long braids, was now cut shoulder-length and fashioned in a stylish manner. She even wore a lot of make-up which brought out her pretty brown eyes. However, Chloe's wide, slightly lopsided smile had remained unchanged, and just like before, it still made Anastasia smile whenever she saw it.

"Likewise," Chloe said as she looked at Anastasia. "Oh my gosh," she added for the second time that day. "You're like insanely beautiful now, but then again, you always were."

Anastasia had to bite her tongue. She didn't want to bring down the mood by stating how deceiving appearances could be. Instead, she forced herself to smile and said, "Right back at you, Chloe. You look amazing."

Chloe blushed, obviously delighted with the compliment. "It's going to be so much fun having you around again – just like old times!"

"You knew I was coming?" Anastasia asked in surprise.

"Of course I did. Your grandfather told me to keep an eye out for you. He remembers how close we were."

Anastasia wondered what exactly she meant. Was her grandfather asking Chloe to keep watch over her or to merely anticipate her arrival? Even though she was curious, she decided that it would be too embarrassing to inquire further.

"I can show you where your classes are," Chloe offered, "and we'll have lunch together for sure."

Anastasia hardly heard Chloe as she looked toward the school's entrance, searching for Gorgeous. Even with all the excitement of seeing her friend again, she hadn't forgotten about him. Unfortunately, she was disappointed to discover that he'd left. Although it wasn't likely, she'd hoped that he was waiting for her.

"Um, is everything alright?"

"What?" Anastasia asked, returning her attention to Chloe.

"You were looking for someone," she said with a mischievous smile. "Who is he?"

"No one," Anastasia replied too quickly.

Chloe laughed. "If you say so."

"Can you show me where the office is?" Anastasia inquired, desperate to change the topic. "I don't have my timetable yet."

"You don't even need to ask," Chloe replied, linking arms

with Anastasia and leading her through the school's front doors. She chatted excitedly as they went, but Anastasia had trouble concentrating on what she was saying; all she could think about was seeing Gorgeous again.

"Here we are," Chloe said, interrupting Anastasia's thoughts as they came to a stop outside a door marked *Office* in large white lettering.

"Thanks," Anastasia said gratefully. "Hopefully, this will be the only time I'm escorted to the office."

Chloe laughed before reaching for Anastasia's hand and giving it a gentle squeeze. "I'm really glad you're back," she said with a smile. "We'll catch up later, okay?"

Anastasia nodded and then watched as her friend disappeared into the crowd of students, who were hurrying to class as the morning bell rang. Chloe was as sweet and helpful as ever, making it crystal clear that she still had a heart of gold.

Returning her attention to the office, Anastasia opened the door and stepped inside. It was a bright, spacious room furnished with two large oak desks for the administrative assistants and a line of comfortable-looking chairs for the students. Potted plants and cut flowers added color to the office as did the decorative plaques featuring motivational quotes which hung on the walls.

Since one of the assistants was on the telephone and the other was already helping a student, Anastasia sat down near two girls, who were likely waiting to speak with an assistant as well. Right away, she noticed the girls casting her curious glances. Anastasia was going to introduce herself when they suddenly started to whisper about her.

"She must be new because I've never seen her before, and of course, I know everyone in this school."

"I saw her arrive this morning with Mr. Lockhart. She's

probably his granddaughter."

"No, she's too old to be his granddaughter. She must be his daughter."

"Then where has she been all these years?"

The girls' gossiping was cut short when the assistant called one of them to her desk. Although the girls hadn't been talking about Anastasia in a mean-spirited way, their behavior was just plain rude. It was like she was there for their entertainment, and that made her angry. However, she decided to let it go because she didn't want a confrontation on her first day at school, especially since she sometimes had trouble controlling her anger.

Continuing to sit there while now feeling annoyed, Anastasia had to wait twenty minutes before the assistant was able to see her.

"How can I help you?" inquired the assistant, whose nameplate upon her desk read, *Lisa*. She was middle-aged, and from the expression on her face, completely overwhelmed, as if uncertain about how to perform her clerical duties.

"I'm new here, and I need my timetable," Anastasia explained.

"Can I have your name?"

"Anastasia Lockhart."

Biting her lip like she was concentrating hard, Lisa turned to her computer, clicking the mouse every few seconds or so. Obviously needing help, she looked at her co-worker, who was still on the phone, chatting like it was a personal call. It was clear that Lisa hadn't been well-trained, if at all.

Anastasia repressed a sigh, thinking about how her day wasn't getting off to the greatest start. She hated being late, even if it wasn't her fault, and she knew that it wouldn't make a good impression on her first period teacher. Nevertheless, she waited politely until Lisa managed to find and print her timetable several minutes later.

With her timetable finally in hand, Anastasia hurried along the empty hallway, her footsteps echoing eerily as she went. It was disconcerting trying to navigate in an unfamiliar place, especially with time not on her side. When she found her chemistry class, which was on the second floor and at the end of a long hallway, she was over half an hour late.

"May I help you?" the chemistry teacher asked in an unfriendly tone as Anastasia entered the classroom. She'd been writing on the whiteboard just moments ago and was clearly unhappy with the interruption.

"Ms. Stevenson?" Anastasia asked, reading the name on her timetable. As she stood at the front of the classroom, she was fully aware that all eyes were on her.

"Yes?"

"My name's Anastasia. It's my first day."

"Very well," Ms. Stevenson replied, while returning her attention to the whiteboard and continuing to write. "I'm almost done assigning the lab work for today. You'll need to find a partner."

Anastasia looked around the classroom, noticing how each long desk seated three students. All the seats were taken, with the exception of one desk at the back. That's where a boy and girl sat, but they didn't seem interested in offering her the third chair. Instead, the girl cast Anastasia a challenging look, while the boy whispered sensually in her ear. It was obvious that they were a couple.

"Will you be joining our class or not?" Ms. Stevenson asked impatiently, upon seeing that Anastasia was still standing there. "If you are, there's an empty chair beside Jack and Jill." She pointed straight to the boy and girl at the back of the class.

The students lost interest in Anastasia as they began working on the day's experiment. For the most part, they were noisy and handled the equipment and chemicals with little care. Anastasia glanced at Ms. Stevenson to find her leaning against the wall and texting on her cell phone. She was a young teacher who was obviously interested in her paycheck above all else – including everyone's safety.

Reluctantly, Anastasia headed toward Jack and Jill, but they were too busy whispering sweet nothings to notice her presence. Even their experiment remained untouched. It was easy to see that they were in their own world with no outsiders allowed.

"Should I be expecting Mother Goose anytime soon?" Anastasia joked in a friendly manner, hoping to break the ice.

Jack and Jill stopped whispering and looked up at Anastasia as if she was crazy. Apparently, they didn't like her sense of humor.

"You know, get the whole nursery rhyme gang together," Anastasia tried again.

"We get it," Jill snapped. Sighing loudly, she turned her attention to the experiment.

"Hey," Jack finally greeted Anastasia in a nonchalant tone.

In response, Anastasia smiled at Jack. Unfortunately, this only caused Jill to narrow her eyes, as if warning her to back off.

Reading this couple was far too easy for Anastasia. Jill's nastiness stemmed from her insecurities, which was completely ironic since Jack was so in love with her that he couldn't see any of her flaws. She was pretty sure that this was the first serious relationship for the both of them.

Finally sitting down, Anastasia watched as Jill filled a glass beaker with distilled water before placing it on the Bunsen burner and turning the flame to the highest setting. She wanted to tell Jill that, according to the instructions on the whiteboard, they should be using 150ml of water, not just 50ml. However, Anastasia couldn't handle any more icy stares, so she remained silent.

As the water began to boil rapidly, Jack whispered something dirty to Jill. Although Anastasia couldn't hear everything that he was saying, it made Jill blush and push him playfully.

"You're so silly," Jill cooed, while placing her hand flirtatiously on his thigh.

"And you're so beautiful," Jack murmured, kissing her cheek and then her lips.

Feeling more than a little awkward, Anastasia busied herself with reading the whiteboard. She wanted to get this experiment done as quickly and painlessly as possible. Anastasia reached for the chemical container and was about to pour a small amount into an empty beaker when Jill suddenly stopped her.

"Don't touch anything," she commanded. "This is *my* experiment."

Reaching her breaking point, Anastasia snapped back, "Fine. You do all the damn work."

"Gladly," Jill retorted, while pouring an unmeasured amount of the chemical directly into the boiling water.

Predicting a negative consequence to Jill's hasty actions, Anastasia quickly backed away. Jack and Jill, on the other hand, merely stared with wide eyes as the mixture reacted badly. Seconds later, the beaker broke in half, causing the liquid to spew all over the desk. Several students gasped, and even Ms. Stevenson looked shocked, although she took her time coming to see them.

"Are you guys okay?" Anastasia asked Jack and Jill, noting how they still looked shaken-up.

"We're fine," Jill replied, recovering quickly. "Why would you do that?" she asked loudly and clearly.

"Excuse me?" Anastasia was hardly able to choke out.

"I told you to follow the instructions on the whiteboard," Jill said.

Sternly, Ms. Stevenson turned to face Anastasia. "Did you do this on purpose?"

"I didn't do anything!" Anastasia exclaimed. "Jill's lying!"

"No, she's not," Jack interjected. "Anastasia was being careless, and now she's trying to blame someone else for her mistake."

As silence filled the classroom, Anastasia realized that no one else had seen what really happened, or if someone had, they weren't going to speak up. Defending herself was pointless; she knew that the more she talked, the guiltier she would appear.

"You're no longer allowed to participate in the lab experiments, which means you'll lose marks," Ms. Stevenson informed Anastasia. "Now excuse me while I call the janitor. He has a mess to clean up."

As if timed perfectly, the bell rang, signaling the end of class. Anastasia mustered all her confidence as she walked out of the classroom with her head held high. However, inside she felt like crying. She was undeniably angry at the false accusation, but it was more than just that. Anastasia wanted Cedar Falls to be her fresh start; instead, it was starting to feel exactly like Toronto.

The cafeteria was bustling with upbeat, noisy students who were enjoying their sixty minutes of mid-day freedom. It was exactly the type of environment Anastasia wanted to avoid. Everyone seemed so happy and carefree, and that alienated her since she wasn't in the same state of mind. Unfortunately, she'd made plans to meet Chloe in the cafeteria, and she knew that ditching her to eat alone in some hallway corner wouldn't help in her attempt to be perceived as normal.

In search of Chloe, Anastasia scanned the crowd. She finally found her sitting at a prime location table which had a great view of the trees outside and just the right amount of sunlight streaming onto it. However, her heart sank when she saw who she was sitting with – it was the queen bee she'd seen outside the school earlier that day. There was another girl with them, and she too looked perfectly primped and rich. Believing that befriending the popular crowd would only draw unwanted attention and segregate her from the majority of students, Anastasia prepared to leave. Whenever she saw Chloe next, she'd have to make up some excuse about getting lost and being unable to find the cafeteria. After all, she didn't want to hurt her feelings.

"Anastasia!" Chloe called, waving to her.

Cringing, Anastasia waved back and slowly made her way toward the table. She could feel people watching her as she went, probably wondering what she'd done to deserve such an honor. Quickly, Chloe pulled out a chair and smiled widely, obviously delighted to see Anastasia. She just couldn't help but ponder why; surely she realized that Anastasia didn't belong there.

"Ladies, this is Anastasia Lockhart," Chloe introduced her. "She's a childhood friend of mine."

"Hey," Anastasia greeted, trying to sound as friendly as possible.

The two girls smiled at Anastasia. One of them looked sincerely interested in meeting her, but there was something about that queen bee which seemed rather cold; not that Anastasia was surprised.

"This is Marissa Brookes," Chloe said, gesturing toward a

girl with chin-length strawberry-blonde hair, light freckles, sparkling blue eyes, and a tiny, perfect nose. Marissa definitely had a unique look, but she was charmingly beautiful.

"And this is Kate McKinley," Chloe continued, smiling at the queen bee. Kate looked even more beautiful up-close. From her skin to her posture, everything about her appearance seemed flawless. However, behind those pretty hazel eyes was a challenging stare.

"Welcome to Cedar Falls," Kate said in a dignified tone, as if it was her right to decide who enters the town.

"Anastasia is from Toronto, but she'll be staying here for a while," Chloe informed them.

"I love Toronto!" Marissa exclaimed. "My family and I go shopping there every spring. I'm addicted to their clothing boutiques. They definitely have a better selection than Cedar Falls."

Not completely sure how to respond, Anastasia merely smiled at Marissa. She knew little to nothing about Toronto's fashion scene, but she didn't want to say so.

"Fashion's my thing," Marissa continued with a sweet smile, almost as if she could sense Anastasia's slight unease. "I immediately noticed your outfit. It's so chic and modern."

Kate snorted and then said bitchily, "In a gothic sort of way, I suppose."

Anastasia looked down at her clothes. She wore a black knitted cowl neck sweater, dark blue skinny jeans, black boots, and some jewelry that consisted of an antique-looking key pendant necklace and a chunky charm bracelet. Her outfit didn't differ that much from what the other students were wearing.

"Is black nail polish fashionable in Toronto?" Kate asked with wide, not-so-innocent eyes. "I'd love to know. It's important for me to keep abreast of developing trends."

Kate's tone was filled with sarcasm, but she smiled as she talked, making it seem like she was being sincere. However, Anastasia knew better, and she wasn't about to let Kate get away with talking to her in that manner.

"Yes, everyone's wearing it," Anastasia lied, while proudly showing off her nails.

"Black can be classic or daring," Marissa informed them. "One can never go wrong with it."

Anastasia couldn't have cared less about the color of her nail polish. What she did care about, though, was that she'd stopped Kate from visually dissecting her. By the sneer on Kate's face, Anastasia knew that she was expected to bow down to her. Well, that certainly wouldn't be happening anytime soon.

"How are your classes so far?" Chloe asked Anastasia, most likely noticing the growing tension.

"Horrible," Anastasia replied honestly as she unwrapped her club sandwich and began to eat. "Do you guys know some hormonally-charged couple named Jack and Jill? They were practically rolling on the science floor — it was disgusting! They're also such liars. You wouldn't believe what they said about me."

Kate cleared her throat loudly. "As a matter of fact, I do know Jack. He's my cousin."

"Oh," Anastasia muttered, casting a glance at Chloe and Marissa, who looked sufficiently awkward.

"He's also a preacher's son," Kate snapped. "So, I highly doubt he's capable of lying."

There was so much irony in Jack being the son of a preacher that Anastasia hardly knew where to begin her mockery. She quickly bit her tongue, though, and decided to keep her less-than-stellar opinions about organized religion to herself. Cedar Falls was a very religious town, and the church had a large following which included her grandparents.

"So, your last name is Lockhart," Kate began, as if preparing for another attack. "Is that right, Anastasia?" She continued quickly, not waiting for a response. "That must make you Kendall's daughter."

Blood rushed to Anastasia's cheeks. The thought that some of her mother's former friends would recognize her and ask a lot of prying questions had crossed her mind. After all, the physical similarities between the two of them were very pronounced. However, she'd never expected anyone who was her own age to start inquiring about her mother.

"You know my mother?" Anastasia asked, pretending like it was no big deal.

"Her reputation precedes her," Kate answered smugly. "This town never forgets."

"Then what a petty town this is," Anastasia said through clenched teeth and in a tone that was barely audible.

Of course, Kate heard her and was more than happy to respond in a sweetly insincere manner. "Don't fret about it. Cedar Falls has many other conversation starters – for example, Frost. Now there's a real freak story."

Marissa, who had looked confused for the last minute or so, suddenly seemed alert. Chloe, on the other hand, still appeared uncomfortable. Although they'd never talked about her mother when they were young, Anastasia knew that Chloe would've heard the scandalous details from her parents.

"What's Frost?" Anastasia asked, desperate to have the negative attention taken away from her.

"Not what – who," Chloe replied.

"Frost is so cute," Marissa gushed. "He's got this totally sexy bad boy thing going on," she added to Anastasia.

"Be quiet," Kate hissed. "Never let anyone hear you say

that. It'll permanently destroy your reputation."

"Sorry," Marissa muttered as she concentrated on eating her lunch in an obvious attempt to conceal her embarrassment.

Kate shook her head in disapproval as she spoke to apparently anyone who would listen. "Frost is such a loner. He acts different from the rest of us, like he doesn't even want to fit in. It's so strange, but I guess I shouldn't complain. After all, a guy like that has no right to be a part of this town. It's best for everyone if he just stays away."

Anastasia was taken aback by Kate's harsh bigotry, especially as she continued to insult Frost in an almost rant-like state. Although she had a lot of nasty things to say about him, she never actually explained why she disliked him so much. Anastasia thought this was very odd, and she assumed that there was more to the story than Kate was willing to reveal. Regardless of what was going on, she wished that Kate would shut up. After all, she'd just learned the hard way that it was never a good idea to talk poorly about someone, even if they did deserve it.

When lunch finally came to an end, Anastasia couldn't get out of the cafeteria fast enough. Although Chloe had insisted that Anastasia join them again tomorrow, there was no way she was going to suffer through another lunch like today. Somehow, she'd just have to make her own friends.

As Anastasia walked through the school's Humanities wing in search of her English class, she noticed that the hallways were a lot busier. Even more prominent was the impoliteness of many of the students. One girl had allowed a door to slam shut in her face, while another had bumped into her and not apologized. Being treated this way by strangers gave Anastasia a new vantage point in regards to her own recent behavior. In Toronto, she used to hurry through her days, not truly caring about other people. Instead, she spent her time dwelling on her seemingly meaningless and hopeless existence. It was a selfish and ugly way of life, and she didn't want to be that kind of person anymore. Starting today, she decided to take small steps in the right direction. She held doors open for other students, and she didn't yell at the girl who'd bumped into her.

Anastasia's good behavior seemed to reap immediate rewards as she suddenly saw Gorgeous walking straight toward her, almost like he'd appeared out of nowhere. As he drew closer, her heart beat faster, and it felt like her body was starting to melt. His smile was perfect, his intense eyes were locked on hers, and she couldn't help but fantasize about the chiseled body that was likely underneath his jeans and dark blue sweater. Everything about him, from the slight stubble upon his face, to his self-assured yet humble demeanor, made him appear more mature than the other boys at Cedar Falls.

He was now only a few feet away from Anastasia, but his smile had faded and it looked like he'd lost his confidence. He cast a somewhat timid glance at her and then disappeared into a classroom. Anastasia was disappointed that he hadn't spoken to her, and she was even more upset to learn that her classroom was right next door to his. Couldn't karma have helped her just a bit more and put them in the same class? At this rate, she'd never get to know him. Not that it would make a difference, though. He was probably one of the most popular boys at Cedar Falls, and that meant he'd be interested in someone like Kate – not her.

Sighing, Anastasia hurried into her English class. By this point, she wasn't surprised to find yet another disappointment awaiting her. In the middle of the class sat Jill, and it was clear from her expression that she wasn't ready to play nice. Quickly, Anastasia found a seat at the front of the class.

"Good afternoon," the teacher greeted as he entered the classroom and began unpacking today's material onto his desk. He was probably in his mid-thirties, and with light brown hair, green eyes, a good physique, and a sexy Irish accent, he was very eye-catching. "Welcome," he said, turning his gaze to Anastasia. "According to my records you're Anastasia Lockhart."

"Yes," she said quietly, wishing that he hadn't said her last name out loud. If Kate knew about her mother, then maybe other students did, too.

"I'm Mr. O'Donoghue," he said, offering his hand to her. "I'm sorry to say you've picked quite a time to join us. We're half-way through Milton's Paradise Lost, and we have a test scheduled for next Monday. I'm sure I'll find a way to get you caught up, though."

"That's okay," Anastasia said, after releasing his hand. "I read Paradise Lost when I was twelve, but I still remember it well."

Mr. O'Donoghue was impressed, but a few students laughed. Anastasia's face reddened slightly. It probably wasn't the best idea to add that it was one of her favorite classic novels.

"You've humbled me," Mr. O'Donoghue admitted. "I didn't study any of Milton's work until university."

Mr. O'Donoghue stepped away from Anastasia's desk and began presenting his prepared material. He was a talented, lively lecturer, and it was apparent that he was passionate about his job. After just forty-five minutes in his presence, it was clear to her that his greatest skill was making literature accessible, especially for such a challenging book.

"So, that brings me to the question of how do we read these characters," Mr. O'Donoghue said, bringing his lecture to an end. "Let's start with the character of Satan. How does Milton represent him and why is it significant?"

"Satan is the representation of evil," Jill answered without raising her hand. "There's no good in him, so he must be destroyed."

"That's a good start," Mr. O'Donoghue said generously, "but is there any other way Milton portrays him, and why does he do so?"

The class fell silent, and no one raised their hand.

"Anastasia, you look pensive," Mr. O'Donoghue noted. "Mind sharing your thoughts?"

"I think Satan is the most complex character in Paradise Lost," Anastasia began. "He's portrayed almost human-like because of his jealousy, anger and drive. That's what makes him the most relatable character in the whole book. Also, he's the first one to be introduced to the readers, and he has a goal that he's determined to achieve. According to most epics written during Milton's time, wouldn't that make Satan the protagonist?"

"Excellent observations," Mr. O'Donoghue commented. "Can anyone respond to the question Anastasia has raised?" When no one spoke up, he faced her once again. "Care to answer your own question?"

"He's both the protagonist and antagonist because he started as an angel but then succumbed to his jealously for God's Son. He had a choice, but he made the wrong one. Milton wrote a cautionary tale. Since we possess traits similar to Satan's, we too can fall from grace."

"That's a very insightful interpretation," Mr. O'Donoghue praised Anastasia, before addressing the whole class. "If everyone wrote with that level of analysis, you'd all be getting A's."

The bell rang, and for the first time that day, Anastasia

didn't want the class to be over. Reluctantly, she placed her notebook and pen into her backpack. That's when she experienced a creepy feeling, as if someone was breathing down her neck.

"Satanic bitch," a female voice whispered in Anastasia's ear.

Tears instantly stung Anastasia's eyes. She didn't need to turn around to find out who had spoken. The voice unmistakably belonged to Jill.

"Anastasia, can I see you for a moment?" Mr. O'Donoghue asked.

After her nasty comment, Jill had been one of the last students to leave the classroom. Anastasia and Mr. O'Donoghue were now alone, and as she walked toward his desk, she had to force back her tears. She was neither Satanic nor a bitch, but being called such things hurt very deeply.

"I'm confused," Mr. O'Donoghue began in a serious tone. "I have your mid-term English grade from the last school you attended. Either you're failing or one of their administrative assistants is prone to typos."

"I know I'm failing," Anastasia said quietly.

"From what I saw today, you have the potential to be an outstanding student," Mr. O'Donoghue said, instead of prying any further into her previous academic mishaps. "I run a literacy group that meets three times a week during lunch. Basically, we get together to discuss books, but we also offer tutoring services and often organize literary events in the community. I think this would be a great opportunity for you, especially since you'll be getting extra credit."

"Sign me up," Anastasia hurried to say. Joining the literacy group was a no-brainer; it would allow her to pass the class, while giving her a legit excuse as to why she could no longer have lunch with Kate. Anastasia smiled at Mr. O'Donoghue.

He had no idea how much he was really helping her.

The school day had come to an end, and Anastasia was now walking down a deserted snow-covered road. The bright sun still shone in the spotless blue sky, and as she looked at the cedars which lined the road, she noticed how the snow fell like confetti every time a slight breeze stirred the branches. It was a beautiful mid-afternoon, but Anastasia was beginning to feel uneasy. She'd been walking for too long, and her surroundings were no longer familiar. Somewhere along the way, she must have made a wrong turn, causing her to become lost.

Anastasia was embarrassed to admit that she needed help, especially since she'd been so adamant about walking home. Nonetheless, she retrieved her cell phone, knowing that she'd have to call her grandfather. She tried dialing, but the call failed immediately – she wasn't getting any reception out here. Realizing that she could be in serious trouble, panic seized her.

"I'm going to get through this," Anastasia whispered to herself. Those were the words she'd often used for comfort whenever she felt sad or scared. Right now, though, she knew that she had to think rationally. Although a car hadn't passed for the last twenty-five minutes or so, there was a set of tire marks on the road. She could follow those tracks, hoping that they'd lead to some type of help, but turning around and retracing her steps seemed like a better option.

Anastasia hurried in the direction she'd come, praying that she would be able to find her way back. If she didn't arrive home soon, her grandparents would start to worry. They had always been overprotective, insisting to know where she was at all times. Her grandparents were the exact opposite of her mother; she never seemed to care where Anastasia was or who she was with.

Amidst the silence of the woods, Anastasia suddenly heard the faint sound of approaching footsteps. She spun around, feeling equally anxious and relieved as she waited for someone to appear from over the undulating road. Slowly, Gorgeous was revealed, walking straight toward her. His presence in her time of need and amongst such beautiful scenery made her momentarily question if she was merely dreaming.

"Are you lost?" he asked, stopping right in front of her.

"I..." Anastasia tried to respond, while staring so intently upon him that everything else seemed to become a blur. "I'm so lost," she finally admitted, forcing her gaze from him and onto her surroundings. "Can you give me directions to Evergreen Road?"

"You're far from home," he noted. "Let me take you there."

"Thanks, I'd really appreciate that," Anastasia said, before he began leading her forward. She smiled at him, even though he was looking straight ahead with a serious expression upon his face.

"You shouldn't be out here," he warned, "especially alone."

"You were alone, too," Anastasia pointed out.

He smirked at her comment and then cast her a quick, interested glance. "I guess you're right."

"I'm not trying to pry," Anastasia began hesitantly, after a slight pause in their conversation, "but why *are* you out here?"

"It's where I live."

"I didn't see a house."

"You're inquisitive," he stated in a friendly manner, despite the flicker of fear in his eyes. "I promise you there's a house back there."

"I'll take your word for it then," Anastasia replied in a slightly flirtatious tone.

"That's entirely up to you."

Anastasia's heart fluttered as he smiled at her, their eyes lingering on each other for several moments. She felt the overwhelming urge to kiss him, but when he broke his gaze, she realized that she was being way too hasty.

"My name's Anastasia, by the way," she said, wondering why he hadn't introduced himself first.

He looked away, almost as if he no longer wanted to be there. "I'm Frost," he responded.

Anastasia had to hide her surprise. How could this be the boy who Kate had insulted so mercilessly? Frost was extremely handsome, and he looked like he could be the captain of any sports team. According to all the high school clichés she'd ever heard, that would put him at the top of every girl's boyfriend wish list.

"Frost is an unusual name, but I like it," Anastasia said, trying desperately to forget everything that Kate had said about him. "What does it mean?"

"The state of freezing."

"That's not what I'm asking," Anastasia said with an amused smirk, all the while thinking that's exactly how she would've answered if she were him.

Suddenly, Frost stopped dead in his tracks and stood still and tense. It was as if he'd heard something, even though the woods were as quiet as ever.

"Frost, what's wrong?" Anastasia asked, studying his concerned expression.

"Shhh..." he whispered, while staring into the woods in an intense manner. "We're in danger."

Startled by Frost's words, Anastasia scanned the surrounding area but saw nothing out of the ordinary.

"Why?" she demanded. "What's out there?"

When Frost didn't reply, Anastasia stepped forward. Quickly, he put his arm in front of her, stopping her from going any further. Frost then nudged Anastasia behind him and kept a tight grip on her arm.

"A cougar is watching us," Frost said in a low tone. "We have to show him we're not afraid."

Anastasia's heart pounded so hard that it felt like it would rip from her chest. She never knew there were cougars in Cedar Falls, far less had she ever seen one. However, what she did know was that cougars could be very dangerous, and that she and Frost had nothing with which to defend themselves.

"Where is he?" Anastasia asked, her voice hardly a whisper.

"Don't make eye contact," Frost said hastily, despite the fact that his own gaze hadn't shifted from the woods for several moments. In a swift motion, he raised his arms above his head in a gesture that mimicked a violent protest. "Hey!" he called, his voice growing louder as he continued. "Go away! Get out of here!"

The woods seemed to come alive as the cougar started to run. Anastasia only saw a flash of brown fur in between the trees, and even that was enough to make her shiver. The cougar had been close but was now fleeing from them, and as he went, branches shook and twigs snapped in half. After the cougar had disappeared into the wilderness, everything was still and quiet once again.

Frost maintained his grip on Anastasia's arm as he hurried her forward. His pace was so fast that she had to run just to keep up. Since the cougar had left them unharmed and was probably a mile away by now, Anastasia wondered why Frost still looked so alarmed.

"I think we can slow down," Anastasia said several minutes later, finally resisting Frost's pull.

Frost released Anastasia's arm and reduced his speed slightly. "We have to keep moving," he advised. "Cougar's stalk their prey, and he could return at any moment."

"How did you know the cougar was there?" Anastasia asked one of the many questions which were circulating in her mind.

"If you spend enough time in the woods, you'll get to know its rhythm, especially when something is wrong."

"What do you mean?" Anastasia inquired. She was tired, still a bit shaken-up and definitely not in the mood for cryptic language.

"Stay close to me and you'll be safe," Frost promised.

Nothing else was said as they trekked onward. Twenty minutes later, Anastasia began recognizing her surroundings. As her grandparents' house finally came into view, she realized just how lost she'd really been. If Frost hadn't found her, she didn't want to think about what could've happened, especially with that cougar roaming the woods. He'd saved her, and they both knew it.

"This was the place I was looking for," Anastasia joked as she stopped outside the Lockhart residence.

Frost smirked, but his expression soon changed when he looked upon her house. He appeared uncomfortable as his eyes settled on the living room window. "I should go," he said abruptly, before turning around to leave.

"You can come in," Anastasia said, causing Frost to pause momentarily. "You should rest a little, and I can get you something to eat."

In the background, a door swung open and then someone shouted out to Anastasia. She turned around to see her grandfather hurrying toward them.

"Thanks, but that's not a good idea," Frost replied as he rushed to leave. "I'll see you around."

"Don't you want a ride home?" Anastasia called after him. It would be dark soon, and she knew that he shouldn't be walking alone. Unfortunately, Frost was already too far away to hear her.

"Anastasia, what's going on?" Mr. Lockhart demanded, once he'd reached her side. He sounded angry, but his expression was clearly one of relief. "What were you doing with that boy?"

"He walked me home," Anastasia began to say.

"Frost is nothing but trouble," he interrupted. "How many times do I have to tell you to stay away from him?"

"Maybe if you told me why, it would sink in better," Anastasia responded in frustration.

Mr. Lockhart sighed. "You're a smart girl, Anastasia. You know that Mr. Stone is his father. As for his mother, no decent woman would marry a man like that. We do *not* associate with those types of people."

Anastasia questioned the accuracy of her grandfather's criticism. He was obviously threatened and angered by Mr. Stone's successful business, so maybe his judgment was clouded. Either way, she felt very defensive of Frost.

"Well, I guess Frost has beaten the odds," Anastasia said, almost glaring at her grandfather. "I was lost, but he brought me home. He sounds like a real jerk, huh?"

Mr. Lockhart narrowed his eyes at Anastasia. "I'm picking you up every day after school," he said, as if it was a cruel punishment.

Anastasia didn't have a chance to respond as her grandfather marched into the house. She was about to follow him when she noticed her grandmother watching from the living room window. Upon being spotted, her grandmother hurried away. However, it was too late; she now understood why Frost had left so quickly. He knew that her grandparents not only disliked his father but his whole family, too. Suddenly, Anastasia's life seemed a lot more complicated.

Later that night, Anastasia ran a hot bath for herself. It had been a very long day filled with many unexpected events, and she was in dire need of some relaxation. Not all of her day had been hard, though. She smiled while thinking about Frost. He was different from the other boys she'd known, probably because she couldn't read him. Frost was a mystery – one that she was eager to unravel.

Anastasia was about to step into the water when she remembered that her Dead Sea bath salts were still in her bedroom. It was her only indulgence and well worth every penny. Wrapping a white towel around herself, she headed to her bedroom. That's when she heard her grandparents talking quietly in the kitchen. Upon hearing her name, Anastasia crept closer and listened.

"It was foolish of me to let Anastasia walk home from school," Mr. Lockhart said. "She hasn't been in Cedar Falls for four years – it's no wonder she got lost!" With a deep sigh he added, "Anything could've happened to her, Rose. What the hell was I thinking?"

Sympathetically, Mrs. Lockhart placed her hand on top of Mr. Lockhart's. "You were allowing Anastasia to make her own choices. It's important that she feels in control of her life."

"No," he replied sharply. "What's important is keeping her safe. We need to set strict boundaries and make sure she stays within them."

"Of course there should be rules," she agreed, "but she also needs some freedom." Taking a deep breath, she added,

"You shouldn't have told her to stay away from Frost. It will only encourage her to rebel."

"You gave Kendall freedom and she ruined her life," Mr. Lockhart pointed out angrily. "I won't let the same thing happen to Anastasia."

"Please be gentle with her, Fredrick. You know Anastasia is troubled."

Too hurt to listen any longer, Anastasia hurried back to the bathroom. She slammed the door behind her and then started to cry, not caring if her grandparents heard. If anyone could see the goodness inside of her, she thought it would've been them. Unfortunately, all they saw was a girl with issues, and now she was their burden. Knowing what her grandparents really thought about her made Anastasia feel like a freak who was alone in this world.

Part Three

Cruel Intentions

The clock hadn't struck seven yet, but Anastasia stood outside her house, waiting in the cold, dreary early morning weather. She was desperate to avoid her grandparents, and as they slept, she'd written them a brief note stating where she was going and with whom. Anastasia hadn't spoken to her grandparents since overhearing their frank discussion about her, and she wanted to keep it that way for as long as possible. It had become second nature for Anastasia not to talk about what was really bothering her — even though that only caused more trouble.

Finally, the ride Anastasia had been waiting for appeared in the distance. Seconds later, a stylish light blue car stopped outside her house. As the driver rolled down the window, loud music could be heard coming from inside.

"Get in, bitch!" Chloe called out jokingly.

As Anastasia entered the car, she immediately noticed the sleek, spotless interior which featured leather upholstery and branding just about everywhere. The car was obviously new and expensive, and this caused Anastasia to wonder what type of lifestyle Chloe now led. Although her father owned a dental practice in town, he'd always been somewhat frugal. Anastasia hadn't seen him in years, though, and by the looks of Chloe's car, he'd definitely changed his money-saving ways.

"Do you like it?" Chloe asked, while running her fingers over the silver swirl pattern on the steering wheel cover. "My parents bought it for my sweet sixteenth. I thought I was going to faint when they unveiled it at my party."

"The car's amazing, Chloe," Anastasia replied, while thinking about her own sixteenth birthday. She'd spent it alone and crying, wanting to just disappear. Looking back, she couldn't even remember what had upset her so much. "I wish I could've been at your party," she added with a small smile, trying to erase the disturbing memory.

"I wish you were there, too," Chloe said in an almost sad tone as she drove away from the Lockhart residence. "You probably didn't know this," she continued after a moment's pause, "but I used to consider you my best friend. We had so much fun together, and I felt like I could tell you anything. I missed that. I missed you."

"Children grow up," Anastasia pointed out, attempting to control the emotions that were surfacing because of her friend's words.

"True, but you completely disappeared."

There was no point in denying it; Anastasia had cut Chloe out of her life, and she'd done so without providing a reason. In fact, Anastasia was surprised that she was being so friendly. All those missed calls and unanswered letters must have really hurt Chloe at the time.

"My intentions were never cruel," Anastasia said softly and sincerely.

"I kind of knew that, but it's nice to hear you say it." Chloe took her eyes off the road for a second to smile at Anastasia. "So, can you guess where I'm taking you for breakfast?"

"Dale's Diner," Anastasia replied, without missing a beat. Having eaten there countless times, it'd always been one of her and Chloe's favorite places.

"Since you'll be spending your lunches with Mr. O'Sexy now, I thought we might as well have breakfast together."

"Mr. who?" Anastasia asked with a laugh.

"Come on, Anastasia," Chloe began in a teasing manner, "don't pretend you haven't noticed Mr. O'Donoghue's smoldering good looks. I seriously considered joining the literacy group just so I could stare at him."

"Now that's creepy."

"It's only creepy if I follow through on it," Chloe said with a playful shrug as she parked her car outside Dale's Diner.

A bell chimed as Anastasia and Chloe entered the diner, and immediately, she noted that everything was exactly how she'd remembered. With wood furnishings, forest green walls and numerous photographs of nature scenes and animals, it was still charmingly rustic and very inviting.

"Our old table is empty," Chloe pointed out, while leading Anastasia through the busy diner. "Let's get it before someone else does."

As Anastasia sat down, nostalgia settled in. The waitress who took their order wore the familiar black and green uniform, and Dale was still running around, trying to complete a dozen tasks at once. It was like no time had passed at all.

Anastasia was about to comment on this when she overheard part of a strange conversation between two men who sat a few tables away. She instantly recognized them as Leo and Mike — brothers who ran their own handyman business in town. They also happened to be friends with her grandfather.

"At first I thought people were making a big deal out of nothing," Leo spoke loudly. "I mean, pets go missing all the time and a couple of dead deer isn't anything to worry about.

But then I saw it with my own eyes – a large buck brutally savaged by goodness knows what. Something's not right in these woods, and I'm going to find out what's going on."

"I bet the police already know what it is," Mike said angrily, in between bites of his hash brown. "They're always sneaking around and hiding things – all on *our* tax dollars. It's a conspiracy, I'm telling you."

Although Anastasia rolled her eyes at Mike's paranoia, she couldn't help but feel a little concerned by Leo's words, especially after what she and Frost had encountered in the woods. "Should I be worried?" she asked Chloe with a slightly forced laugh, knowing that her friend had heard the conversation, too.

Chloe shrugged, as if she was indifferent. "Lately, there's been a lot of talk about some wild animal, but since I never go into the woods, I'm not worried. Besides, the adults here are always gossiping about something. I really don't give it much attention anymore."

Before Anastasia could say anything else on the matter, the waitress brought them their food. Although she knew that she should tell Chloe about what had happened yesterday after school, she was too embarrassed to admit that she'd gotten lost. She also didn't want to divulge the subsequent events which included her grandfather's reaction to finding her with Frost.

"Thanks," Anastasia and Chloe said simultaneously to the waitress, before reaching for their cutlery and starting to eat.

"Don't tell Kate what I'm having for breakfast," Chloe said, stabbing a large sausage with her fork. "She so wouldn't approve."

"Who cares?" Anastasia replied with a snort. "Last time I checked, you were your own person."

Chloe sighed. "I know you and Kate didn't exactly hit it

off, but being her friend is worth the effort. You get invited to the coolest parties, and being around her makes you feel special."

"I get it," Anastasia said as she poured maple syrup over her blueberry pancakes. "Seriously, I do." She didn't bother to voice her observation that Chloe only appeared interested in what Kate could do for her.

"Then you'll come to Kate's sleepover on Saturday night?" Chloe asked with a smile. "It would be the perfect opportunity for you to get to know her better. Marissa will be there, too."

"I guess I can make it," Anastasia said hesitantly. She didn't want to spend any more time with Kate, but Chloe was trying so hard to be helpful that saying no to her seemed impossible.

Excitedly, Chloe talked about all the fun they would have – not only at Kate's sleepover but for the rest of the school year as well. Although Anastasia tried to pay attention, it was difficult to think about anything else other than the fact that Frost had just walked into Dale's Diner. Was it possible that he was getting hotter each time she saw him?

As if Frost could sense that someone was watching him, he turned sideways and looked at Anastasia, smiling but appearing hesitant to approach her. She gave him a reassuring nod, causing him to step forward. Unfortunately, he must have been too busy staring at her to notice that he'd stepped right in front of a waitress.

The waitress, who was in a hurry to serve customers, didn't have enough time to stop. As she collided into Frost, the tray of food she was carrying crashed to the floor. Silence filled the diner as everyone stopped what they were doing to stare at Frost, the waitress and especially the broken dishes and splattered food which now littered the previously spotless diner.

Anastasia felt her face redden for Frost as he hurried to help the waitress. Hoping to lend a hand as well, she stood up, only to be stopped by Chloe.

"Don't get involved," she advised. "He's trouble."

Seeing that the staff was now taking care of the mess, Anastasia sat back down. She watched as Frost apologized profusely and offered to pay for the food and dishes. After Dale generously told him to forget it ever happened, Frost hurried to leave. Anastasia wanted to follow him, but she thought doing so may further embarrass him.

"Well, that was awkward," Chloe muttered.

"You said he was trouble," Anastasia spoke quickly. "Why?"

"You first," Chloe bargained, while looking very serious. "Why were you so eager to help him?"

"Because he helped me," Anastasia said softly, hoping that Chloe wouldn't make any further inquiries.

Chloe was obviously taken aback. "Didn't you hear what Kate said about Frost yesterday? He's a complete outcast." She shivered slightly before continuing. "Frost was found deep in the woods as a baby. It was the middle of winter, and when Mr. Stone came upon him, Frost was almost frozen to death. That's how he got his name."

"That isn't funny," Anastasia said, not believing the story.

"I'm not joking. There was this big investigation, but the police couldn't find Frost's biological parents. After that, Mr. and Mrs. Stone adopted him."

"If this *is* true," Anastasia began, still very skeptical, "why didn't I know Mr. Stone had a wife and son?"

"They didn't come into town much — how strange is that? I even heard that Frost was homeschooled before attending Cedar Falls High, probably because his parents were afraid he'd be bullied."

"Poor Frost," Anastasia muttered, while trying to process all the information she'd just received.

"Frost's origins make him a freak," Chloe said softly, as if she truly believed in what she was saying. "Imagine how crazy his real parents must've been to abandon their baby in the woods. Compared to them, even Mr. Stone looks normal." Chloe reached across the table to gently squeeze Anastasia's hand. "You can't hang out with Frost. It'll only make you an outcast, too."

Anastasia felt anger swelling inside of her. How dare Chloe say these things about Frost and then try to dictate her life. It was petty, cruel and, unfortunately, true. If Anastasia was to fit in, she couldn't associate with Frost. Trying desperately to ignore the fact that she was a complete hypocrite, she cast Chloe a fake smile. "So, what time should I be at Kate's house on Saturday night?"

"I'll pick you up around six," Chloe answered, before signaling the waitress and asking for their check. She then quickly retrieved her expensive-looking wallet. "Breakfast is on me," she said firmly.

"Thanks," Anastasia responded with a sincere smile, remembering how Chloe had always been generous. She was a good friend and, despite their vast differences, one that Anastasia wanted to keep.

Fifteen minutes later, Anastasia and Chloe entered the halls of Cedar Falls High. At first, everything appeared to be normal, but Anastasia soon got the feeling that she was being watched. All around her, students whispered. However, when she looked at them, they stopped talking and turned away. Although she couldn't hear what they were saying, she knew that it was about her.

"I know you're the new girl, but this is ridiculous," Chloe said, obviously sensing the strange atmosphere. "What's going on?"

"I have no clue," Anastasia responded, feeling more self-conscious than ever.

"Let me walk you to class," Chloe offered, with a concerned expression on her face. "I'm going that way, too."

Anastasia nodded gratefully. "Let me grab my chemistry textbook first," she said, before turning a corner and almost bumping into a small group of students who were gathered around her locker. "Excuse me," she muttered in annoyance.

With Chloe by her side, Anastasia stopped in front of her locker. That's when she noticed the dark blue rose which was carefully placed through the loop of her combination lock. Tied to the rose with a thin black ribbon was a handwritten note which read, *Welcome to Cedar Falls.*

"It's *so* wrong," a girl spoke loudly, while glaring at Anastasia.

"Can I help you with something?" Anastasia snapped as she stepped toward her.

The girl cast Anastasia another unfriendly glance before walking away. The other students began to leave, too, whispering as they went.

"Is this the reason people are staring at me?" Anastasia asked in an exasperated tone, more to herself than Chloe. "It's just a rose!"

"I doubt that's the only reason," Chloe stated as she took the rose and examined the note. "I don't recognize the handwriting. Who do you think it's from?"

"I don't know," Anastasia answered quickly, even though she suspected and hoped it was from Frost. Knowing that Chloe wouldn't be too happy about that prospect, she kept her thoughts private.

"Well, I have a guess, and it would explain this negative attention you're getting." Chloe looked closely at Anastasia and then asked slowly, "You're not dating Frost, are you?"

"Seriously, Chloe? I only met him yesterday."

"Then let people know it's not true before the rumors get any worse." Chloe handed the rose back to Anastasia. "Whoever did give this to you is thoughtful – he removed the thorns."

Admiring the rose, Anastasia noted its beauty and how special it was because of its scarcity. If the rose really was from Frost, she couldn't help but think how perfectly it epitomized him.

"Coming?" Chloe asked as she began to leave.

Quickly, Anastasia retrieved her textbook and then gently placed the rose in her locker. She'd never received a flower from a boy before, and she wouldn't allow anyone to ruin the moment. Smiling slightly, she hurried along the hall with Chloe and then said goodbye as they reached their separate classrooms.

As expected, chemistry class was boring and lonely. She was forced to sit with Jack and Jill again, but at least neither of them spoke a single word to her. They were far too busy playfully touching each other and doing anything besides their school work. Jack and Jill weren't the only students who were distracted, though. Hearing her name whispered around the classroom made it difficult for Anastasia to concentrate on the formulas that Ms. Stevenson wrote on the whiteboard. She was about to raise her hand and ask for extra help when her cell phone vibrated, alerting her of an incoming text message.

I was wrong about the rumors, the message from Chloe read. *They're about Mr. O'Donoghue. Everyone thinks you're hooking up with him.*

Feeling sick and overcome with confusion, Anastasia stared at the message for several moments, praying that it would somehow change to read anything other than what it did. Who would start such a rumor and why? It had absolutely no foundation, but sadly, Anastasia knew that the most vicious rumors usually had no accuracy.

A new text message from Chloe caused Anastasia's cell phone to vibrate again. *This is harsh, but I thought you should know what's being said. I'm so sorry this is happening to you.* There was a link below the message which directed Anastasia to a very active social media page. To her sheer horror, there were hundreds of posts about her and Mr. O'Donoghue. Someone had even created a poll which asked voters if they thought Mr. O'Donoghue would end up in jail. As Anastasia continued to scroll through the page, she felt like crying. It seemed like everyone had an opinion on the disconcerting topic, but the consensus was the same: Mr. O'Donoghue was a pervert, and Anastasia was a slut.

Anastasia was about to shut her cell phone off when she saw the post, from an anonymous user, that had started it all. *Seems like that new girl, Anastasia, and Mr. O'Donoghue have really hit it off. He was totally flirting with her during class, and she stayed with him afterwards – behind closed doors, of course! Here's a tip for Anastasia and Mr. O'Donoghue: what you're doing is illegal!*

"Will Anastasia Lockhart please report to the principal's office?" a voice suddenly came from over the P.A. system.

Several students turned around in their seats to stare at Anastasia, causing her face to flush with embarrassment. She couldn't believe this was happening, especially since it was only her second day at Cedar Falls High. It was like some twisted form of karma kept her from leading a normal life.

"The principal's waiting for you, Anastasia," Ms. Stevenson warned in a stern tone.

"In case you don't know, his office is located beside the front doors," Jill told Anastasia with a very smug smile.

Feeling heavy-footed and almost numb, Anastasia slowly rose and walked out of the classroom. As she made her way down the empty hallway, dread overcame her. She knew that this had to be about Mr. O'Donoghue. What else could it possibly be? Anastasia reminded herself that she hadn't done anything wrong, but unfortunately, that thought did nothing to ease her nerves. This was going to be bad.

Like an ominous sign, a door marked *Principal's Office* in large black lettering came into view. Anastasia took a deep breath and then knocked upon the door. Seconds later, it opened to reveal a tall, heavy-set man with thick black hair and glasses which were several sizes too big.

"Come in, Anastasia," he said, before stepping aside and opening the door wider.

The office was inviting, spacious and accentuated by a variety of thriving potted plants; however, Anastasia couldn't help but feel on edge. She took the chair the principal offered to her and then squirmed anxiously. Anastasia wanted to get whatever this was over with as quickly as possible.

"I'm Principal Keith," he said, while sitting down behind his large desk that was cluttered with stacks of paper.

Anastasia merely offered a small smile in response.

"You're not in trouble," Principal Keith reassured her in a tone which was gentler than expected for a man with such an imposing physical appearance.

"Why did you want to see me?" Anastasia asked, trying to keep her voice steady and her expression one of naivety.

"It's come to my attention that unprofessional behavior may be occurring between a student and faculty member. Do you know anything about this matter?"

Remaining silent, Anastasia thought about how she should

respond. If she claimed to be ignorant of the matter, it might look like she had something to hide. On the other hand, if she confessed to knowing about the rumor, that would also appear suspicious.

"Anastasia?" Principal Keith interrupted her thoughts.

"I..." Anastasia replied, unable to say anything else.

"You can be honest with me," Principal Keith reassured her for a second time. "My job is to ensure a safe and healthy environment for all students. I'm here to help you, Anastasia."

The old Anastasia would have played dumb just to avoid any trouble which could potentially befall her. However, she now wanted to be a stronger and better person. After all, the innocent Mr. O'Donoghue was the one with the most to lose, and that wasn't fair. "I've heard the rumors," she finally admitted, "and they are absolutely *not* true."

"Why would people lie about something so serious?" Principal Keith inquired, suddenly sounding as if he was interrogating Anastasia instead of helping her.

"I have no idea how or why the rumors about me and Mr. O'Donoghue were started," Anastasia said hastily, with growing frustration. She cringed after speaking, realizing that she had said too much.

"Has Mr. O'Donoghue ever displayed any behavior which made you feel uncomfortable?"

"No!" Anastasia cried. "Didn't you hear me the first time? It's not true – none of it!"

"Calm down," Principal Keith advised. "These questions are routine for this type of investigation."

"Investigation of what? Nothing happened!" Anastasia assumed the impromptu meeting with the principal would be the peak of this nightmare, but with an actual investigation, the rumor would only become more public and humiliating.

For once in her life, couldn't telling the truth make things simpler?

"Serious allegations have been brought forth by both staff and students. While your account of the events is important, I must take into consideration other factors. I have no other choice but to file a report with the school board."

"So, basically you don't believe me," Anastasia seethed, before running out of the office.

The first class of the day had just ended, and the hallways were now filled with students who were hurrying to get to their next class. Anastasia was also in a hurry, but she was heading toward the nearest exit. She flung the front doors open and then leaned against the cold brick, finally allowing the tears to flow down her face.

Anastasia needed to talk to someone, and not knowing who else to call, she retrieved her cell phone and dialed. "Grandma?" she choked out, after the person on the other end had answered. "I need you."

It felt like an eternity, but Anastasia's grandmother arrived at Cedar Falls High in less than half an hour. As soon as she pulled into the parking lot, Anastasia ran toward her car and then jumped inside. She had waited outside the whole time, and without her coat, she was freezing. However, that seemed like a much better fate than re-entering the school and facing the students and staff who thought she was capable of having such an inappropriate relationship.

"Please, take me home," Anastasia immediately begged her grandmother, who looked at her with great concern.

Without asking a single question, she drove home. However, when they arrived in their driveway, Anastasia burst into uncontrollable tears. Her grandmother hugged her and didn't let go until several minutes had passed. She then retrieved a small package of tissues from her purse and wiped away Anastasia's tears.

"I don't know what I've done to deserve this," Anastasia sobbed, calming down only slightly. "There's a horrible rumor and it's so not true. I..." Her voice cracked as she began to cry again.

"Shhh...take your time," Mrs. Lockhart said soothingly.

Taking a deep breath and forcing the tears to stop, Anastasia continued. "Before I tell you what the rumor is, you have to promise that you'll believe me when I say it's a lie."

"I believe you," she replied without hesitating.

"People are saying I'm dating my English teacher." As Anastasia said the words out loud, she realized how ridiculous they sounded.

Mrs. Lockhart didn't look the least bit shocked. "I've heard crazier rumors," she admitted. "Small towns have many great attributes, but ironically, privacy isn't always one of them. People talk, and sometimes what they say isn't nice or true." She paused for a moment. "Don't ever allow anyone to define who you are – make that decision for yourself."

"I know you're right, but how can I possibly go back to school? I can't face my English teacher. What if he thinks *I* started the rumor?"

"If you stand your ground, the truth will come out, but if you run away..." Her voice trailed off as she smoothed Anastasia's hair and smiled. "I know you can overcome this."

"Why are you being so nice to me?" The words tumbled out of Anastasia's mouth before she knew what she was saying.

This time, Mrs. Lockhart did look shocked. "My dear, how can you ask such a thing? You know I love you."

Conflicted, Anastasia said nothing.

"Oh, Anastasia," she said, while wrapping her in a hug again. "I've been giving you space because I thought that would help you adjust. I hope you weren't thinking I didn't care."

"It's my fault," Anastasia replied quickly. "I'm sorry if you thought I wanted space because I don't. I love you, Grandma."

"Let's go inside. I'll put the kettle on and..."

"No," Anastasia interrupted firmly. "You should go back to work. I'll be fine. I just need a little time to recuperate if I'm going to return to school tomorrow."

Mrs. Lockhart smiled at Anastasia. "You truly are a strong girl," she said proudly, before kissing her forehead.

Alone in her house, Anastasia stood in the bathroom, washing her tears away. She dried her face on a soft towel and then looked into the mirror. Despite the horrible morning Anastasia had experienced, she smiled slightly at her reflection, feeling a glimmer of hope for better things to come. Her relationship with her grandmother was on the right track and heading toward a stronger bond than ever. All it took was for Anastasia to be honest instead of trying to hide behind some tough façade. It was a huge step, but she knew that the hardest challenges were still ahead of her.

When Anastasia exited the bathroom, she heard a knock upon the front door. Uncertain of who could be there, she hurried down the stairs and then looked through the peephole. She was surprised to find Frost standing on her porch and what appeared to be his dark blue SUV parked on the road. Seeing that he was about to leave, Anastasia quickly opened the door.

"Please don't leave." Anastasia hadn't meant to say those words, especially in such a needy tone, but they had just come out like some unstoppable force.

Frost turned around and smiled. "I hope you don't mind me dropping by, but I saw your grandmother taking you home." He blushed slightly. "I wanted to make sure you were alright."

"I'll live," Anastasia promised.

In silence, Anastasia and Frost looked at each other. She noted how everything about him seemed unique, and it all stemmed from those light blue eyes which gazed so kindly upon her. No one had ever looked at her like that before.

"I also came to apologize," Frost said, now looking at the ground as if he was deeply ashamed. "I was the one who gave you the rose."

"What you did was nice – thank you," Anastasia replied, trying to act normal even though she was delighted to confirm her suspicion of who had given her the rose.

"I was going to tell you this in a note and put it in your locker," Frost explained awkwardly, "but I realized that would only cause more trouble."

"Never," Anastasia said with a small smile. "You can put notes in my locker anytime." Trusting her instincts, she opened the door wider. "Do you want to come in?"

Frost looked conflicted. "I'd love to, but I know your grandfather doesn't like me."

"His feud with your father isn't our problem." To ease the slight tension, Anastasia added in a teasing manner, "You better come in or the cougar might get you."

"I'm not afraid of the cougar," Frost said quickly.

"Admitting you're scared doesn't emasculate you – it makes you human."

"Okay, I was scared, but only because the cougar was there and so were you."

This time, it was Anastasia's turn to blush. "I guess I'll

have to join you outside then," she said, while grabbing one of her grandmother's coats which hung nearby and then closing the door behind her.

They began walking along Evergreen Road, admiring the scenery. Although the day had started with a gray sky, the clouds now rolled by, allowing the sun to appear every so often. Cedar Falls truly was a beautiful place, and as Anastasia took a deep breath of the fresh, chilly air, she temporarily forgot that danger lurked in the woods.

"I love it here," Frost stated. "I wouldn't want to live anywhere else."

"It has some good things to offer," Anastasia said, casting Frost an interested side glance.

Pleased, Frost smirked. "I hear Toronto has a lot to offer, too. Why did you come to Cedar Falls?"

"You really don't know? I assumed my sordid trysts with Mr. O'Donoghue weren't the only rumor now circulating about me. Give them a little scandal, and people like to keep on digging."

"I don't trust gossip," Frost said gently, as if to ease Anastasia's growing agitation. "That's why I'm asking you."

"Sorry," Anastasia said through a sigh. "To be honest, it was my mother's decision to send me here."

"Tell her I say thank you."

Blushing yet again, Anastasia turned her face away. "So, you never told me the real meaning of your name," she said casually, hoping that he would open up to her. She cringed afterwards, realizing that she may have sounded insensitive.

"Unfortunately, those rumors *are* true," Frost answered, his expression suddenly changing to one of anger.

"I can't imagine," Anastasia said sympathetically.

"Well, I can. I have these memories of lying in the woods, cold, crying and filled with fear and confusion."

"That...that's impossible," Anastasia interjected in shock. "You were just a baby."

"Then explain how I remember it." When Anastasia couldn't offer a response, he continued. "The Stones have given me so much, and I'm extremely grateful for them, but a part of me still wants to find my biological parents."

"It's natural to want to know where you came from," Anastasia said gently.

"No," Frost sneered, his jaw clenching with an anger he was obviously trying to control. "When I find them, I'm going to look straight into their eyes and say exactly how I feel. I hate them, and they should damn well know it."

With wide eyes, Anastasia stood back and looked at Frost. He'd turned into a spiteful, vengeful person, and although he had every right to be mad, it just made him ugly. Anastasia didn't like what she saw, especially since it differed so vastly from his usual demeanor.

"I need to get back to school," Frost said abruptly, while heading in the direction they had come.

"Of course," Anastasia said softly, sad that he had to leave. The truth was she liked being around Frost, even when he acted a little bipolar.

After walking Anastasia back to her house, Frost faced her and said apologetically, "I shouldn't have unloaded that on you."

Gently, Anastasia touched Frost's arm while looking into his eyes. "I'm glad you feel like you can talk to me," she whispered as she leaned her body closer to him.

Frost smiled at Anastasia and then wrapped her in his arms. Although she'd hoped for a kiss, she settled into his arms, feeling warm and safe. She let out a content sigh, noting how he had a unique scent to him; almost like a mixture of the woods and rich spices. Finally, Frost released his grasp on

Anastasia, causing a wave of sadness to come over her.

"I'll see you soon," Frost promised, before heading back to his SUV.

From her porch, Anastasia gave Frost a small wave and then watched as he disappeared down the road. As she stood there, her mind circulated with thoughts. Anastasia had seen how Frost's anger affected him; it mirrored her own behavior, especially toward her mother. Suddenly, she realized that unlike Frost's parents, her mother had never truly abandoned her. It may have felt that way upon learning she would be going to Cedar Falls alone, but perhaps her mother only made that decision to help Anastasia. In hindsight, she could see that she'd done nothing to make the situation any easier for her mother or even herself.

Swallowing her pride, Anastasia retrieved her cell phone and began to compose a text message. Although she wasn't ready to disclose everything that had happened in the last forty-eight hours, she believed that her mother deserved more than just one word replies.

Mom, I know we haven't talked much since I arrived in Cedar Falls, but I'm still getting used to being here. Grandma and Grandpa are doing fine. Grandma's been asking about you. How's everything in Toronto?

Anastasia re-read the message, noting how it was bland and almost formal. However, it was civil and showed that she'd made an effort – that had to count for something. Taking a deep breath, she sent the message, and within a minute, she received a response. Although her mother's message was also unexciting and mostly filled with details about her workday, at least they were talking, and that's something Anastasia hadn't been able to say for the longest time.

❄ ❄ ❄

Part Four

The Sweetest Temptation

With her head held high, Anastasia ignored the stares and whispers as she walked down the hallway of Cedar Falls High the next day. In her mind, she kept repeating her grandmother's words – the truth will come out – and that gave her strength. Also a great comfort was Chloe, who had driven her to school and was still by her side, acting as if it was no big deal to be associating with her. Just like when they were young, Chloe was once again proving herself to be a loyal, trustworthy person, and Anastasia couldn't be happier about having her as a friend.

"How are you holding up?" Chloe asked Anastasia quietly, obviously not wanting to embarrass her.

"Ask me again after English," Anastasia replied through a sigh, cursing the fact that it was her first class of the day.

Chloe cast Anastasia a sympathetic look. "Think of it this way – seeing Mr. O'Donoghue now means you don't have to worry about it all day."

"I know you're right. Thanks for being so..."

Before Anastasia could finish her sentence, a tall, skinny and somewhat nerdy-looking boy slung his arm around her shoulder and whispered loudly into her ear, "I hear you're always ready for a good time – does that apply to students, too, or are you only interested in teachers?"

Anastasia was so taken aback by the boy's sudden

appearance and derogative words that she just stared at him with wide eyes. Luckily, Chloe was quick to react.

"I'm surprised *you* of all people listen to rumors, Sean. I remember some pretty nasty ones about you. Something about paying your cousin to go with you to last year's school dance. And what about the one of you spying on girls in the change room?" Chloe stepped closer to Sean, whose face was now bright red. "The difference between you and Anastasia is that the rumors about her *aren't* true."

"I...I was only joking with her," Sean stuttered, causing the gawking bystanders to laugh at him.

"You're so not funny," Chloe said, shaking her head in disgust.

Finally finding her voice, Anastasia angrily pushed Sean away from her and hissed, "Go to hell."

"Sean's a total wannabe," Chloe told Anastasia as they continued down the hallway at a slightly quicker pace. "Don't pay any attention to him."

"It's not just him, though," Anastasia said, coming to a stop a few feet from her English classroom. "It's what *everyone* is thinking."

"Not the important people," Chloe promised. "Listen, I have to get to class. I know you have the literacy group at lunch, so I guess I won't see you until after school – or maybe at the assembly during last period. Either way, text me any time if you need to talk, okay?"

"Thank you," Anastasia said, before giving Chloe a quick hug and then watching her walk away.

With a deep breath, Anastasia entered the classroom and took her usual seat. The stares and whispers were even worse in the class, and when Mr. O'Donoghue arrived, she had to muster all her confidence to look him in the eye. She was positive that he'd heard the rumors, and more than likely, he'd already been questioned about it by the principal.

"Good morning," Mr. O'Donoghue greeted them like it was an ordinary day. "I'd like to begin this class with a discussion rather than a lecture." Retrieving a piece of chalk, he wrote in big letters, *Lies and deceit*. As if his statement wasn't bold enough, he underlined his words, causing the chalk to scrape noisily over the blackboard.

Why is he doing this? Anastasia thought, resisting the urge to slide down in her seat. She highly doubted this was the lesson he'd originally prepared for today's class.

"Lies and deceit," Mr. O'Donoghue said, pausing briefly before continuing, "is one of the many themes Milton uses in Paradise Lost. Yet, I would argue it is the most important because of its effects on the characters and plot. Do you agree with me, and if not, why?"

As usual, no one raised their hand, and although Anastasia had several thoughts to share, she didn't feel comfortable speaking up. She knew that it was much easier to merely fade into the crowd of silent students.

"You all must agree with me then — terrific!" Mr. O'Donoghue said in a good-natured tone, even though Anastasia suspected that it was somewhat forced. "Satan perfectly epitomizes this theme because he is constantly deceiving others, especially by the use of disguises. He's also the one who tells the most lies. However, it's not until Satan combines these two elements that he causes the most damage. Can anyone give me an example?"

This time, a girl raised her hand. "When Satan disguises himself as a snake and lies to Eve so she'll eat the forbidden fruit."

"Excellent answer," Mr. O'Donoghue praised the girl. "What this teaches us is that anonymity and lies are a dangerous combination, and this lesson is as prevalent today as it is in Milton's epic. Examples, anyone?"

Knowing exactly what Mr. O'Donoghue was trying to prove and gaining strength from his courage to take a stand, Anastasia raised her hand, finally ready to speak her mind. "The Internet is a prime example of a disguise. Anyone can hide behind their computer or phone, using it as a means for spreading lies that have absolutely no foundation. What they don't realize is that their vicious deceit has consequences, and while they may be anonymous for now, the truth *will* be revealed."

The class became deadly silent, and this time, it was a smile that Anastasia had to hide.

"That's exactly what I was thinking," Mr. O'Donoghue commented, casting Anastasia a reassuring smile. Turning to the rest of the class, he continued, "Although Satan is clearly at fault for being the originator of the lie, the other characters are also responsible when they decide to believe him. Like Eve, we all have the choice whether or not to believe what we're being told, so remember to always choose wisely." He paused and then added with a smirk, "I guess this was a lecture after all."

By the time English class had come to an end, Anastasia was in better spirits, making it easier for her to handle the next couple of classes and even the literacy group meeting. Still, she was glad when it was time for the assembly because it meant that she might see Chloe, and a friendly face was always welcome, especially in an environment like this. Anastasia also thought about the possibility of running into Frost and that made her heart flutter. If only she hadn't promised Chloe that she'd stay away from him – it had been such a childish thing to do and obviously something that she wouldn't be able to uphold.

Wanting to put her books away so she wouldn't have to carry them to the assembly, Anastasia headed toward her locker. After reaching it, she opened the door and found a folded note which fell onto the floor. Picking it up, she immediately recognized the handwriting as belonging to Frost.

Anastasia,

I'm still thinking about the conversation we had yesterday. I've never been able to open up so easily to anyone before, and it's the first time I felt like I could be honest without fear of being judged. I hope I can return this favor to you since being the new girl in town — especially in a place like Cedar Falls — must be hard. I'm not a fool, and I know the things people say about me, but I have a feeling you've already looked past that. If I'm right, meet me in the woods behind the school while everyone is at the assembly. I'll be waiting.

Frost

A shiver of excitement ran throughout Anastasia's body. She knew that it wasn't a good idea to miss the assembly or venture into the woods, but she didn't care. Waiting until the hallway was empty, she grabbed her coat and then hurried through the back door.

The early afternoon sun was high in the sky, shining brightly and making the snow-covered trees and ground sparkle as if it was a winter wonderland. Amongst the beautiful scenery, Anastasia noted a pair of footprints leading deep into the woods. She followed them and soon came upon Frost, whose back was turned to her as he stared into the distance.

As if sensing her presence, he turned around, smiled and

said, "You came."

"There was no need for you to doubt that," Anastasia replied, smiling back at him. "So, what are we doing out here?"

"Why tell when I can show?" Frost said, guiding her forward.

After a few minutes of walking, they came to a bend in the woods. Anastasia heard ducks quacking nearby, and when they turned around the corner, she saw a small frozen pond filled with colorful mallards. When the ducks saw them, they began to quack louder.

Frost led Anastasia to a flat rock that made the perfect seat for two. Since the sun was shining upon it, he only had to sweep away a light dusting of snow before gesturing for her to sit down. As they both did so, the ducks waddled excitedly toward them.

"They're so pretty," Anastasia commented, especially noting the brilliant hues of green on some of their feathers, "but why do they stay? It's not like there's anything here for them."

"That's where you're wrong," Frost said, retrieving a small bag from his coat pocket. "They fly here almost every day, knowing they'll be fed. That sounds like a sweet deal to me." He opened the bag, offering the contents to her.

Anastasia took a handful of the bread crumb, peanut and bird seed mix, and then gently tossed it toward the eager ducks. She'd been starting to wonder what that bulge in Frost's pocket was, and she would've never guessed it was duck feed. She almost snickered at the thought.

"I've never skipped school to do something like this," Anastasia said, taking more of the mix and sprinkling it a couple of feet in front of her. "Now I truly know what a badass you are."

"I promise you're not missing anything important. They have these assemblies every month, and it's basically an excuse for the principal and teachers to tell each other what a wonderful job they're doing – in front of an audience, of course."

"Of course. Otherwise, what's the point?"

Frost smirked before quickly turning serious. "Sometimes I can't stand being in school. People think they know you, but they don't."

Soothingly, Anastasia placed her hand on Frost's knee. "You never have to pretend around me. I understand what you're going through at school, probably better than anyone else."

"I have secrets, Anastasia."

"We all do. So, why don't you start by telling me one of yours?"

Appearing hesitant, Frost looked at the ground, as if he was contemplating something very serious. However, when he lifted his head a moment later, his disposition had changed and he now wore a smile, although Anastasia sensed that it wasn't completely sincere.

"Well, it's not exactly scandalous," Frost began slowly, "but one of my biggest passions is music. I've been playing the guitar since I was ten, and I even write my own lyrics – not that they're any good."

"I'd love to hear them," Anastasia pried gently.

"I have been working on something new." Looking somewhat shy but still keeping his gaze on Anastasia, Frost began to sing in a low, husky voice:

As if by chance
It only took one glance
Girl with green eyes, let's not say our goodbyes

I know life's rough
But I feel you're tough
Wish you could see, how good you look to me
Then all your tears
And even all those fears
Will disappear, forever far from here

Silence fell over the woods once Frost had finished singing, and his cheeks flushed a pale shade of red. "I know it's not perfect, and I swear I play the guitar better than I write."

"It's beautiful," Anastasia whispered, deeply touched by the sentiment of Frost's lyrics.

"The inspiration just sort of hit me," Frost whispered back.

Swept up in the moment, Anastasia's pulse quickened, and ever so slowly, she leaned in closer.

"The assembly will be over soon," Frost pointed out, standing up abruptly. In one swift move, he poured the rest of the mix onto the pond for the ducks.

"Um, yeah," Anastasia replied, feeling a little rejected and confused.

As they began to walk back to the school, Anastasia thought about the mixed signals Frost was giving her. He was interested in her – the song certainly proved that much – but there seemed to be something holding him back. Not wanting to consider the hurtful possibility that she liked him more than he liked her, she concluded that he didn't have much experience with girls or was even just shy.

"I really like spending time with you," Frost said, as if he could sense her worries, "and I think you won the ducks over, too."

"Then we'll have to do it again," Anastasia said.

"Definitely."

When they reached the school, Frost opened the door, allowing Anastasia to enter first. As soon as she walked into the building, she collided with another student who'd been on her way to exit. Although they'd hit into each other hard, Anastasia was more concerned about who was standing in front of her rather than her pain.

"Chloe," Anastasia gasped. "What are you doing here?"

Chloe was silent as she looked at Anastasia and Frost, her expression of surprise very much apparent. "I was starting to worry about you," she answered, regaining her composure. "I hadn't heard from you since the morning, and when I couldn't find you at the assembly, I thought maybe you'd gone outside to get away from everyone."

"That's so sweet, but I'm fine."

"I can see that," Chloe muttered, her eyes averting to Frost for a second. "Anyway, are you ready to go home?"

"Yeah," Anastasia replied, before casting Frost a small smile as if to say goodbye.

As Anastasia and Chloe walked away, the hallway began to fill with noisy students, who were eager to leave school for the day. However, a silence hung over the two girls, neither of them willing to discuss what had just happened. But even without words, Chloe's feelings were crystal clear — she wholeheartedly disapproved of Anastasia's new relationship.

❋ ❋ ❋

It was six o'clock on Friday night as Anastasia and Chloe drove to Kate's house. They were going to her sleepover, and Anastasia wasn't dreading it as much as she would've thought. In fact, she was looking forward to spending time with Marissa. Although Anastasia had only seen Marissa once in the last three days, she'd been very kind and told her not to worry about the rumors because they would soon pass. As for Kate, Anastasia hadn't seen her at all, and she was fine with that. She'd pretend to like her for Chloe's sake, but that would be the extent of Anastasia's relationship with Kate. She just didn't want or need any more fake friends.

"Kate's house isn't much further," Chloe said, coming to a stop at the street sign and then making a left turn.

"Do you guys hang out there a lot?" Anastasia asked, wondering just how close Chloe and Marissa were to Kate.

"Whenever we have the chance," Chloe admitted. "I'm always hounding Kate to have more parties. You'll understand why when we get there."

As they neared Kate's house, the roads began to look familiar. It didn't take Anastasia long to realize that these were the roads where she'd become lost. That meant Kate's house was close to Frost's. However, it was hard to believe that any other family lived nearby as Kate's brightly-lit multi-million dollar house came into view. Their immaculately kept property was likely several acres and there wasn't a single neighbor in sight. Anastasia's suspicion that Kate came from Cedar Falls' wealthiest family was instantly confirmed.

"You can close your mouth now," Chloe joked as she stopped her car on the flagstone driveway that was free of snow, probably due to the labor of a groundskeeper. "It's a nice place, huh? Just wait until you see inside."

Anastasia tried to suppress her jealousy as they walked toward Kate's decorative glass front door. She wasn't usually obsessed with material items, but it was hard to see someone she didn't particularly like have so much, especially when her financial situation had never been good.

Exactly three seconds after ringing the whimsical-sounding bell, Kate opened the door. "Welcome to my house," she greeted with an air of superiority. "Come in."

Unsurprisingly, the interior of the house was as grand as the exterior, but Anastasia pretended not to notice. "Thanks for inviting me," she said diplomatically.

"It was her idea," Kate commented, while wrapping her arms around Chloe's shoulders and giving her a gentle squeeze. "Isn't she the sweetest?"

"Totally," Anastasia replied sarcastically, analyzing how Kate appeared almost desperate to be in control. It was like she viewed Anastasia as a threat, but that couldn't possibly be true. The only person Anastasia had ever been a threat to was herself.

"Is Marissa here?" Chloe asked as she awkwardly broke from Kate's embrace.

"She's picking up the pizza," Kate answered with a roll of her eyes. "I told her delivery is the only way to order fast food, but she wouldn't listen. She has a crush on one of the pizza boys, though, so I guess she's hoping he'll ask her out. It's kind of pathetic, huh?" Quickly, Kate turned to Anastasia. "So, have *you* had any luck with the Cedar Falls hotties?"

"Not at all," Anastasia lied. The truth was she hadn't been able to stop thinking about Frost. Every day he would leave sweet notes in her locker to express his growing affection for her. This had given Anastasia something to look forward to, making school a much more pleasant experience.

"Odd," Kate muttered in a leading tone of voice. "Anyway, did you guys hear about the fiasco at Dale's Diner a few days ago? Supposedly, Frost totally lost it for no apparent reason and began destroying the place."

"That's not what happened," Anastasia corrected Kate, deeply annoyed that yet another false rumor was being spread. It was a perfect example of how easily a situation could be misconstrued, and she was getting more than a little sick of this reoccurrence.

"How would you know?" Kate pried, her eyes narrowed in suspicion.

"We were getting breakfast there and saw the whole thing," Chloe intervened. "Honestly, it wasn't a big deal."

Kate said nothing else about the matter, but from the way she studied Anastasia, it was obvious that her curiosity had been piqued. She stood a little taller and with her hands on her hips, as if trying to put Anastasia in her place. Instinctively, Anastasia straightened her posture and looked right back at her. It was definitely a passive-aggressive staring contest, even though Anastasia had no idea what had prompted it.

The doorbell rang again, breaking the silence. Reluctantly, Kate shifted from her self-dignified pose to answer the door. On the other side stood Marissa, who had a friendly smile on her face and a large box of pizza in her hands.

"Let's get this party started," Marissa said excitedly as she stepped inside.

Unintentionally, Anastasia raised her eyebrows, hardly considering their small gathering to be a party. If these girls could see some of the parties she'd been to in Toronto, they'd be shocked. Not that she wanted to relive those nights. In fact, Anastasia was more than happy with a quiet, uneventful sleepover.

For the next hour, the girls sat in Kate's luxurious living room, while chatting, eating pizza and enjoying the upbeat music coming from the super expensive sound system. Anastasia was having a great time catching up with Chloe and getting to know Marissa. Chloe had so many funny stories to share, and Marissa's sweet and charming personality made it impossible not to like her. Unfortunately, Kate was being more unfriendly than ever; she'd hardly said anything since

Marissa arrived, but no one seemed to notice far less care. Against her will, Anastasia felt bad for Kate, sensing that she was being used for her money and popularity.

"So, how about a round of *never have I ever*, girls?" Marissa asked with a mischievous smile, interrupting Anastasia's thoughts.

"Never have I ever?" Anastasia repeated, while furrowing her brow.

"Don't make that expression, honey," Kate advised in a condescending manner. "You'll get premature wrinkles." She paused slightly before adding, "Never have I ever is a game. You say you've never done something even though it's a lie."

"I'll go first," Marissa said eagerly. "Never have I ever been asked out by a hot pizza boy!"

"That's great!" Anastasia said, sincerely happy for her new friend. "What's his name?"

"Mitch," Marissa replied with a wide smile. "While I was waiting for the pizza, we started to talk and that's when he asked me to go to a movie tomorrow night."

"Great!" Kate said mockingly. "Now you two can get matching initial accessories!"

"What are you talking about?" Marissa demanded, obviously hurt.

"You can do so much better than some pizza boy."

"You don't even know him!"

"Let's keep it that way," Kate snapped.

Any sympathy Anastasia had felt for Kate instantly disappeared. She was rude, conceited and didn't care about other people's feelings. It was no wonder that even her friends didn't like her – she was such a bitch.

"It's my turn," Kate continued, staring straight at Anastasia. "Never have I ever seen Anastasia and Frost meeting secretly behind the school and acting *very* friendly."

Anastasia's face flushed. How the hell did Kate know about that? One look at Chloe's surprised expression assured her that she'd said nothing about the matter.

"Seriously?" Marissa asked with wide eyes, apparently forgetting how upset she was with Kate. "What's it like to talk to him?"

"You've never talked to Frost, like *ever*?" Anastasia asked in shock, realizing that the segregation in Cedar Falls was worse than she'd initially thought.

"Of course not," Kate replied for Marissa, "but that doesn't mean we're not curious. After all, every town needs a freak, and I'm starting to wonder just how weird Frost really is."

"He may be different but that doesn't make him weird," Anastasia argued, trying to control her anger.

"I'll believe that when I see it," Kate said in her signature leading tone of voice. "Perhaps we should pay Frost a visit and see what he's like when he thinks no one is watching. It's the only way to reveal someone's true nature."

"By spying on him?" Anastasia was horrified by the idea.

"Consider it a field experiment," Kate said nonchalantly as she began to get ready.

"I heard Frost lives deeper in the woods than anyone else in Cedar Falls," Marissa commented with a shiver.

"This doesn't sound like a good idea," Chloe added.

"With my parents out of town, I can't leave you guys alone in my house. So, it looks like you're coming with me, bitches." With that said, Kate grabbed her coat and then sauntered out of her house, causing Chloe, Marissa and Anastasia to hurry after her.

As Kate drove down the deserted road on route to Frost's house, Anastasia began to feel uneasy. She'd only come to keep Chloe and Marissa safe, but what protection could she really offer them? Anastasia was a city girl who knew very little about the way of the woods.

All too soon, Kate pulled over at the side of the road and then instructed in a bossy tone, "Everyone out!"

"Here?" Marissa asked, her eyes wide with fear.

"It's not like I can park in his driveway," Kate snapped, before getting out of the car.

Obediently, Chloe and Marissa exited the car. Not wanting to be alone, Anastasia followed them just in time to see Kate disappear into the woods. She gulped. It was a still, cloudless night, and the full moon shone brightly, casting creepy shadows everywhere. The air was frigid, and the sound of Kate treading quickly over the snow seemed to echo eerily throughout the woods.

"We shouldn't let her go alone," Marissa said, her voice almost shaking.

Anastasia nodded, while quickly deciding that the best way to get out of this situation was by convincing Kate to return home. With Chloe and Marissa by her side, she took a deep breath and then entered the woods. Using the light from the moon, Anastasia navigated in between the trees, following the sound of Kate's footsteps until she found her.

"This is stupid," Anastasia said, after the three of them had caught up to Kate. "Everyone is saying there's a potentially dangerous animal on the loose, and I swear I saw something in the woods." Hesitating, she finally added, "Frost was with me and he claims it was a cougar."

Kate's speed increased, but she seemed to be driven by anger instead of fear. She was like a girl possessed, hell bent on getting to Frost's house as quickly as possible. Confused, Anastasia wondered what was wrong with Kate – and with all of them for following her in the first place.

"Anastasia's right," Chloe said firmly. "This isn't safe."

"There are no dangerous animals in Cedar Falls," Kate retorted. "It's just a myth to keep kids out of the woods."

"Are you sure about that?" Anastasia snapped, gesturing toward a large live-catch trap that was positioned off to the side, less than twenty feet away. It was the smell of the bait — a chunk of raw meat — that had allowed her to make the disconcerting discovery. She could only guess that Mr. Stone had been the one to set the trap.

"We're almost there," Kate remained steadfast, although Anastasia was certain that she heard a quiver in her voice.

Within minutes, the comforting glow of lights appeared nearby, illuminating a medium-sized house. Under Kate's command, they crept closer until they were outside a window at the back of the house. A light flickered in the room, and the curtains were parted ever so slightly, probably making it difficult but not impossible to see inside.

Kate gestured for the three girls to stay back, before leaning closer to the window and peering in. She was silent for several moments, even though something had definitely caught her attention. "Frost is in there," she finally spoke in a hushed tone.

Unable to control her curiosity, Anastasia stepped forward and looked over Kate's shoulder. Her pulse raced as she saw Frost sitting in front of a fireplace, topless and tuning his guitar. The flickering glow from the fire danced over Frost's body, highlighting his muscular build. When he put his guitar down and stood up, both Anastasia and Kate ducked. However, they continued to watch as Frost stretched his upper body before reaching for a notebook that lay upon the mantle. He then sat back down, interchanging between writing in his notebook and strumming on his guitar.

"Damn," Kate muttered, most definitely unintentionally.

"Let me see," Marissa demanded impatiently.

"Shhh..." Chloe warned sternly, despite pushing forward in an attempt to peek in the window.

Knowing how wrong this was, Anastasia backed away. Frost had gone from being talked about because people thought he was a freak, to being spied upon because of his hot, unbelievably toned body. Either way, he was constantly being dehumanized. Anastasia was disgusted by her friends' treatment of him, but she was also ashamed that she'd stooped to their level.

"Wow," Marissa muttered, almost pressing her face against the glass.

"This isn't right," Anastasia began to say. However, she was interrupted by the sound of heavy footsteps fast approaching.

"Hey!" a loud voice suddenly echoed throughout the woods.

Spinning around, Anastasia saw a man hurrying toward them. As he came closer, she felt her heart leap into her throat – it was Mr. Stone. She blushed deeply, mortified that he'd caught them spying on Frost.

"It's okay," Mr. Stone assured Anastasia as he slowed his pace. He was now only a few feet away from her.

"Move," Chloe said desperately, while pulling Anastasia away from Mr. Stone.

Anastasia turned around to see that Kate and Marissa had left the window and were already running deeper into the woods. Not thinking twice, Anastasia and Chloe followed their lead and began to run.

"Come back!" Mr. Stone called after them. "It's dangerous out there!"

Ignoring Mr. Stone's warning, the four girls continued running and didn't stop until their lungs ached and they had stitches in their sides. Several times, Anastasia had called out to Kate, begging her to stop, but she'd just kept on going. Now shivering in the cold, unforgiving night, they were far from their car and likely lost in the middle of nowhere. The prospects did nothing to instill confidence in Anastasia.

"We need help," Chloe said breathlessly, confirming Anastasia's fear.

Quickly, Anastasia retrieved her cell phone and was disappointed, although not surprised, to find that she had no reception. One by one, Kate, Chloe and Marissa discovered that their cell phones also didn't work.

"What are we going to do?" Marissa moaned, almost in tears. "I'm cold and scared and..."

"Shut the hell up," Kate scolded harshly. "I can't think with you whining."

Marissa started to sob and, instinctively, Anastasia hugged her. She'd always hated to see anyone upset or hurt, especially when that person was as nice as Marissa. Kate's abusive attitude was getting out-of-control, and Anastasia was about to speak up when Chloe beat her to it.

"You're not helping the situation," Chloe bravely told Kate, while stepping forward.

"I don't see you doing anything!" Kate retorted.

"It's your fault we're out here!" she shot back.

As the arguing continued, another sound coming from nearby caught Anastasia's attention. She sensed that someone was in the woods, creeping around them as if they didn't want to be seen or heard. Anastasia's heart pounded as a feeling of dread washed over her. When she heard a branch snap, she knew for certain that someone was out there.

Suddenly, a shrill cry ripped through the woods, mere seconds before a cougar pounced on Chloe and tackled her to the ground. It happened so fast that no one had a chance to move. Instead, they watched in horror as the cougar sunk his teeth into Chloe's arm, causing her to cry out in pain. Then he started to drag her away.

Kate and Marissa screamed, while running in the direction they had come. This startled the cougar and made him retreat slightly, giving Anastasia a chance to run to Chloe's side. She was shocked that Kate and Marissa had left, but thankfully the commotion they made while fleeing, along with Chloe's ongoing cries of pain, were enough to make the cougar turn around and disappear into the woods.

"Help me!" Chloe screamed in agony as she lay on the ground, clutching her arm just above where the cougar had bitten.

Desperate to help Chloe but unsure of what to do, Anastasia crouched beside her and touched her shoulder, hoping to provide some sort of comfort. It obviously didn't help. Chloe was shaking, probably from a combination of pain, shock and lying on the freezing ground. Anastasia's eyes traveled to Chloe's arm, her stomach churning as she saw the damage that the cougar had done. The sleeve of her coat had been ripped off, and it looked like she was bleeding heavily, although it was impossible to see the depth of the wound due to the lack of light.

"It's going to be okay," Anastasia promised Chloe. "I'll get you out of here, but first we need to find Kate and Marissa."

"Please stay!" Chloe cried, grabbing onto Anastasia as if to prevent her from leaving. She then whimpered, proving just how painful it was to move.

"I'd never leave..."

"Kate and Marissa did," Chloe interrupted, her grasp on Anastasia tightening as she looked up at her with wide, terrified eyes.

"I'm not them," Anastasia said firmly. "We're leaving together."

Ever so gently, she began to lift Chloe up, causing her to cry out in agony yet again. Anastasia winced at the sight and sound of her friend's pain, feeling utterly powerless to help her. She knew that they had to get back to the car, but it was clear that Chloe wouldn't be able to walk such a distance, even if they could find their way.

"Everything hurts," Chloe moaned, while being incompliant with Anastasia's ongoing efforts to pull her up.

"Please, Chloe," Anastasia begged. "We can't stay here in case the cougar comes..."

An angry growl came from somewhere in the woods, cutting Anastasia off mid-sentence. It seemed so close, but despite her best efforts, she couldn't see anything. Both she and Chloe became deathly quiet, listening as the cougar paced noisily around them.

"Where...where is he?" Chloe whispered breathlessly.

"Everywhere but nowhere," Anastasia whispered back, noting how every time she thought she'd pinpointed the cougar's location, it quickly changed. It didn't take her long to realize that they were being circled.

Hurriedly, Anastasia rose to her feet and made herself as tall and large as possible. She remembered what Frost had done the last time they'd encountered the cougar; he'd portrayed himself as the predator instead of the prey, and that was exactly what she had to do.

"Get out of here!" Anastasia yelled as loudly as she could, while waving her arms in the air.

"What are you doing?" Chloe asked fretfully, in between gasps of pain as she hardly managed to sit up. "Don't make him angry."

"Get lost! Leave!" Anastasia continued to shout, ignoring Chloe in the process.

As the cougar sounded closer, Anastasia knew that her

defense mechanisms weren't working – she just didn't know why. When Chloe's whimper drew Anastasia's attention back to her, she finally understood the cougar's behavior; he had tasted Chloe's blood and wasn't going to leave without some more. She had been marked as the prey.

"You have to get up now!" Anastasia cried as she pulled Chloe onto her feet and then struggled to support her.

The woods became still, as if even the wind was afraid to stir. Anastasia listened for the cougar but heard nothing other than her racing heart and Chloe's soft whimpering. Maybe he had finally left. Maybe she and Chloe really would be alright.

Growl...

The startling noise came from behind Anastasia and Chloe, making them turn around ever so slowly. They now faced the cougar, who inched closer in a hunched position and continued to growl in a menacing tone. Although he was a slender, medium-sized animal, he still looked strong and very dangerous. The cougar's ears, which lay almost flat to his head, along with his bared fangs, perfectly conveyed an aggressive disposition. Instantly, Anastasia knew that she and Chloe were in serious trouble.

Upon hearing a hurried rustling in the distance, Anastasia's fear heightened – another cougar must be entering the scene, preparing to devour her and Chloe equally. She felt her knees weaken and her chest ache from all the panicking. Still, she wanted to fight back, not only for her sake but for Chloe's, too. She spotted a fallen branch nearby, and after telling Chloe to steady herself, Anastasia grabbed for it.

The cougar hissed and lowered his body, as if getting ready to attack. Then the strangest thing happened – the cougar stumbled sideways and let out a painful whine. Turning around, the cougar tried to slink away; however, he appeared so groggy that he just collapsed. Several seconds passed, but the cougar remained on the ground, motionless and quite possibly dead.

"Are you okay?" someone suddenly shouted.

Turning in the direction of the voice, Anastasia saw a guy hurrying toward them. As he drew closer, she was surprised to discover that it was Frost. Even more shocking was the fact that he carried a gun.

"Are you hurt?" Frost asked, placing his hand on Anastasia's shoulder and looking closely at her.

"I'm okay, but Chloe was attacked by the cougar and she..."

"Anastasia," Chloe interrupted with a weak moan, right before she fainted.

Frost hurried to help Chloe, while Anastasia stood on guard, holding her tree branch in one hand and his gun in the other. Working quickly, he loosened the collar of Chloe's coat and checked for a pulse. Frost then unzipped his own coat and ripped a piece of his shirt, tying the strip of fabric tightly around her wound.

"How bad is she?" Anastasia asked, almost not wanting to know the answer.

"Her pulse is slow," Frost replied as he placed his arms under Chloe's shoulders and legs and then gently lifted her up. "She's losing a lot of blood. We need to get her to the hospital. Are you able to run?"

Anastasia took one last look at the limp, stationary cougar and then threw her branch on the ground. She nodded to Frost, before following him through the woods. Anastasia ran as fast as possible, but she could tell that she was holding Frost back. Nevertheless, he stayed by her side until they reached his house.

Immediately, Frost guided Anastasia to his SUV. He placed Chloe in the back seat and instructed Anastasia to keep a firm grip on her so she wouldn't fall over. Frost then took the gun from Anastasia and hurried to start the SUV. Seconds later, they were speeding down a darkening road that she'd never seen before.

From the cougar attack to rushing Chloe to Cedar Falls Hospital, everything had happened so fast that it felt unreal. Anastasia now sat in the hospital's waiting room with Frost, anxiously anticipating an update on Chloe's condition, while also obsessively repeating the night's events in her mind. However, all that currently mattered was Chloe's well-being.

Why is the doctor taking so long? Is that a good sign or a bad one? These questions tortured Anastasia as she fidgeted uncomfortably in her chair. She'd always hated hospitals with all the ill people and strange machines which sounded as scary as they looked. It seemed too artificial, as if life relied solely on science and technology.

Frost placed his hand on top of Anastasia's, obviously sensing her inner turmoil and wanting to offer her comfort. However, his hand was so warm that Anastasia immediately jerked away from him. Curiously, she looked at Frost, noting his embarrassed expression and sudden unease.

"Do you have a fever?" Anastasia asked, while realizing how cold her own hands were due to the frigid temperature she'd been exposed to as well as her current state of nervousness.

"I'm fine," Frost replied so quickly that it was unconvincing. "I wish *you* would see a doctor, though."

Defiantly, Anastasia shook her head. "All I care about is Chloe. I'm not leaving until I know she'll be alright."

"She's lucky to have a friend like you," Frost said softly.

Anastasia smiled at the compliment, allowing some of her tension to ease. "She was even luckier to have you there tonight. Thank you, Frost. I seriously don't know how I could ever repay you."

This time it was Frost's turn to shake his head. "I'm not looking for anything in return. I'm just glad I could help, even though I know you're a woman who can handle herself." For the second time that night, he looked embarrassed. Quickly, he smiled playfully and then added in a teasing manner, "After all, that was a pretty jagged branch you were holding."

Despite everything, Anastasia laughed. "I guess the unluckiest one was that cougar. At least the people of Cedar Falls can relax now that he's dead."

"I didn't kill the cougar – I used a tranquilizer," Frost hurried to explain. "When you were calling Chloe's father and your grandparents, I called my dad and told him everything that had happened. As we speak, he's transporting the cougar hundreds of miles away. This will be safer for everyone, and the cougar will have a better chance for survival."

"I didn't realize Cedar Falls Woods were that big," Anastasia commented in surprise.

"You wouldn't believe the secrets that these woods keep."

Wrinkling her forehead, Anastasia wondered what Frost had meant, but she was wary of asking for clarification. After all, it was a pretty odd statement to make. Finally, Anastasia broke the awkward pause by simply asking, "So, why go to such lengths to move the cougar? Why not just kill him?"

Frost seemed to cringe at Anastasia's insensitivity. "That cougar is still very young, and his parents were killed by poachers. It was starvation that caused him to act so dangerously bold." He paused for a moment before adding, "I don't believe any creature is innately bad. They are just shaped by their circumstances."

Anastasia saw the irony in Frost's words. He could have easily been talking about the both of them, in fact maybe he was. It made her more than a little uncomfortable that Frost could see the real her. She studied him, trying to figure out what he was all about. She'd thought spending more time with him would make it possible for her to read him like she did so well with others, but she still had nothing. Giving up, Anastasia sighed. She'd just have to get to know him the old-fashioned way – not that it would be much of a burden.

"How do you know so much about animals?" Anastasia asked. "Like, how to deal with them and know what they're thinking? Are you an animal whisperer or something?"

Frost laughed faintly before answering. "Let's just say I have a great affinity with nature and all its creatures, well, maybe except humans."

A nearby commotion caused Anastasia and Frost to turn their attention toward the administrative desk, where a man was practically yelling at the medical assistants. He was of average height and weight, had thinning light brown hair and was dressed in dentist scrubs. Anastasia recognized him as Mr. William Fairbanks – Chloe's father. She hurried to his side, with Frost at her heels.

"Mr. Fairbanks," she said quickly. "It's me, Anastasia."

Mr. Fairbanks spun around to face Anastasia. "Is my daughter okay? No one will tell me – it's complete incompetency on the hospital's behalf." He glared at the assistants, who were hurrying to help several other people.

After guiding Mr. Fairbanks away from the desk, Anastasia spoke in a soft manner, hoping to calm him down. "The doctor took Chloe away almost an hour ago. I'm sure someone will let us know what's going on soon."

"How could you be so stupid?" Mr. Fairbanks snapped at Anastasia. He then looked at Frost, as if seeing him for the first time. "You better not have touched my daughter or I swear I'll..."

"Mr. Fairbanks, what are you talking about?" Anastasia spoke sharply, no longer caring if they were making a scene.

"Kate and Marissa called me right before you did. They were worried sick because you took Chloe to meet Frost in the woods."

"Ex...excuse me?" Anastasia choked out, shocked by what she'd just heard. Perhaps Kate on her worst behavior could tell such a lie, but Marissa? Anastasia had thought that Marissa was so much better than this. "That is *not* what happened," she continued, before Mr. Fairbanks could speak. "It was *Kate* who dragged us into the woods, and it was *Kate* who fled when your daughter was attacked by the cougar. As for Frost, he saved us – Chloe would be dead if it wasn't for him!"

From the way Mr. Fairbanks trembled, Anastasia knew that he was overcome with worry and was most likely not thinking clearly. However, he had no problem narrowing his eyes at her and saying in a cruel tone, "My Chloe was fine until you came back."

"Ms. Lockhart," said the nurse, who Anastasia had spoken with earlier, "the doctor is finished with Ms. Fairbanks. Would you like to..."

"I'm Chloe's father," Mr. Fairbanks interrupted. "I want to see her – alone."

"Certainly, Mr. Fairbanks," the nurse replied. Before she led him toward Chloe's room, she turned to Anastasia and said softly, "She's going to be fine."

Anastasia nodded appreciatively to the nurse and then let out a sigh of relief. It felt like she'd awakened from a nightmare to find everything a lot less scary. However, now that she knew Chloe was out of danger, she had the energy to get angry at Mr. Fairbanks. He had no right to treat her, and especially Frost, so poorly. In fact, it wasn't even like him.

Mr. Fairbanks always used to be kind and patient, but that obviously wasn't true anymore.

"We should probably leave," Frost advised, interrupting Anastasia's thoughts. "We can see Chloe tomorrow morning, but right now, I'm taking you home. You need to rest."

"Thanks," Anastasia said as they began to leave the waiting room.

Anastasia and Frost hadn't gone far when her grandfather entered the hospital. She knew that trouble was brewing as he spotted them almost immediately and then marched forward. From the expression on his face, it was clear that he was anything but happy.

"I should have known you were involved," Mr. Lockhart said, while pointing a finger accusingly at Frost.

"Grandpa, what are you doing here?" Anastasia asked, stepping in front of Frost in hopes of preventing yet another verbal fight. "I said I was fine. You didn't have to come."

"Of course I had to come, Anastasia, because you're obviously not fine. What has *he* done to you?"

"Oh my gosh!" Anastasia exclaimed, completely exasperated. "What is wrong with you people that you have to constantly blame Frost for everything?"

"We can talk about this at home," Mr. Lockhart said as he held onto Anastasia's arm and tried to lead her away.

Anastasia resisted her grandfather's pull and instead looked at Frost. At this moment, she desperately needed guidance, for someone to tell her if she should stay and defend Frost or allow her grandfather to silence her by taking her home.

"Go with your grandfather," Frost said, as if he could read Anastasia's thoughts.

"Stay out of this, boy," Mr. Lockhart warned Frost angrily. "And leave my granddaughter alone. She doesn't need any more reasons to mess up." With those harsh words spoken, he began to usher Anastasia out of the hospital.

As Anastasia went, she couldn't concentrate on anything other than the fact that this was so embarrassing – that is, until she passed the administrative desk and heard the assistants' hushed conversation, which had obviously taken priority over their hectic jobs.

"I've filed the doctor's preliminary report," one of the older assistants said, appearing slightly shaken-up, "and it's exactly what I thought it would be – almost identical to the one I filed seventeen years ago."

"That poor girl," her co-worker muttered, looking very pale. "It's a miracle she survived."

"I just can't believe it's happening again. It's like Cedar Falls is cursed."

Anastasia slowed her pace, hoping to hear more of their conversation so she could try to make sense of it. She wondered if the report they were referring to was Chloe's, and by the way the assistants suddenly stopped talking when they noticed her nearby, she guessed the answer was yes.

"Come on," her grandfather said gruffly, while hurrying her forward. It was like he sensed what was going on between Anastasia and the medical assistants, and he clearly couldn't get her out of there fast enough.

It was only 10:30 p.m. as the Lockhart residence lay still, silent and in darkness. Her grandparents had already gone to bed, but Anastasia was wide awake, sitting motionlessly on the rocking chair in her bedroom. The dolls, which had occupied that chair for the last several years, were now scattered on the floor. Anastasia had replaced those dolls with herself, or at least it felt that way. After all, she perfectly epitomized a doll – beautiful but expected to fit a mold that others had created for her. Hell, it even felt like she no longer had a voice.

After arriving home from the hospital, Anastasia's grandfather had lectured her non-stop about how careless and dangerous it was to be in the woods, especially at night and with a wild animal on the loose. She didn't have a chance to explain or defend herself, far less update them on Chloe's condition. In fact, she'd probably still be getting yelled at right now if it wasn't for her grandmother's insistence that he calm down and they all go to bed.

Sighing, Anastasia got up, preparing to spend another sleepless night in bed. If she was going to torture herself by dwelling on the terrifying cougar attack *and* the odd conversation between the medical assistants, she might as well be comfortable.

Anastasia had just slipped into her silk pajamas when she heard a light thud against her window. Frowning with concern, she wrapped her black robe around herself and then proceeded to the window. When she pulled the curtains aside and peered out, she saw Frost about to toss another snowball at her window. Immediately, he smiled in that sheepish manner which never ceased to soften her heart.

Quickly, Anastasia opened her screen-less window, shivering as the cool air blew inside. "You found me," she said quietly, not sure if she was whispering so her grandparents wouldn't hear, or merely because the situation was so romantic that it almost seemed unreal.

"You found me, so it's only natural that I'd find you," Frost whispered back, while stepping forward and then leaning against the windowsill.

"Technically, Kate was the one who found you," she pointed out teasingly.

"Let's ignore that unpleasant fact because *you* were the one

I was trying to impress. You seriously don't think I always sit topless in front of a fireplace, flexing my muscles, do you?" He laughed softly. "Since you went to such trouble to spy on me, I thought I might as well put on a show."

"How did you know we were there?" Anastasia pried.

"Call it a gift, or an extra sense, or whatever you like."

Frost was obviously playing with Anastasia, and she knew that he wouldn't be giving her real answers anytime soon. However, that hardly mattered because other thoughts which were much more pressing currently occupied her mind.

Bringing herself closer to Frost, Anastasia spoke in her most seductive tone, "You do know this is considered stalking, right?"

"Then ask me to leave," Frost replied, not missing a beat.

Anastasia cast Frost a flirtatious half-smile. He was so gorgeous and manly that she felt her knees going weak. Everything about him enticed her, and she definitely couldn't resist her feelings for him. She bit her lip until it hurt, in an attempt to control her mind from wandering to thoughts of what might happen if he came inside. Anastasia wanted Frost, and have him she must.

"Hypocrite," he teased a second later, interrupting her growing fantasies. "I actually came by to see how you were doing."

"Like I said earlier, I'm fine," Anastasia replied, disappointed that he wasn't responding to her flirting. "Aren't you cold out there?"

"No. I like it this way," Frost stated.

"Weirdo," Anastasia continued to tease.

"So they say."

"Not me," Anastasia said, quickly turning serious. "I do want to ask you something, though. What's up with you and Kate? Sorry to say, but it seems like she has some sort of vendetta against you.”

“Oh, she does, all because that little bitch didn’t get her way for once.” Frost instantly appeared to regret his words. “You wouldn’t believe me, so what does it matter?”

“Give me a chance, Frost. You might be surprised.”

He sighed deeply before speaking. “Kate singled me out on my first day at Cedar Falls High. She’d never talk to me during the day, but after school, she wouldn’t leave me alone. At first I was flattered, but soon it became creepy. Tonight wasn’t the first time Kate’s been at my window – it used to be her favorite extracurricular activity until my parents told her parents that it had to stop. I guess she was embarrassed as hell, and she just wouldn’t let it go. Trying to make my life miserable became her new hobby and it continues to this day.”

There was a moment of silence until, despite her best efforts, Anastasia began to laugh. All of Kate’s odd behavior, from her constant need to put Frost down to belittling Anastasia for spending time with him, now made sense. Shakespeare was right when he wrote, the lady doth protest too much. Anastasia just never expected that the truth would be *this* scandalous.

“It’s not funny,” Frost claimed, trying to look stern even though the corners of his mouth twitched with amusement. “It was a very traumatic time for me.”

“I’m sure it was,” Anastasia said, her laughter dying down, “but you’ll be even more traumatized to see the shrine she’s built for you in her bedroom. I’m talking about life-size portraits and a really weird voodoo love doll.”

“Stop that,” Frost said playfully, while gently grabbing her hands, “or I’ll never tell you anything again.”

Frost felt as warm as ever, but Anastasia no longer cared. All that mattered was the fact that his face was just inches away from hers. Being so close to him allowed her to look deeply into his mesmerizing eyes. They were the color of the ocean – beautiful, endless and full of secrets. Unable to resist any longer, Anastasia placed her hand behind Frost's neck and brought his lips toward hers. Their lips hardly brushed together when he gently pulled away to kiss her forehead instead. His kiss lingered, soft and loving, but Anastasia still felt her heart sink with disappointment. She'd thought that he'd wanted this as much as she did. How could she have been so wrong?

"I want to ask you something," Frost muttered, while slowly running his fingers along the side of Anastasia's face in a slightly nervous manner. "Will you be my girlfriend?"

Taken aback, Anastasia stared at Frost. She hadn't been expecting that at all. It was such a sweet gesture, but she found herself apprehensive about the idea. Anastasia hated labeling anything, especially relationships since they always ended in heartache. On top of that concern, she also knew that everyone would be against them dating.

"Please say something," Frost begged, "because it feels like my heart's going to explode."

"I don't make a good girlfriend," Anastasia blurted out, wanting to be completely honest with him. "Trouble follows me wherever I go, and I have issues – a lot of them."

Frost lightly touched Anastasia's lips with his index finger, as if to stop her from speaking negatively about herself. "You're also independent, brave, caring, and needless to say, the most beautiful girl – woman – I've ever seen. You have a lot more going for you than against you."

"How can I say no after that?" Anastasia whispered with a small smile, no longer allowing her fears and past experiences to dictate her present life. "I'd love to be your girlfriend."

As they smiled at each other, Anastasia felt the rush of

their forbidden love. It was special but also dangerous, and if her grandparents ever found out, they would possibly send her back to Toronto. Nevertheless, it was *so* worth the risk.

"I'm afraid our first date will have to wait," Anastasia continued. "I'm so grounded, and I..."

"I get it," Frost interrupted. "This can be our little secret for as long as you like."

"Thank you," Anastasia responded sincerely.

"You have my number – please use it," Frost said as he began to retreat from her window.

"Actually, I don't..." Anastasia started to say. However, her words were cut short as a strong gust of wind appeared seemingly out of nowhere and whipped her hair in front of her face. When the wind died down and she could see clearly again, Frost was gone. Anastasia leaned out the window in search of him, but she still couldn't find him.

Shivering, Anastasia closed the window. Her bedroom was now very chilly, so she hurried to bed, anxious to get under the warm duvet. As she went, a small note which lay on the floor caught her attention. After picking it up, she quickly realized that it was Frost's phone number.

What the hell? Anastasia thought in confusion, while staring at the familiar handwriting. She had no idea how Frost could have put that note in her bedroom. However, if his intentions were to be sexy and mysterious, it was definitely working. Anastasia was charmed by Frost, and she was left wanting more – a lot more.

❄ ❄ ❄

Part Five

Troublemaker

Anastasia entered Cedar Falls Hospital the following afternoon, experiencing an array of emotions. She felt guilty for being so happy about her new relationship status with Frost, even though her concern for Chloe overshadowed everything else. She was also worried about running into Mr. Fairbanks. The last thing she wanted was another fight, or worse than that, to be told she wasn't allowed to see Chloe.

Uncertain of where to find her friend, Anastasia went to the administrative desk in the emergency ward. "I'm looking for a patient who was admitted last night," she said, after reaching the front of a very long line. "Her name is Chloe Fairbanks."

"Let me check," the young medical assistant replied, before turning to her computer. "She's in the ICU, room number thirteen. That ward is right beside us. You can't miss it."

"Thank you," Anastasia said. She was slightly taken aback to hear that Chloe was in intensive care. Yesterday, the nurse had said Chloe was going to be fine, so what was she doing in a ward like that?

Trying to forget about how much she disliked hospitals, Anastasia hurried to the ICU, following the increasing numbers on the doors until she reached room thirteen. She knocked lightly upon the door, but even after several moments, there was no response. Unwavering in her pursuit to see Chloe, Anastasia entered anyway.

The private room, which was painted a sterile shade of white, was small, windowless and very minimalistic. It looked like a place to die rather than to get better, and when Anastasia's eyes fell upon Chloe, who was sleeping in bed, she felt her heart break. Chloe was attached to a scary-looking machine that monitored her vitals, and she had the largest bandage Anastasia had ever seen wrapped around her injured arm. Just as disconcerting was how shockingly pale and weak she appeared.

Sitting in the chair beside Chloe's bed, Anastasia gently reached for her hand, noting how it felt a little cold. She knew it was good for Chloe to get a lot of rest, but she looked so distant and almost lifeless that it scared Anastasia. Unable to stand seeing her like this, she yearned for the times when Chloe was happy and healthy.

"Do you remember when we snuck out to go camping?" Anastasia asked softly, even though she knew that Chloe couldn't hear her. "We were only seven, and it was my last day of summer vacation, so we wanted to spend as much time together as possible."

Anastasia smiled as the memories came to the forefront of her mind, as vivid as though they'd happened yesterday. "You brought your old play tent, and when dusk fell, we trekked into the woods. It seemed like we'd been walking forever when we came upon that pretty little clearing with the most amazing view of the stars. By that point, I was hungry and not having taken my own food, you didn't hesitate to give me half of your sandwich."

For a moment, she stopped talking, thinking about how typical it was for Chloe to behave so selflessly. She then continued, "We must've been out there for hours, just chatting and giggling like the silly girls we were. That was also the night we exchanged friendship bracelets – I still have mine, you know."

Anastasia paused once again, this time suddenly turning somber. "It was all fun and games, but then we started to get cold and scared. Little did we know, your parents and my grandparents had organized a search party, and when my grandpa found us, he was so angry. You tried to take the blame, probably thinking it would make him stop yelling at me. That was the first and only time I'd seen my grandpa mad – until now, of course."

The room became silent again as Anastasia watched Chloe sleep, her gentle breathing making her chest rise and fall in perfect rhythm. More than likely, it was a sedative or painkiller which was offering her the temporary relief. Anastasia knew that Chloe was the last person who deserved to be in this situation, and it all seemed like the cruelest of ironies.

The sound of the door opening startled Anastasia out of her thoughts, and when she turned around, she saw Chloe's doctor enter the room.

"I didn't know Ms. Fairbanks had a visitor," he said in a friendly tone.

"How is she?" Anastasia asked abruptly, completely forgetting her manners.

"I'm afraid I can't release any details about her condition to non-family members," he replied, beginning to flip through a folder which probably contained the information she was seeking. "Mr. Fairbanks is on his way here. You're welcome to stay and ask him."

"Um, it's okay," Anastasia muttered, knowing that she wouldn't get any information from him. "Thanks, anyway."

As Anastasia left the room and walked through the ICU

ward, she realized that she'd have to wait until Chloe was awake to get answers. Unfortunately, that moment seemed like it would never come.

Passing by the emergency ward on her way to exit, Anastasia heard a commotion, like someone was yelling incoherently, while another person tried to calm him down. Within seconds, she saw an occupied gurney being rushed toward the ER by a worried-looking paramedic. As they crossed her path, she was able to get a clear view of the injured man, and immediately, she felt nauseous. She knew that man as Pete — a one-time drunkard who'd since turned his life around and now worked closely with her grandfather at Rural Mart. Pete had obviously just suffered a traumatic accident because half of his face was covered in a blood-stained bandage, and he wouldn't stop talking, although the only words she could decipher were *out-of-nowhere* and *those eyes*.

As Pete and the paramedic disappeared into the ER, Anastasia's mind raced with thoughts about what could've happened to him. From Pete's camouflaged-patterned outfit to his eerie words, she guessed that he'd been hunting in the woods. If that was the case, then maybe he'd been attacked by an animal, just like Chloe. Shivering, Anastasia began to suspect that something very strange was occurring in Cedar Falls Woods.

❋ ❋ ❋

It was an unusually cold Monday morning as Anastasia thanked her grandmother for the ride and then entered Cedar Falls High. Without Chloe, Anastasia felt alone and also a little self-conscious. She couldn't even hang out with Frost because it would create more gossip, resulting in her grandparents discovering the truth about their relationship. No matter what she did, she'd still end up by herself.

Hurrying through the hallway on route to her locker, Anastasia felt that she was being watched. It was a sense that she was very familiar with, but this time it seemed different. From the glares and snarky whispers, Anastasia suddenly realized that, for some reason, these students hated her.

When Anastasia arrived at her locker, she was shocked to find Kate, Jill and another girl she didn't recognize standing there with their arms crossed and sour expressions upon their faces. Marissa also stood beside them, appearing sufficiently awkward and keeping her head down as if she couldn't bear to look at Anastasia. From the corner of her eye, Anastasia saw Frost standing nearby, looking on edge and ready to step in at any given moment. Knowing that he had her back, she walked toward the girls.

"Can you please move?" Anastasia asked the girls, making sure that she concealed her slight nervousness.

"I don't think so," Kate snapped unexpectedly.

"Who do you think you are?" Jill added in an equally harsh tone. "You walk into *our* school and act like you own the place. Well, listen up, *sweetie*, it doesn't work like that. You really crossed the line when you almost killed Chloe."

"When I *what?*" Anastasia practically shrieked. "Chloe's my best friend. I'd never do anything to hurt her!"

Kate snorted. "Get real, Anastasia. Everyone knows that Chloe's *my* best friend. Your odd obsession with her really has to stop."

"Kate and Marissa saw what you did," the other girl spoke up. "You..."

"Oh, wait, I've heard this one," Anastasia interrupted in a sarcastic tone. "I lured Chloe into the deep, dark woods, while Kate and Marissa looked on, totally unable to stop me.

Such a story rings so true, huh?" She then added in a stone-cold tone, "You're the ones who need help. Now get the hell out of my way."

In the background, Anastasia heard Frost stifle a laugh. As Kate's sneer deepened, it was clear that Frost's support of Anastasia greatly angered her. Kate took a step forward right as the bell rang, signaling that class would soon start. The students, who had gathered to watch, along with Jill and the unidentified girl, reluctantly began to leave. However, Anastasia and Kate stood their ground, with Frost and Marissa, respectively, standing by them.

"Is it hard?" Anastasia asked bitterly.

"What?" Kate demanded, obviously pretending not to care.

"Keeping track of your lies. I'm likely not your first victim." Anastasia then turned to Marissa. "You know, I really liked you. I guess my judgment was pretty damn wrong."

Marissa remained silent, but her cheeks reddened and she was visibly ashamed. Instantly, Anastasia wondered why Marissa was so loyal to Kate. She'd never seen Kate display any real kindness or affection – other than for herself – and Marissa usually received the majority of her nastiness. Anastasia realized that Kate either had some serious dirt on her, or she just had no self-esteem. Both of these reasons seemed pretty bleak.

Marching to her locker, Anastasia pushed past Kate. She'd had enough of her bullshit, and she definitely wasn't going to put up with it any longer. Unfortunately, it appeared that Kate wouldn't back down that easily.

"You'll never win," Kate hissed, starting to circle Anastasia as if they were wild animals. She then brought her face close to Anastasia's and whispered in a threatening tone,

"This is *my* school and *my* town. You don't have a chance."

"You may think that you own Cedar Falls, but it's merely a delusion," Anastasia hissed right back. "Rumor has it you're just a sad little peeping tom who can't get a man."

Kate's face turned the deepest shade of red Anastasia had ever seen. Her breathing became shallow, and she almost looked like she was going to have a heart attack. Quickly, Anastasia regretted her words. This wasn't the way to deal with someone like Kate, and even worse than that, she'd betrayed Frost's trust. Anastasia knew that she'd taken things way too far.

"What's she talking about?" Marissa asked Kate.

"Nothing," Kate snapped. "She's the daughter of a whore. Don't believe a word she says."

Or maybe Anastasia hadn't taken things far enough.

Smack!

Anastasia hardly knew what she'd done until it was too late. In anger and retaliation, she'd slapped Kate right across the face. It had felt so good and totally justifiable. After all, she had no right to make such a horrible comment about Anastasia and her mother.

Slowly, Kate took her hand away from her flushed cheek. As her shocked expression lessened, her fury was crystal clear. Marissa tried to comfort her, but she wasn't the least bit interested. In her eyes, Anastasia could see that she was only after revenge.

"You little bitch!" Kate shrieked as she lunged toward Anastasia and shoved her against the lockers.

Pain shot throughout Anastasia's body, followed by an uncomfortable tingling sensation. Her elbows and back were particularly sore since they had been the first parts to make contact with the lockers. Cringing, Anastasia attempted to strike back at Kate, but Frost stopped her mid-attack by wrapping his arms around her waist and pulling her away. He had arrived at her side so quickly that she could do nothing to resist.

"Stop it right now!" a male voice suddenly shouted.

Anastasia, Frost, Kate, and Marissa stood still, watching with wide eyes as Principal Keith marched toward them. Knowing that fighting on school property would be considered a serious offense, Anastasia felt her heart sink. At least Kate had been caught, too. That meant she wouldn't be going down without Kate right by her side.

"What is the meaning of this?" Principal Keith demanded with a very stern expression.

"There was a slight misunderstanding," Frost said, finally letting go of Anastasia and then stepping forward, "but it's been resolved."

"Is that so?" Principal Keith replied, obviously not believing a word Frost had said. "Well, I certainly don't consider fighting in the hallway any sort of resolution. In fact, it's the complete opposite. Anastasia, my office – now."

"What...what about Kate?" Anastasia hardly choked out, overcome with disbelief. "She provoked me. She pushed me." Anastasia knew that she sounded desperate and childish, but this was just so unfair!

"I saw *you* attempting to assault Kate," Principal Keith spoke to Anastasia in a strict tone. "Although I will be questioning everyone involved, disciplining you, Anastasia, is my top priority." He then turned to Frost, Kate and Marissa, still looking very serious. "You may go to class."

"Thank you for helping me, Principal Keith," Kate said with a fake sob, before grasping onto Marissa's arm and quickly walking away.

"You honestly don't have the whole story," Frost warned Principal Keith.

"Get to class, Frost," Principal Keith replied.

Obediently, Frost began to leave, but not before casting Anastasia a supportive look and mouthing to her, *it's okay*. Unfortunately, his kind gestures did little to soothe her worries because she knew that he was so wrong. Her current situation couldn't possibly be any worse.

The minutes ticked by slowly as Anastasia sat in the principal's office yet again. This time she was waiting for her grandfather to arrive so he could be somewhat inaccurately informed of her latest misdeed. As luck would have it, the principal hadn't been able to contact her grandmother; that meant she would have to cope with her grandfather's reaction all by herself – terrific.

A knock sounded upon the door, causing Principal Keith to get up quickly. Anastasia turned around in her chair to see her grandfather being ushered inside. As expected, he looked furious. However, in his eyes, she saw another emotion. Was it shame or disappointment? Both of these guesses made Anastasia feel like crap.

"Hello, Mr. Keith," Mr. Lockhart greeted solemnly, while shaking his hand.

"Mr. Lockhart," Principal Keith replied, nodding toward an unoccupied chair. "I'm sorry we're not meeting under better circumstances."

Mr. Lockhart refused the chair that Principal Keith had intended for him. "What's happened?" he asked instead.

"I caught Anastasia trying to engage in a physical fight with another student. As you likely know, we have a zero tolerance policy in regards to violence."

"I completely understand," Mr. Lockhart spoke quickly, "but did you see Anastasia hit this other student?"

"Like I said, Mr. Lockhart, I arrived on the scene before

anything serious could take place. I'm very particular about patrolling the hallways, especially when students should be in class."

"With all due respect, Mr. Keith, if Anastasia didn't actually hit someone, I don't see the need for quite this much rigmarole."

"That is entirely irrelevant!" Principal Keith remarked, clearly unable to maintain the passive-aggressive debate which he and Mr. Lockhart were engaged in. "There are other witnesses. In fact, it appears that Frost was of great assistance in keeping Anastasia under control."

Remaining silent, Mr. Lockhart shot Anastasia a quick, angry look. She wondered what upset him more — the fact that she was in trouble or that she'd disobeyed his orders regarding Frost. It was probably a combination of both, although she had been pleasantly surprised by his willingness to defend her. Maybe their relationship wasn't as far gone as she'd thought.

"I always consider the welfare of all my students," Principal Keith continued in a matter-of-fact tone. "Although I must protect the victim, I'm also doing what's best for Anastasia in the long run. She's dealing with a tough situation at Cedar Falls High, and that is surely interfering with her decisions, not to mention her studies."

"What tough situation?" Mr. Lockhart almost snapped.

"I'm referring to the allegation of an inappropriate relationship between Anastasia and a faculty member. Although hard evidence is yet to be found, the investigation is still ongoing."

Wincing at the untimely revelation of such personal information, Anastasia slowly slid further down in her chair. She stared at the carpeted floor as if it was the most interesting thing she'd ever seen. Unfortunately, Anastasia and her grandmother's efforts to keep the Mr. O'Donoghue scandal quiet suddenly didn't matter – the secret was out.

"It's not true, Grandpa," Anastasia muttered, trying to control her anger and frustration. She was distraught when he said nothing and instead looked away.

"I'm sure the last few days have been difficult," Principal Keith spoke to Anastasia, softly and almost in a condescending manner, "and I'm more than willing to recommend a wonderful therapist. However, I don't have any other choice but to expel you because of today's behavior."

Anastasia knew that this was coming the moment Principal Keith called out to them in the hallway. However, actually hearing those words made the situation feel that much more real. What was she going to do now? She doubted there were any other schools nearby – not that they'd want her anyway.

"Can I ask you to reconsider?" Mr. Lockhart tried one last time, most definitely losing endurance.

"I'm afraid not," Principal Keith replied, before turning to Anastasia and then adding, "Please remove your personal belongings from your locker and leave immediately."

Humiliated and still very much angry, Anastasia hurried out of the principal's office without saying a word. When she entered the hallway, she almost bumped into Marissa. She wondered what Marissa was doing there but that hardly mattered anymore.

"Anastasia, I'm so..." Marissa began to say. However, she was interrupted by Mr. Lockhart.

"Get your things and meet me in the car," he said gruffly. "I'm too embarrassed to stay here any longer."

Anastasia and her grandfather left in opposite directions, but she soon realized that she wasn't alone as Marissa hurried after her, begging for her to stop so they could talk. Anastasia kept on going, trying to ignore her for as long as possible. However, Marissa's refusal to give up finally broke her down.

"What do you want from me?" Anastasia demanded, spinning around so quickly to face Marissa that they almost collided. "There's nothing left for you to take."

"I...I don't want anything," Marissa stuttered. "What happened with the principal?"

"None of your business," Anastasia snapped, while opening her locker and retrieving the only items which belonged to her – the rose and sweet love notes that Frost had given her. "Do you really think I'd give you even more reasons to gossip about me?"

"It's not like that," Marissa protested.

"Save it, because I'm not interested." With that said, Anastasia marched down the hallway, out of Cedar Falls High and into her grandfather's car.

As expected, the ride home was deathly quiet. This atmosphere was all too familiar for Anastasia, but that didn't mean she was any more comfortable with it. The silence gave her a moment to think, and she couldn't help but wonder where her spiraling life would lead her. Anastasia used to think that the chaos would have to eventually end at some point. However, she now pondered if she really was cursed, forever doomed to cause trouble wherever she went.

"I see Rose got my message," Mr. Lockhart pointed out in a grave tone.

Seeing her grandmother's car parked in the driveway, Anastasia cringed. They had been getting on so well, and she hated to think how this latest incident would negatively impact the progress they'd made. This specific consequence greatly irritated her.

Anastasia's grandfather exited the car, causing her to follow him even though she was feeling particularly heavy-footed. Somehow she managed to walk into the house, and as soon as she did, no words or emotions were held back.

"Is everything alright?" Mrs. Lockhart asked, immediately jumping up from the chair she'd been nervously sitting in and then hurrying toward Anastasia. She studied her face and body, before letting out a sigh of relief. "You don't look hurt, but are you?"

"No, I..." Anastasia tried to respond.

"She's the one who started the fight," Mr. Lockhart interrupted.

"What?" Mrs. Lockhart's eyes widened.

"And she's been expelled for it," he continued, growing angrier by the second.

"Oh, Anastasia."

"Stop it!" Anastasia cried, overcome with fury. "Don't you even want to hear my side of the story? It's like no one cares about what I have to say!"

"How can we trust anything that you say or do?" Mr. Lockhart bellowed. "We've done everything we can to provide you with a safe home and an opportunity to turn your life around. Yet, all you do is keep disappointing us. What other choice do we have, Anastasia? You have to go back to Toronto."

At first, Anastasia's eyes widened with shock, but soon the truth settled in. "Let's face it, *Grandpa*, I was never welcomed here in the first place. You hate the fact that I'm my mother's daughter and that you couldn't save either of us."

Running to her bedroom, Anastasia slammed the door behind her and then began packing as quickly as possible. She wasn't going to spend a moment longer in a place where no one wanted her, but that didn't mean she was leaving Cedar Falls. Anastasia couldn't bring herself to do such a thing now that she was with Frost. Somehow, she'd figure out a way to stay and make it work.

In the background, Anastasia heard her grandparents arguing. She couldn't remember them ever being so upset with each other, and underneath her own anger, she felt guilty for causing trouble. However, she repressed that feeling and instead tried to concentrate on a solution to her current problem. Eventually, her grandparents ceased fighting, but only when the telephone began ringing continuously.

Ten minutes later, just as Anastasia had packed the last item, a knock sounded upon her door. Before she had a chance to say, *come in*, or more likely, *go away*, her grandmother opened the door ever so gently and then stepped inside.

"We need to talk," Mrs. Lockhart said softly.

"Please don't," Anastasia replied, while trying to close her luggage with some difficulty. "I'm not going to fight with you."

"I'm glad we're on the same page," she said, after sitting down on Anastasia's bed and gesturing for her to do the same. "That was your principal on the telephone. He said another student came forth, insisting that you were acting in self-defense. Mr. Keith acknowledges that he was hasty in making a decision and, under the circumstances, has decided to reduce your expulsion to a one week suspension."

"Does it even matter?" Anastasia asked, although she couldn't deny that she was somewhat satisfied to hear the news. "Grandpa doesn't want me here. I'm leaving."

"Your grandfather is a proud man, but that's not always a good trait. He doesn't show his emotions well, and he hates to admit when he's wrong. However, he did ask me to speak with you. We want to forget today ever happened, and your mother doesn't even have to know."

"What's the catch?" Anastasia asked with narrowed eyes.

"We want you to take the job at the library. It will give you direction, responsibility and perhaps help keep you out of trouble." Mrs. Lockhart smiled at Anastasia, making her realize that she did have a choice in the matter. "Oh, and one other thing," she added slowly, as if to heighten the suspense, "you must believe that you're always welcome here – because you are."

As her grandmother wrapped her in a hug, Anastasia realized how much she was loved. Suddenly, everything that had happened today no longer felt so dire, and somehow, she knew that she would get through it.

❋ ❋ ❋

It was the first day of Anastasia's suspension from school, and she only had one objective in mind – to see Chloe and make sure she was getting better. As she walked down the corridors of the hospital, she found herself less apprehensive about being there. Anastasia realized that being exposed to an environment she didn't particularly like actually made it seem not as scary. She guessed that after a while anything could be perceived as normal.

As Anastasia neared Chloe's room, Mr. Fairbanks exited. He hadn't seen her yet, and she contemplated turning around and leaving. However, she was desperate to speak with Chloe, and it's not like she'd done anything wrong. Mustering all her confidence, Anastasia proceeded forward.

Now talking on his cell phone, Mr. Fairbanks was still oblivious of Anastasia's presence. "Can't you get an earlier flight?" he asked in an annoyed tone. "Chloe will be released by the time you arrive, and I know that she needs your support now." He paused for a moment and then sighed. "It's your choice, Gloria – goodness knows you've never listened to me. However, she's your daughter, and I thought that meant something."

After ending the call, Mr. Fairbanks turned sideways, finally noticing Anastasia. He looked startled at first, but he soon approached her with an emotionless expression upon his face. "Anastasia," he greeted, appearing neither angry nor upset to see her.

"I've come to see Chloe," Anastasia said firmly. "She's my best friend, regardless of what you may think."

Mr. Fairbanks nodded. "Chloe told me what happened that night – well, the parts that she can remember. I shouldn't have reacted the way I did, but you have to realize that Chloe's my life. She's the only person I have left in this world, and if anything happened to her, I couldn't cope with it."

"What about her mother?" Anastasia pried, already suspecting that Mr. and Mrs. Fairbanks were no longer together. "Hasn't she been around?"

Sadly, he shook his head. "She's been in Europe for the past two years. Since then, we've only seen her once when she visited for Chloe's sixteenth birthday."

From Chloe's expensive new lifestyle to Mr. Fairbanks uncharacteristic behavior, it all made a lot more sense now. They were both dealing with a massive change and were most likely experiencing feelings of abandonment. She just couldn't believe that Chloe hadn't opened up to her about the separation or, quite possibly, the divorce. It must have hit her really hard.

"I'm sorry to hear that," Anastasia said sincerely, deciding to forgive and forget Mr. Fairbanks behavior toward her and Frost on that dreadful night. "You said something about Chloe's memory – what's wrong with it?"

"She's having trouble remembering the attack. The doctor scanned her brain, and there appears to be no damage. They think it may be a response to the traumatic events she's endured. Perhaps it's a defense mechanism to help deal with the shock."

"Can I see her?" Anastasia asked anxiously.

"Of course," Mr. Fairbanks said, stepping aside.

Quietly, Anastasia entered the room to find Chloe reclining in bed, her eyes closed and her head slightly turned. She still looked pale and fragile, but there was a calm demeanor about her, and her cheeks had a hint of rosiness to them. As if Chloe could sense Anastasia's presence, she opened her eyes and offered a small smile.

"Hey," Anastasia said softly, while sitting in the chair beside Chloe's bed. "How are you doing?"

"I've never felt better," Chloe responded with a smirk.

Anastasia laughed lightly. "Stupid question, huh?"

"No," Chloe replied quickly as she reached for Anastasia's hand, wincing slightly at the movement. "Thank you for caring." She sighed before continuing. "The doctor said I tore ligaments in my arm, suffered a mild concussion and let's just say they had to *really* stitch up my wound."

"You're going to get better, though, and that's what counts."

Chloe shifted uncomfortably in her bed. "It doesn't feel that way." She then hurried to add, "At least one good thing has come from this – I know who my real friends are. You stayed with me when Kate and Marissa left. I'll never forget that."

"I had help," Anastasia replied, causing Chloe to appear confused. "Frost dealt with the cougar, carried you to his SUV and then drove you to hospital. He actually saved both our lives."

Shocked, Chloe looked at Anastasia with wide eyes. "I had no idea," she muttered, her cheeks brightening with embarrassment. "I'm so sorry, Anastasia. I should have never told you to stay away from Frost, and I definitely shouldn't have tried to make you change just to please Kate. I've been such an idiot."

Seeing how upset Chloe was becoming, Anastasia spoke gently, "That's in the past, and it's not like you're the only one to fall under Kate's spell. We've so lost Marissa to her."

"No, we haven't. She came to see me yesterday in such a state that I thought *she* was the one who needed admitted to the hospital. I'm talking waterworks and umpteen apologies. Marissa regrets leaving us on that night, and she's over being Kate's minion."

"Do we believe her?" Anastasia asked cautiously. She liked to think of herself as someone who could forgive others, but Marissa's behavior had been really hurtful.

"Definitely. Marissa spilled a lot of dirt on Kate, and that's going to come at a high price for her." Chloe looked down at her bed sheets, obviously uncertain of whether she should continue speaking or not.

"What have they been saying about me?" Anastasia asked, almost in a teasing manner even though she found none of this amusing.

"Jill started the rumor about you and Mr. O'Donoghue, and Kate encouraged her to do so. Kate told Jill what you said about her and Jack. She wanted to cause trouble for you, and I guess she saw the opportunity in Jill."

"Does Kate really hate me that much?" Anastasia asked, frustrated and upset. "I really haven't done anything to her."

"You're kidding, right?" Chloe asked rhetorically, before continuing. "Your mere presence in Cedar Falls is reason enough for Kate to dislike you. You're everything that she isn't, and she's so threatened by that."

Suddenly, someone knocked upon the door and then

entered. It was a young, attractive hospital worker who was carrying a tray. "Sorry for interrupting, but it's time for Chloe's lunch," he said with a warm smile.

"Hi, Jay," Chloe responded, immediately perking up. She gave her head a little toss so her hair would fall forward. It was beyond obvious that she liked him.

"I'll visit you again soon," Anastasia promised as she stood up and gave Chloe a gentle hug. She was almost out the door when Chloe called to her.

"Thank Frost for me," she said sincerely.

"I'll be sure to tell him," Anastasia responded with a smile.

As Anastasia left the hospital, she felt so much better about everything. Chloe was going to be fine, and it seemed like Marissa had finally seen Kate for what she really was – a manipulative bitch. So what if Kate and Jill hated her? At least she had some real friends, including a wickedly hot boyfriend in Frost.

✳ ✳ ✳

On the second day of Anastasia's suspension, she'd begun to work at the library. She had reasoned it was easier to accept the job and keep her grandfather somewhat content than it was to refuse and start yet another argument. In truth, she wasn't wholly opposed to the idea anyway. She hated staying home all day, by herself and with nothing to do but rehash bad memories. Besides, she could really use the cash.

Cedar Falls Library wasn't the old, musty place that Anastasia had imagined it would've become. In fact, it had recently undergone a makeover and was as nice, albeit not as big, as any library in Toronto. The shelves were stocked full of a wide range of books, and there were a few new computers. There was even a small separate study room, although Anastasia suspected that it didn't get used often.

As for the staff, there were two full-timers, her grandmother and Mrs. Davenport, as well as four other part-timers. Anastasia was mainly being trained by Mrs. Davenport, who was patient, friendly and very much an advocate for literacy. Overall, she was learning quickly, and her time there was mostly positive.

On this particular night, Anastasia and her grandmother were alone in the library, preparing to close early because of the monthly town meeting which would start in just over an hour. Right now, they were busy making sure all the books were properly shelved. This was Anastasia's favorite part of her job because everything was so quiet and it gave her a chance to browse the books. There were so many titles that she wanted to read – although she hadn't done that recreationally for years. It seemed as if a part of the old Anastasia was starting to resurface, and that felt so good.

"Can you flip the sign on the door to closed?" Mrs. Lockhart called to Anastasia as she started to turn off the computers.

Lost in thought about a paranormal romance book that she desperately wanted to read, Anastasia approached the door. She'd just turned over the sign when a figure appeared on the other side. Startled, Anastasia let out a loud gasp, her heartbeat quickening as the late night visitor opened the door and stepped inside.

"Hi, Anastasia," Marissa said shyly as she pulled down the hood which had been covering a large portion of her face.

"Is everything okay?" Mrs. Lockhart asked, while hurrying to Anastasia's side.

"I hope so," Marissa spoke quickly, retrieving a beautifully wrapped box of chocolates and then offering them to Anastasia. "I know this can't even begin to make up for all the things that I've done, but it is a peace offering because I am *so* sorry."

Anastasia suddenly felt embarrassed by her over-the-top reaction to Marissa's arrival, even though it was unexpected. "Can we have a moment alone?" she asked her grandmother, who nodded in understanding.

"Don't tell me you're lactose intolerant," Marissa joked, although her laughter came out nervously.

Finally taking the chocolates, Anastasia said graciously, "You really didn't have to."

"I'm so sorry," Marissa repeated abruptly, becoming very emotional.

From the way her lips quivered to her teary eyes, Anastasia guessed that this was the beginning of the hysterics which Chloe had so generously warned her about. As Marissa continued, she realized that her assumption was dead on.

"I know what I did was wrong, and I don't even know why I did it. Supporting Kate in all her lies was horrible. I didn't even recognize the person I was becoming. I was weak, scared and oh so wrong."

"Calm down," Anastasia advised, concerned that Marissa would actually start to hyperventilate. "Although I can't deny that I'm still kind of pissed, I will be able to get over it sooner rather than later."

"That's all I'm asking for," Marissa readily jumped at the opportunity to get their friendship back on track.

"It helps that you told Principal Keith the truth," Anastasia added. "Thanks."

"You have no reason to thank me," Marissa said as she hugged Anastasia. "I was only trying to right one of my many wrongs."

"Sorry to interrupt, girls," Mrs. Lockhart said, while approaching them, "but I have to lock up now. Do you need a ride home, Marissa?"

"No, I have my car." She then turned to Anastasia. "We'll talk soon, right?"

"Sure," Anastasia replied with a smile.

After Marissa left and Anastasia's grandmother closed the library, they headed home. With the waning moon still somewhat bright, Anastasia looked upon the woods. They were beautiful at night – from the safety of a moving car, of course. However, she experienced a weird sensation, as if someone or something was watching her. Chalking it up to mere paranoia stemming from that horrifying night in the woods, Anastasia averted her eyes to the road ahead. She was actually proud of herself for not having any other post-traumatic stress symptoms, and she wanted to keep it that way.

Their house soon came into view, and as Anastasia and her grandmother exited the car and then headed inside, they discussed what work would need to be done at the library tomorrow. Unfortunately, their conversation quickly came to a stop when they saw her grandfather pacing angrily in the living room. Notably, the love notes which Frost had written for Anastasia, along with the dried blue rose, were placed on the coffee table.

"Is that another gift from lover boy?" Mr. Lockhart asked harshly, while pointing toward the box of chocolates. "You have a lot of explaining to do, young lady."

Anastasia felt her face burn with embarrassment. She couldn't believe that her grandfather had read such personal notes. Anger rapidly set in as she realized how he had retrieved them in the first place; he must have snooped throughout her entire bedroom because she'd made sure that those notes were *very* well-hidden.

Looking confused, Mrs. Lockhart picked up a single piece

of paper. She read some of it before hurriedly placing it back on the table. "Oh, Fredrick," she said to her husband, "how could you?"

"Don't turn this around on me," he raised his voice. "I had to find out from the principal that a teacher is accused of dating our granddaughter. Can you blame me for wondering what else she's been keeping from me? And I was right," he added, while thumping his fist upon the coffee table, "she's seeing Frost behind our backs."

"Frost and I haven't done anything wrong," Anastasia protested, "but going through my stuff definitely is!"

"Although you may not believe it now, I *am* doing what's best for you."

"No, you're not!" Anastasia cried. "Frost is the most kind, caring and amazing guy I've ever met – I'd never leave him."

"Enough!" Mrs. Lockhart exclaimed before Mr. Lockhart could snap back. She turned to Anastasia. "You shouldn't have kept your relationship with Frost a secret. We need to know that you're being honest with us. That's all I ask of you." She then faced her husband. "You had no right to snoop through Anastasia's personal belongings. I'm sure you've lost a little bit of her trust tonight."

"Make that a lot of trust," Anastasia mumbled.

"Anastasia is allowed to see Frost, if she so wishes," Mrs. Lockhart continued. "However, there are to be no more secrets. If this family is going to work, we need to talk openly with one another. Is everyone in agreement?"

Neither Anastasia nor her grandfather said a word. Instead, they both nodded.

"Good," Mrs. Lockhart commented as she began to leave the living room. "Now get ready for the meeting, Fredrick. I don't want to be late."

With a little satisfied smirk, Anastasia collected her notes and rose, while her grandfather looked on silently. She was surprised and very happy that her grandmother had stood up for her. It proved that Anastasia really could rely on her, and that security was priceless.

Quickly, Anastasia headed to her bedroom, still partially embarrassed that her grandfather had read the notes, but more so excited to see Frost. She knew that he would be coming to her window, just like he always did. It was actually a miracle that her grandparents hadn't caught him yet – not that she was complaining. After all, a girl had to have some secrets.

Once her grandparents had left for the town meeting and she'd had the chance to freshen up, Anastasia waited by her window, feeling the rush and butterflies she always experienced whenever she was about to see Frost. When she saw him approaching from across her backyard, she quickly opened the window. By now, she was so used to the encroaching cold breeze which accompanied their nightly encounters that she hardly noticed it anymore.

"Hi, beautiful," Frost said with a wide smile, before leaning over the windowsill and kissing her on the cheek.

"Hey, I've got some news," Anastasia said, tugging playfully at the collar of Frost's coat and giving him a secretive smile.

"Oh, yeah?" Frost said, raising his eyebrows with piqued interest.

Anastasia nodded. "We don't have to hide our relationship any longer. My grandparents know we are dating, and to tell the truth, I'm really relieved."

"That's great, Anastasia, and also a little ironic. Last night, I told my parents we're dating." Hurriedly, he added, "I know I should've talked to you about it first, but the words just sort of came out. They're happy about it and would love to have you over for dinner sometime soon."

"Its fine," Anastasia reassured him, noting how cute he looked when he was nervous. "Actually, it's better than fine, and I can't wait to officially meet your parents."

"Good," Frost said with a sigh of relief, "because it's not easy to keep a secret." He appeared thoughtful for a moment and then continued. "Anyway, I thought we could go for a drive tonight. Are you interested?"

"Definitely," Anastasia answered, eager to try something different. "Meet me on the porch."

Closing the window, Anastasia hurried to the foyer to retrieve her coat and boots. After putting them on, she stepped outside to find Frost waiting for her.

Frost didn't say a word as he reached for Anastasia's hand, his heat slowly spreading throughout her body as they walked toward his SUV. She'd originally thought his unnatural warmth was odd, but now it felt comforting, even though she still had no explanation for its cause.

"Won't people see us?" Anastasia asked, wondering what had prompted Frost's sudden desire to go out. "I'm still grounded until Monday, you know."

"Supposedly, a lot of people go to the church for the town meeting, and it's the only time your grandfather and my dad will be together in the same room. Trust me, it's the perfect opportunity to hang out without being seen."

Frost released Anastasia's hand so he could open the car door for her, but still, she felt a wave of disappointment over their broken touch. She entered the SUV, and after he'd closed the door behind her, he swiftly got in and put the key into the ignition. Anastasia couldn't help but note how he always acted like a gentleman.

"Speaking of your grandfather," Frost continued as he

drove down the street, "how are things between the two of you?"

"Oh, they're great," Anastasia replied sarcastically. "I love being told how to behave and especially who my friends should be. It's also really healthy that the only time we talk is to argue."

"Things sound pretty good then." Frost kept a straight face even though he was obviously teasing her.

"Shut up," Anastasia said, smiling slightly in spite of herself.

"Seriously, Anastasia, I'm sure your grandfather wants the best for you. He just doesn't realize what that is yet."

"Maybe," Anastasia admitted, "and I do wish our relationship was better, even if only for my grandma's sake since all this fighting is so unfair to her. But when nothing I say or do pleases him, I start to wonder what's the point in trying."

"If something's important to you, then you should never give up on it."

Anastasia thought about Frost's words as she stared out the window, taking in the spooky scenery. The woods seemed alive as branches swayed in the wind, creating constantly moving shadows on the road. She even saw some type of bird – probably an owl – swooping among the trees. Unfortunately, the owl flew so fast that she had no time to point him out to Frost.

"I know you're right," Anastasia said, breaking the silence as she turned her head away from the window. She much preferred looking at Frost, anyway. "I've really made an effort with my mom, and I can already see the change in our relationship. We text every day, and we're more open with each other now. She even admitted to feeling alone and overwhelmed for these past four years, so I guess we've found our common ground."

"You'll never have to feel alone again," Frost promised, taking one hand off the wheel for a few seconds so he could lovingly caress Anastasia's knee. "As for being overwhelmed, I'm here to share all your burdens."

"I'm here for you, too," Anastasia said quickly. "Always." Looking at Frost, she couldn't suppress her smile. He made her feel protected and wanted, as if he needed her as much as she needed him. Despite knowing him for a short period of time, she'd never felt so strongly about any other guy.

"Actually, I think I can ease one of those burdens right now," Frost said, casting her a mischievous grin. "Not having you at school meant I had some spare time to do a bit of detective work. Turns out the investigation into your alleged affair with Mr. O'Donoghue has been closed due to insufficient evidence."

"Are you serious?" Anastasia asked with wide eyes, although she knew that Frost wouldn't joke about something like this.

Frost nodded. "I'm sure the news will be all over school by Monday morning – just in time for your return."

Anastasia was silent for a moment as she processed the news. "You have no idea how relieved I am to hear all of this," she said slowly, "but how did you find out?"

Frost shrugged as if it was no big deal. "I know how much this thing with Mr. O'Donoghue has affected you, so I made it my mission to get answers."

"Well, whatever you did, thank you," Anastasia said, deciding that it was pointless to dig into the matter any further. "You know, something else is kind of bothering me. This may sound stupid, but I feel like my grandparents didn't want me at the town meeting."

"What makes you say that?" Frost asked, his voice

suddenly a little strained.

"I think I'm an embarrassment to them. What other reason would they have for not inviting me?"

"You have to stop thinking so negatively about yourself, Anastasia. Anyone would be lucky to have you in their life."

Anastasia blushed, not used to hearing such sweet words from a boy. "You're right – *again* – and I need to start taking more control of my life. I loved going to those town meetings when I was young, so invitation or not, we're going tonight."

"That's not a good idea," Frost said uneasily. "The plan was *not* to be seen, remember?"

"We won't actually go inside the church, just secretly observe from the outside," Anastasia reassured him. "Come on, it'll be fun."

"Yeah, maybe," Frost muttered.

As Frost started in the direction of the church, he became very quiet, making Anastasia wonder what could be wrong. After all, it was just a harmless town meeting.

"We don't have to go, if you really don't want to," Anastasia said in concern.

"If this makes you happy, then I'm in," Frost replied, giving her a small smile.

When they reached the church, Frost parked behind a long line of cars at the side of the road. Although Anastasia remembered the town meetings as always being busy, this was ridiculous. From the church and school parking lots and all the way to the street, there were cars everywhere, making it seem like the whole town was in attendance.

"Is it always like this?" Anastasia asked with a furrowed brow as they exited the SUV and began to make their way toward the church.

"My knowledge of town meetings comes from my dad, who only started attending when he opened his business,"

Frost admitted. "So, I wouldn't really know, but this does seem a bit excessive."

Coming to a stop in front of the church, Anastasia looked up to see the steeple reaching high into the night sky, crowned by a large, stark cross that appeared almost menacing. It was hard to take her eyes off the imposing symbol, but when staring upwards started to make her feel dizzy, she slowly turned her attention to the oversized two-door entrance. Just like the rest of the building, the doors were impeccably maintained, despite being over a hundred years old, and featured the occasional design of a Biblical figure.

Ever so carefully, Anastasia began to open one of the doors. She cringed as it creaked loudly, but thankfully, no one would've heard the noise because of the heated argument that was occurring within the church. Anastasia peeked from behind the door which was slightly ajar, curious as to what could cause such a commotion.

As expected, the church was packed with people, several of whom had to stand since all the pews were full. It seemed like everyone was engaged in a discussion, but it was her grandfather and Mr. Stone's voices which rang out the loudest and clearest.

"Dammit, Fredrick, why won't you listen to me?" Mr. Stone yelled, obviously reaching his breaking point. "We have a *cougar* problem. I've been aware of the issue for a while, and I have traps set up. My son and I already dealt with one of them."

Mr. Lockhart sneered at Mr. Stone. "If you think this town will put their safety in your hands, then you truly are crazy. You're a man who's always had a lot to hide, so how can we trust you now? We don't know what happens in that little isolated cabin of yours, practically in the middle of nowhere.

For all we know, you could be trying to protect the beast."

Mrs. Lockhart stood up and said something to her husband, which Anastasia couldn't hear. Mr. Stone heard, though, and he was quick to comment.

"For everyone's sake, I hope you at least listen to your wife. You're going to start a panic. Is that what you want?"

Mr. Lockhart hesitated for a moment, but Anastasia knew that he wouldn't remain quiet for long.

"You might want to hear this," Anastasia whispered to Frost. "They're talking about the cougar, and it's getting kind of weird."

When Anastasia didn't receive a response, she turned to Frost, who was leaning against the closed door and looking off into the distance, as if he wanted to leave.

"I can hear just fine," Frost finally stated in a melancholy tone.

"Don't be sad," Anastasia said gently, stepping in front of Frost and reaching for his hands. She assumed he was upset that her grandfather and his father were fighting again, and she felt bad for dragging him to the meeting to hear it. "They'll learn to get along someday, and if they don't, we'll just have to make them." She smiled, hoping her words would help Frost feel better – they obviously didn't.

Anastasia was about to suggest that they go back to her house when suddenly, Frost's grip on her hand tightened as he looked at something over her shoulder. Spinning around, Anastasia saw a man walking toward them, and as he drew closer, she realized that it was Pete. Half of his face was still covered in a bandage, and he limped slightly, as if he was recovering from a bad fall.

Pete ascended the stairs to the church, and upon seeing Anastasia, he gave her a small but friendly nod, likely recognizing her as his boss' granddaughter. However, when he spotted Frost, who'd been uncharacteristically slumped behind Anastasia, the two exchanged an odd glance which lasted for several moments and left Pete looking startled and even a little frightened. Finally proceeding forward, Pete opened the church door, but before entering, he gave Frost another glance, his expression now one of confusion.

"Um, is there something you're not telling me?" Anastasia asked Frost, utterly bewildered by Pete's behavior.

"Not that I can think of," Frost replied a bit too fast.

Suspicious, Anastasia cracked the door open to see Pete heading to the front of the church. As people began to notice his presence, the chatter died down, and even her grandfather and Mr. Stone's ongoing bickering came to a stop. However, it wasn't until Pete had reached the front and started to speak that the church became deadly silent.

"I've had an encounter," Pete's voice echoed around the church, "and as much as I want to forget it ever happened, I've been left with more than just bad memories." He paused to gently touch his bandaged face, but even that seemed too painful as he quickly drew his hand away. "Five days ago, I was hunting deep in the woods, near a tributary of the Great Rapids. I'd spotted unusually large animal tracks leading to the creek, and after following them, I discovered the ice had been brutally smashed, likely for access to the flowing waters below. Certain that the animal wouldn't venture far from his water source, I scoured the area until I heard the unearthly growl coming from behind me. Before I knew what was happening, I was pinned to the ground. With my rifle as my only aid, I fought back and was able to escape with my life, but not before the beast tore his claws into my face."

Slowly, Pete began to unwrap his bandage, and when it was completely removed, there were several gasps of surprise and disgust. Although Anastasia was too far away to see his face clearly, she could imagine umpteen stitches in the shape of three claw marks. As murmurs rose from around the church, Pete held up his hand, as if he had one last thing to say.

"I was taken by such surprise that I didn't have the chance to get a good look, but the one thing that is forever engraved in my mind are those eyes."

"If we're going to keep our families and ourselves safe, then we need a plan," Mike spoke up, taking a stand at the front of the church. "A way to ensure that every inch of Cedar Falls Woods is searched."

Several people applauded Mike, while others began to discuss among themselves what actions should be taken.

"My brother's right," Leo said, standing up. "We've been tracking this problem for a while now, but we need more help. We can't just allow these attacks to keep on happening."

"It's time we killed the beast!" Mike cried out passionately, causing an almost unanimous roar of support from the crowd.

"We need to leave before this meeting really gets out-of-control," Frost said, taking hold of Anastasia's arm and hurrying her away from the church.

"I want to know what they're talking about," Anastasia protested, struggling to keep up with Frost's increasingly fast pace. "What I heard back there wasn't normal."

"You shouldn't have been listening."

"Well, I was. So, what the hell is going on?"

"You know what this town is like," Frost said with spite. "They judge what they don't understand and then believe it's their God-given right to do something about it."

"Are we still talking about the cougar?" Anastasia asked, after they'd reached the SUV and he'd urged her to get inside.

"What else would we be talking about?" Frost answered,

driving away quickly. He looked angry and even a little scared.

"You tell me. Pete was attacked the day *after* Chloe. You'd already taken care of the cougar by that point. Do you think he came back?"

"Yeah, that's what happened," Frost replied in an unconvincing tone.

"Frost, I need to know you're telling me the truth."

Likely noting the expression of concern upon Anastasia's face, Frost reached for her hand. "You *are* safe, Anastasia. As usual, the town is being paranoid and blowing everything out of proportion. It would be best if you just forgot this night ever happened."

Silence fell over them as Frost drove Anastasia back to her house. The more she thought about his words, the more sense they made. Although Cedar Falls definitely had a wildlife problem, that town meeting had been beyond absurd – almost like something out of a movie. They truly were paranoid, with Mr. Stone being the only one who sounded normal. Relaxing a little, Anastasia realized that if she was going to live in this town, then she'd just have to put up with all the craziness.

Part Six

Myth of the Werewolf

Anastasia's breath caught in her throat as Frost ran his fingers over her neck and then up along her face. He always touched her in a sweet and gentle manner, especially when they were alone – like right now. Anastasia seemed to have a mesmerizing effect on Frost, as if nothing else mattered whenever he was with her. He appeared to be most content while merely looking at Anastasia and holding her in his arms. Those feelings didn't go unrequited; she cherished moments like these, and when they were apart, her heart was heavy and yearned only for him.

At this moment, Anastasia and Frost were parked outside Cedar Falls High, cuddling in his SUV. Her suspension had come to an end, and she knew that it was time to face everyone inside. She took strength in her goal of doing well in her courses, and it was also a great relief to know that the case against Mr. O'Donoghue was closed. However, that wouldn't stop people from talking about her, and now that her relationship with Frost was no longer a secret, the school would surely be abuzz with gossip.

"We should probably go inside," Anastasia said bravely, albeit reluctantly, while beginning to break from Frost's embrace.

"Please don't go," Frost muttered softly into Anastasia's ear, unwilling to release his grasp. "We can spare a few more minutes."

Anastasia didn't need to be asked twice as she settled back into Frost's strong arms and placed her head upon his chest. She listened to his heartbeat, noting how it rapidly increased as she slipped her hand under his sweater and then ran her fingers along his firm, hot chest.

"You're so warm," she commented. "How?"

"It's what you do to me," Frost replied, before kissing her forehead.

Sighing, Anastasia stared at Frost's beautiful eyes, while smoothing his soft, unruly hair. She could see and feel the deep affection he had for her, but every so often, she suspected that there was something he wasn't telling her. It didn't make sense, especially since he was usually so open with her. Still, sometimes he was just *too* mysterious.

"You still owe me a first date," Anastasia pointed out, hoping to finally bring normalcy to their relationship. She wanted to make Frost feel secure, so he would be completely honest with her – that is, if he wasn't already.

"How about this weekend?" Frost suggested in his huskiest voice, as if attempting to seduce her. "We can go someplace that's really nice, maybe out-of-town."

"As long as I'm with you, Dale's Diner would seem like paradise." Anastasia cringed slightly after speaking. She wasn't used to being so affectionate and honest with her feelings. Luckily, Frost didn't seem to mind at all.

"I'd prefer to stay away from Dale's, at least until someone else body checks a waitress."

"It wasn't that bad," Anastasia said with a light laugh.

"Even so, I want to take you to Hartfield," Frost protested. "There's this beautiful little restaurant that overlooks the water. My mother used to work there, and I loved just sitting on the patio, watching as the sun set."

"Hartfield," Anastasia repeated. "I've never heard of that town."

"It's on the other side of Cedar Falls Woods." Frost then added with a smirk, "Trust me, it's there."

"It sounds far away."

"Distance only matters if we're apart." Slowly, Frost reached for Anastasia's hand, while looking into her eyes until she felt herself melting. "I know our relationship has been a bit unconventional, and that's what makes it so special. We're *both* different, Anastasia, but that doesn't mean we can't have it all. Our first date *will* be perfect."

Anastasia smiled, even though she didn't entirely understand what Frost was trying to say. It seemed like he had something to prove, which was very out-of-character for him. "I know it will be," was all she said, before leading him from the SUV.

Holding hands, Anastasia and Frost walked into the school. As expected, the students were divided into small groups, whispering as if they had just heard the biggest secret ever told. However, Anastasia soon realized that hardly anyone was paying attention to her or Frost. Had the time finally come for the student body to get over her? She certainly hoped so.

After Frost had walked her to class and said goodbye, Anastasia was left to face her least favorite period — chemistry. Somehow, she managed through it, even with Jill giving her cut-eye for the better part of the time. She just kept reminding herself that Jill and her little friends were the ones with the problem, not her.

As the morning progressed, Anastasia began feeling more confident in her decision to return to Cedar Falls High. She now realized that she had every right to be there, and surprisingly, a couple of her classmates even seemed to be warming up to her. Still, when lunchtime arrived, it was nice to be around someone who actually cared for her.

"Hey, sexy," Frost greeted as Anastasia sat at the table he'd saved for them. "I see you made it through the first half of the day."

"Did you have any doubt?" she asked with a pretend pout.

"Never," Frost replied, while reaching for Anastasia's hand. "Damn, you look so beautiful."

Upon Frost's simple touch, a shiver of excitement ran throughout Anastasia's body. She wanted him so badly, and she knew that he felt the same. Despite the busy cafeteria, her focus was solely on Frost, until everything else seemed to blur around him.

"Let's ditch this place and eat in my car," Frost suggested.

"Perv," she teased.

"That's not what I'm after and you know it. I just like being alone with you."

"You don't have to convince me," Anastasia said with a soft laugh, quickly gathering her backpack and lunch. She was about to stand up when Marissa slammed her lunch tray on the table and then sat down.

"I can't believe Kate," Marissa fumed. "She's spilled like every secret I've ever had. How can she be so heartless?"

Repressing a groan over their interrupted plans, Anastasia cast Frost a pleading look. He responded with a small, comforting smile. Although she wanted to spend time with Marissa, did it really have to be at this very moment?

"Are you really that surprised by Kate's behavior?" Frost asked Marissa, blatantly but compassionately.

"Well, no," Marissa admitted after a moment's pause. "I guess our friendship was purely superficial." Sighing, she unwrapped her sandwich and began eating, obviously unaware of Anastasia and Frost's desire to be alone. "So, have you visited Chloe since she was released from the hospital?"

"Of course," Anastasia replied, now eating her own lunch. "She's doing really well, but it's going to be a while before she can come back to school."

Marissa nodded. "Thank God she's okay."

Suddenly, two girls passed nearby, allowing Anastasia to overhear a disturbing part of their conversation. "The werewolf of Cedar Falls is back," one of the girls said in a shaky voice. "Chloe was attacked during a full moon – what else could it possibly be? My dad said the exact same thing happened seventeen years ago."

With wide, frightened eyes, the other girl nodded. "Have you heard the latest? Someone spotted a large wolf in the woods last night. If it really was the werewolf, that means we're in danger, with or without the full moon."

"And don't forget about what happened to Pete – we don't need more evidence than that."

"Are you two for real?" Anastasia interrupted the girls. She wasn't usually so rude, but what they were saying was too absurd to ignore. "Chloe and Pete were attacked by a cougar, not some mythological creature."

"You were the one who was with Chloe on that night," the girl stated, while looking closely at Anastasia.

"Yeah, so I should know," Anastasia retorted.

Adamantly, the girl shook her head. "We don't get cougars here, but we do have wolves. Cedar Falls is home to a different kind of wolf, though – one that's bigger, deadlier and all evil."

Anastasia couldn't help but snort. "Tell Kate this is her most pathetic ploy yet. Does she really think she can scare me back to Toronto with some fairy tale?"

"Kate doesn't even talk to us," the girl said slowly, casting

Anastasia an odd look.

"Did you see the werewolf?" the other girl pried. "You can tell us the truth – we believe."

"I was there, too," Marissa hurried to speak up. "It happened so fast that I can't be certain of what I saw. It was something wild, though, and ferocious. I've never been so scared in my whole life."

"Seriously?" Anastasia asked Marissa. "Don't tell me you believe in werewolves."

Shrugging, Marissa looked at the floor. "I don't know what to think, but a lot of people have been speculating on what could've attacked Chloe and Pete, and their conclusions are all the same. I don't want to dwell on it, though – too many bad memories."

"You should have told me what people were saying," Anastasia said to Marissa in an annoyed tone.

Marissa looked sheepish. "Sorry, Anastasia. I didn't want to upset you, and I guess I was kind of preoccupied with my own problems."

"Tell everyone the truth, Frost," Anastasia said, turning to face him. She was surprised to find him looking nervous and even somewhat pale. "Frost, are you feeling alright?"

"What?" Frost asked, seemingly snapping out of his thoughts. "Oh, yeah, I'm fine." He then directed his attention toward the two girls who were still standing near their table. "I saw the animal that attacked Chloe, and it *was* a cougar – there's absolutely no doubt about that."

"I'm not going anywhere near those woods for a very long time," one of the girls said, looking unconvinced by Frost's explanation.

"Me either," her friend nodded in agreement.

Without saying another word, the two girls walked away, leaving behind an unsettling atmosphere and many unanswered questions. However, Anastasia was more concerned about Frost. He seemed to be lost in his thoughts yet again, and he was clearly worrying about something.

"What's wrong?" Anastasia asked him gently.

"Nothing," Frost responded abruptly, while turning an undue amount of attention toward finishing his lunch.

Narrowing her eyes, Anastasia studied him. It was evident that he was hiding something, but what could it be? She knew that Frost loved Cedar Falls Woods, so maybe he was concerned that it would be negatively impacted by all this werewolf rigmarole. Yet, if that was the case, why couldn't he be honest? This was a prime example of how Frost's behavior sometimes didn't make sense, at least to Anastasia.

"I know you guys don't believe in werewolves," Marissa said, breaking the silence, "but please be careful anyway. You just never know."

Despite her very best efforts to stay rational, Anastasia shivered slightly. She now listened to her classmate's whisperings, discovering that it revolved around the attacks on Chloe and Pete and especially the werewolf. It seemed like everyone had a theory, supported by some freaky evidence that they vowed to be true.

Memories from Anastasia's first night in Cedar Falls suddenly circulated in her mind. She could've sworn that she'd seen a shadowy figure in her backyard, and whatever it was had caused her frightening, life-like nightmare about a wolf. Knowing that she was being foolish and that these thoughts were solely driven by paranoia, Anastasia forced herself to be realistic. Nevertheless, she couldn't quite shake the eerie feeling which had quickly engulfed her.

That night, Anastasia waited by her window like she always did. She was cozy in dark plaid flannel pajamas and fuzzy black socks; it was a winter-appropriate bedtime outfit which her grandmother insisted she wear after finding Anastasia's skimpy nightie in the laundry room. Surprisingly, Frost found her just as attractive in these pajamas, causing Anastasia to happily adapt to the ensemble. Now, as she sat comfortably in the rocking chair, which had been placed by the window, and peered outside, she realized that the only thing that could make the night better was Frost's presence.

Glancing at the clock, Anastasia read 11:55 p.m. Frost was never late, and she wondered if he would show up at all. She checked her cell phone for what seemed like the hundredth time, but there was still no message from Frost. She had already called him twice, only to receive his voicemail. Where the hell was he?

Suddenly, the sound of footsteps came from upstairs, startling Anastasia in the process. She tensed slightly, while wondering what was going on. Her grandparents were always asleep by 11 p.m. and didn't rise until 7 a.m. This routine, which seemed to be set in stone, was the very reason why Anastasia and Frost's evening encounters had never been discovered.

Slowly, Anastasia rose from the rocking chair and crept out of her bedroom. She'd just entered the foyer when her grandparents came down the stairs, whispering in serious tones. Anastasia retreated until she was out of view; however, she made sure that she could still hear what they were saying. She also watched them, noting how the glow from a nightlight made them look like creepy shadow people.

"Why do *you* have to be the town hero?" Mrs. Lockhart demanded. "You're too old for this."

"Shhh...don't wake up Anastasia," Mr. Lockhart scolded as he opened the closet to retrieve his coat and boots. "You know that I'm not trying to be a hero. There are several other men out there who are tracking this thing. And for the record, I'm not too old."

"Those other men aren't my husband. Please, Fredrick, I can hardly sleep because of worry."

Mr. Lockhart sighed before stepping forward and kissing his wife's forehead. "I don't have a choice. The werewolf has to be killed."

Anastasia muffled her gasp. If her grandfather was so convinced the werewolf was real that he'd risk his life to find him, then it must be true. With a pounding heart and feeling almost sick, she realized that all his odd behavior came down to the werewolf – he was just trying to keep her safe. Suddenly, a terrifying thought entered her mind. What if Frost had been on his way to see her when he was attacked by the werewolf? For all she knew, he could be lying in the woods, hurt and scared, or worse, he could already be dead. These thoughts panicked Anastasia, resulting in an insatiable need to uncover exactly what was going on.

"Go to bed, Rose," Mr. Lockhart continued. "Take one of those sleeping pills, and when you wake up tomorrow morning, we'll hopefully have a better idea of where the beast is hiding."

"Be careful," Mrs. Lockhart begged as he exited the house.

Mr. Lockhart stopped outside the open door to glance at his wife. "I promise," was all he said before disappearing into the night.

Anastasia waited impatiently as her grandmother walked up the stairs. When she heard the bedroom door closing, she hurried to the closet and then put on her coat and boots. Within seconds, she was outside, searching for her grandfather, Frost and answers.

It was a bitterly cold night, and the crescent moon offered little light. Even the small, twinkling stars seemed further away than usual. Still, Anastasia soon found her grandfather scurrying toward the shed at the side of the house. Staying hidden behind a tree, she watched as he unlocked the shed, entered and returned a moment later with a rifle. As a child, Anastasia remembered being strictly told to stay away from that locked shed; now she knew why.

Her grandfather proceeded to hurry toward the road, passing so close to the tree which Anastasia was hiding behind that she could hear his rapid breathing. It was clear that he was nervous, and this gave her an eerie feeling; she'd never seen him frightened before. As he went, she remained hidden, watching until he disappeared from her sight.

Ever so carefully, Anastasia crept over their front lawn and along the side of the road. She quickly spotted her grandfather about a hundred feet away. It looked like he was waiting for someone; perhaps other werewolf hunters, Anastasia guessed. Her suspicion seemed to be confirmed as a truck sped by, hardly giving her enough time to retreat behind the trees yet again. Her grandfather swiftly entered the truck, and then they drove away, leaving Anastasia unable to follow him any longer.

The frigid conditions were starting to get the better of Anastasia as she shivered uncontrollably. She'd never experienced coldness quite like this before, and her exposed skin, although minimal, was already starting to feel like it was burning. She realized that not having a car meant she wouldn't be able to find Frost without seriously risking frostbite. Reluctantly, Anastasia turned back, knowing that's what Frost would want her to do. After all, he was more than likely sound asleep in his warm bed, while she panicked unnecessarily.

Anastasia had only taken a few hurried steps when a rustling came from a dense patch of nearby trees. She stopped and listened, terrified that she was being followed. The rustling ceased, but she could hear the faint sound of someone breathing. Slowly and numbly, Anastasia turned around, her heart racing as she scanned the area. That's when she saw something so shocking that she couldn't even scream. There, less than ten feet away, was a pair of eyes staring straight at her, as if seeing into her very soul. These eyes belonged to an animal – there was no doubt about that. However, from the way his eyes shone and how the rest of his body remained unseen, Anastasia knew that this wasn't any ordinary animal.

Not wanting to stay a second longer, Anastasia ran as fast as she could. She was trying to return to her house, but somehow, it seemed so far away. Anastasia was entering a state of desperation, and she had to know if the creature was following her. She turned around, while continuing to run, and was horrified to see what could only be a werewolf chasing after her. The werewolf appeared like a mere shadow, with the exception of his shining eyes, and he was big – too big.

Before Anastasia knew what was happening, she tripped and fell to the ground, hitting her head hard. It throbbed with pain, causing her to wince. As she lay there, stunned, freezing and staring up at the moon and stars, everything began to spin. Among this celestial blur appeared a beautiful white werewolf with bright blue eyes. He seemed to gaze upon Anastasia in concern, but she couldn't be sure. Then everything went black.

Anastasia awoke with a start, only to find herself in bed and dressed solely in her flannel pajamas and fuzzy socks. Her bedroom was still dark, and as she looked at the clock, she discovered that it was only 4:30 a.m. Vague memories from late last night circulated in her mind, confusing her in the process. The last thing she remembered was lying on the ground with that mesmerizing werewolf looking over her. She'd been scared of the werewolf and was running away from him – that much she was sure of. However, it was the image of those eyes which had truly been imprinted in her mind. There was something kind and gentle about them, but it was more than just that – those eyes had belonged to Frost.

Reasoning that it had been a dream similar to the one she'd had during her first night in Cedar Falls, Anastasia got out of bed to get a glass of water. She was momentarily perturbed to discover that her head felt heavy, but since her throat also felt dry, she concluded that it was due to an oncoming cold. She decided to ignore the symptoms because her immune system usually fought off colds in no time. Besides, she had more pressing issues to think about; despite imagining her grandfather as a werewolf hunter and even the werewolf himself, one thing remained true – Frost had never shown up to her window last night.

✳ ✳ ✳

The temperature in Cedar Falls kept decreasing until it was too cold to even snow. Although the sky was clear and a pretty shade of blue, the air was motionless, making it uncomfortable to breathe. It was the following morning, and the weather had forced Anastasia to stay inside her house, watching from behind the door. She was waiting for Frost to pick her up – that is, if he was even planning to come. She was desperate to get an explanation from him, or at the very least, find out if he was alright. Unfortunately, his unusual tardiness was only causing her to become more frustrated and even anxious. When Frost's SUV finally pulled into her driveway, she hurried toward it, trying to ignore the frigid air which nipped at her face.

"Sorry," Frost mumbled as she entered the vehicle.

"For what?" Anastasia asked, willing to give him the benefit of the doubt.

"I know I'm a little late."

"If you're referring to last night, I'd say you're more than just a little late." Anastasia continued before Frost could respond. "You always come to my window at night, so when you didn't show up, I was worried. Hell, you weren't even answering your cell phone."

Looking perplexed, Frost was silent for a moment. He then faced Anastasia, speaking quietly, "I'm sorry. I'd never intentionally worry you."

"Where were you?"

"Working at my dad's hardware store until 11 p.m.," Frost hurried to explain. "It's unbelievably busy with people buying extra locks and other supplies to secure their houses, all because of some werewolf legend." He paused, as if thinking about something serious. Then, he added remorsefully, "I actually don't think I'll be able to come to your window anymore – at least for a while."

"What about this weekend?" Anastasia asked, overcome with disappointment. "Are you too busy then?"

"Nothing will stop us from being together. We *will* have that date."

Studying Frost, Anastasia noted the bags under his eyes and his constant yawning. She knew that he hadn't slept well, if at all. Since not showing up to her window was the first time he'd truly let her down, she decided to forget about it.

"Don't make a habit of standing me up," Anastasia said sternly, while leaning in for a kiss nonetheless.

Their lips touched for a mere second before he pulled

away and said, "We better get to school." He then drove away, being unusually quiet.

Anastasia repressed a sigh. She was starting to wonder if he found her attractive. Although Frost constantly told her how pretty she was, his inaction spoke louder than words; they hadn't even shared a proper kiss yet. It was beginning to get so pathetic that Anastasia couldn't bring herself to dwell on it any longer.

"So, what are your thoughts on this werewolf mania?" Anastasia asked casually, despite being really curious to hear his opinion. Although she hated to admit it even to herself, the gossip and her dreams were starting to become unnerving.

Frost never had a chance to reply as he suddenly broke hard, causing the SUV to swerve slightly to the left. Anastasia gasped, quickly turning her gaze away from Frost and onto the road ahead of them. She caught a glimpse of a white tail as a deer dashed into the woods.

"Are you okay?" Frost asked hurriedly.

"Yeah, fine," Anastasia answered, her heart rate returning to normal.

A few seconds later, two men emerged from the woods, riding on snowmobiles. Upon seeing Frost's SUV idling on a skewed angle, they came to a stop and dismounted. As they took off their helmets, Anastasia realized that it was Leo and Mike.

"Werewolf hunters," Frost seethed under his breath.

Before Anastasia could say a word, Frost exited the SUV and marched toward Leo and Mike. Quickly, she followed him. Anastasia had never seen Frost look so angry, and it worried her. She remembered the night she'd first laid eyes upon him; he'd been the mediator, not the one initiating the fight.

"What the hell are you playing at?" Frost asked in a strained voice, obviously trying hard to stay calm. "We could've been killed by that deer."

"Calm down, son," Leo responded. "We didn't see any deer."

"I did, and he almost rammed into us," Frost argued.

"We came from a designated snowmobile trail," Mike spoke up. "We haven't done anything wrong."

"I've been traveling this road for years," Frost snapped. "I've never had an issue with the wildlife until people like you started trampling through the woods, disturbing everything in your path. Give up this stupid werewolf hunt before someone really gets hurt."

"I don't know if you're some type of tree-hugger or just plain nuts," Mike snapped right back, "but it's *the people* like me and my brother who are trying to keep Cedar Falls safe."

"You're all making a big mistake," Frost warned.

"And you're in our way," Mike retorted, before putting his helmet back on and returning to his snowmobile.

"This hunt is happening whether you like it or not, Frost," Leo added. "There's been too much evidence against the beast. He has to be destroyed."

Anastasia watched as Leo and Mike mounted their snowmobiles and then rode off into the woods. "That was totally uncalled for," she remarked, finally finding her voice.

"I know," Frost said gruffly. "They make me sick."

"I was referring to you!" Anastasia was flabbergasted by Frost's behavior. Although he had her heart, that didn't mean she'd allow him to act like an ass. "Dammit, Frost, they had rifles!"

"Sorry," Frost muttered for the third time that day. "I shouldn't have put you in that situation." He hurried back to his SUV, looking very distraught.

What's going on here? Anastasia pondered, hardly noticing the freezing air or frosted woods which surrounded her. *Just when I start to get my life in order, everyone else goes completely crazy!*

✳ ✳ ✳

It was a Thursday afternoon as Anastasia exited the pharmacy with a pack of honey and lemon throat lozenges in hand. Her usually strong immune system had failed her, leaving her throat dry and itchy and her nose congested. Even her head ached slightly, causing her to conclude that she had a sinus cold. Nevertheless, she refused to spend any extra time in bed, adamant about not missing school, work and especially that forthcoming date with Frost.

The sun was beginning to set as Anastasia headed toward her grandmother's car, which she'd borrowed to run this errand, but before she could enter, she noticed a flyer under her windshield wiper. She retrieved the flyer and unfolded it, expecting to find some type of home improvement service offered at a discounted price. Instead, what she read was so bizarre that it startled her.

The township of Cedar Falls requests all citizens to render items of pure silver to the community collection station at #1 Main Street. No item is too big or small, with every collected piece to be melted and made into bullets. This is an urgent request in response to the serious wildlife situation occurring in Cedar Falls Woods. Volunteers with animal tracking skills are being recruited on an ongoing basis. Those with military backgrounds are especially encouraged to respond. Please apply in person.

"What the hell?" Anastasia muttered to herself. Although she wanted to believe this was just a prank, the official letterhead of the township made it look pretty damn real. As for the contents, well, she was no ammunitions expert, but she suspected that bullets didn't have to be made from pure silver. That would only be necessary if, according to folklore, they wanted to kill a werewolf.

Anastasia shook her head, as if trying to erase the thoughts from her mind. She then entered the car, determined to stay rational. Since first hearing about the werewolf in the school lunchroom three days ago, the town had become increasingly obsessed with the supposedly mythological creature. In fact, she feared that chaos would soon break out if things continued as they were.

She had only been driving for a few minutes when, after turning onto a usually quiet road, she spotted a small group of people standing at the edge of the woods. Two cars were nearby, both idling with the headlights still on and the doors left wide open, like they'd exited in haste. Worried that someone might be hurt, she parked her car and rushed toward them.

Anastasia's presence immediately frightened the group, which included two young identical twin boys, a man and woman in their late forties and an elderly couple. They were all wide-eyed and breathing heavily, but unlike the others, the twin boys looked more excited than scared.

"Is everyone...?" Anastasia didn't have the chance to finish her sentence as the middle-aged man interrupted her in an almost frantic tone.

"Did you see him, too?"

"I don't know what you're..."

"I tried to get my camera," the man interrupted once again, "but he was gone so fast."

Suddenly, one of the boys growled and leapt at Anastasia, his arms extended and his fingers bent as if he was mimicking a clawed animal. When she let out a small gasp, he laughed and then announced proudly, "I just saw the werewolf!"

"I saw him first," his brother argued, giving him a hard shove.

"Stop it," the woman, who must've been their mother, scolded. "Now is *not* the time."

Concerned and confused, Anastasia glanced at the elderly couple, who had remained quiet up until this point.

"You should go home, dear," the elderly woman advised. "We should all go home. It's not safe for us to be here."

Their attention returned to the snowy ground at the edge of the woods, exactly where they'd been looking before Anastasia arrived. Even the twins fell silent, mesmerized by whatever was on the ground. Gently pushing past the man and woman, who were blocking her view, Anastasia came to a stop and directed her gaze downwards. What she saw almost made her cry out in horror.

Barely illuminated by the fading sunlight were wolf tracks so massive that they couldn't possibly belong to an ordinary wolf. They were also embedded very deep into the snow, evidence of the creature's extraordinary weight. Yet, most shocking of all was how the short trail of wolf tracks turned into barefooted human prints which led into the dark woods.

"You...you saw this happen?" Anastasia stuttered in disbelief, unable to take her eyes off the prints.

The man nodded, speaking before anyone else could. "My wife, kids and I were driving down this road, with my in-laws following in the car behind us. Then, out-of-nowhere, the largest wolf I've ever seen ran right in front of us. I almost hit him, and for a split second he stopped, looking at me with terrified eyes that seemed to glow in the beam of my headlights. The next thing I knew, he resumed running, but before he could disappear into the woods, he transformed...into a human!"

The man was starting to become overexcited again, causing his wife to soothingly put her arm around him.

"I thought I'd gone crazy," the man admitted, "but I wasn't the only one to see him – we all did. Then we found these..." His voice trailed off as he reached for the digital camera, which hung around his wrist by a strap, and then began taking pictures of the tracks.

"If only we'd seen who he was," the woman said, shaking her head sadly, "then all of this could've been over."

Completely overwhelmed by what she'd just seen and heard, Anastasia began to back away, her mind racing with thoughts. The werewolf was real, and as much as she wanted to convince herself otherwise, nothing would change the fact that the evidence was right in front of her eyes. This whole time she'd thought the town was crazy, unwilling to even consider the possibility of the werewolf's existence, and as a result, she'd become exactly what she despised – narrow-minded. Well, not anymore.

Turning around, Anastasia ran to her car, and as she went, she heard the elderly man calling out to her.

"To stay safe, you must stay far away from the woods!"

Anastasia shivered as she started her car and sped away. Didn't that man realize it was impossible to follow his advice since *all* of Cedar Falls was surrounded by woods? There was nowhere to run and definitely no place to hide. And the worst part was that the werewolf could be anyone.

These thoughts caused panic to slowly seize Anastasia, but she fought hard against it. She knew that to save her sanity and avoid the hysterics which many members of the community had fallen victim to, she'd have to remain level-headed. She forced herself to reason that at some point, all animals were unknown to humans and these first encounters were likely as scary as this one. Humans had just stopped looking, so who knew what else was out there?

When she reached her house, Anastasia hurried inside, determined to get answers from her grandparents. She wanted to know everything they knew about the werewolf, including why they had tried to hide his existence. From forbidding her to walk home from school to not inviting her to the town meeting, it all made sense now, especially her grandfather's weird behavior.

"Grandma!" Anastasia called as she made her way through the foyer. "Grandpa! Are you guys here?"

When she didn't receive a response, she looked in the living room and then the kitchen, only to find them both empty. However, she soon spotted a note attached to the refrigerator which read, *Your grandmother and I have gone into town to run some errands. We might be late. Don't go out again.*

Anastasia couldn't help but scoff at the note. It seemed like her grandparents were never home anymore, and they always used some stupid excuse to explain their absence. Tonight was the perfect example; her grandparents knew that she'd been going into town, so they could've easily asked her to do their errands – not that there really were any.

More suspicious than ever, Anastasia ran up the stairs and toward her grandfather's study. Along with the shed at the side of the house, this was the only other place her grandparents had declared off-limits. That's what made it the perfect location for hiding something, especially if they wanted to keep it from her.

Stopping in front of the closed study door, Anastasia tried to suppress her guilt as she turned the doorknob, which squeaked slightly, and then stepped inside. She'd always been a good girl who'd only imagined what was behind this door, and now that she knew, it was a huge letdown. The room would've been bare if it wasn't for two file cabinets, a small desk and a chair.

She switched on the light, knowing that she would need it if she was going to find a logbook, photographs or just about anything which may give her insight into the Cedar Falls werewolf. Unfortunately, having the light on meant she'd have to search fast because if her grandparents came home early, they'd be able to see the study window aglow from outside.

Anastasia opened one of the file cabinets and rifled through its contents, finding nothing other than decades of tax returns. "Don't they know you only have to keep the last seven years?" she muttered, rolling her eyes as she shut the bottom drawer.

Annoyed that she'd spent several minutes on the first cabinet, Anastasia wasted no time proceeding to the next one. Luck was definitely not on her side as she discovered it was filled with pay stubs, all neatly placed in his and her sections and organized in chronological order. "Hoard much?" she commented with a groan, growing even more frustrated as she closed the last drawer.

She looked around the room, wondering if she'd missed anything, but the last place to search would be the desk, and with only one short, narrow drawer in the middle, she doubted it would contain much more than stationeries. Regardless, she reached for the drawer and upon trying to pull it open, she realized that it was locked. She frowned. Suddenly, it seemed a lot more interesting.

Trying to think like her grandfather, Anastasia kneeled on the floor to look under the desk, hoping he'd somehow hidden the key there. Unfortunately, he hadn't. With a disappointed sigh, she stood up, but as she did so, she noticed the calendar lying on his desk. Quickly, she lifted the calendar, smiling proudly as a small silver-colored key was revealed. Her grandfather always said the best hiding places were the most obvious ones, so she'd been confident that the key would be in his study.

Retrieving the key, Anastasia unlocked the drawer and slowly pulled it open. Inside she found a thin white folder marked, *Confidential*, and a tape recorder sitting on top of it. After placing the recorder onto the desk, she opened the folder and then let out a startled gasp. It was a copy of Chloe's medical report from the night she was attacked. She couldn't fathom how her grandfather had obtained this information or even why he would want it.

Anastasia scanned through the report, thinking it might give her some answers, but most of it was written with medical terminology that she didn't understand. It wasn't until she came to the last page that she saw a highlighted paragraph and, from her interpretation, it stated that Chloe's wounds were inflicted by a cougar.

Finished with the report, Anastasia put it back in the folder before picking up another one, which she assumed would also be Chloe's. As she began to read, she was shocked to see that the medical report actually belonged to Pete. Flipping through the pages, she soon found another highlighted paragraph, with this one sourcing Pete's injuries as coming from an unidentified mammal. It went on to suggest that the closest species capable of inflicting such wounds was canis lupus – the wolf.

"Oh my gosh," Anastasia muttered, finally accepting that, unlike Chloe, Pete had indeed been attacked by a werewolf.

Hurriedly, she shoved the folder back into the drawer and then grabbed the recorder. The sole tape was already in it, and when she pressed play, the room was filled with chilling words spoken by a man with a very deep voice.

It was late — really late — when I heard that first howl. Silence followed for the next couple of minutes, then it came again, this time closer. He sounded angry, or maybe he was in pain. Either way, all I could be certain of was that I needed to see this thing. I ran outside, wearing not much more than a nightshirt and boots, but I didn't care as long as I had my rifle. I waited for the howls to start again, and they did — right behind me. Before I could move, I felt him breathing down my bare neck. I prepared to fire, knowing that speed and aim were the only two things that could keep me alive, but when I turned around, he was gone. It was like he was never there, even though he definitely had been. Then, from far in the distance, he howled as if mocking me. That was my only experience with the werewolf, and to be honest, I hope it's my last.

Almost instantly, another voice came from the recorder, this time that of a young girl.

Everyone says the werewolf is bad, but I don't think so. Last summer, when I was camping with my parents, I got lost in the woods really late at night. I was so scared until I heard a gentle whimper and saw the prettiest eyes. I knew he was my friend and that he wanted to help me, so I followed him. He brought me back to my campsite and after he left, I heard him howl like he was happy. Of course, when I told my parents, they thought I was lying because they never saw him, but I know the truth.

Even though Anastasia wanted to listen to more, she switched the recorder off, knowing that she'd stayed in her grandfather's study long enough. She quickly put everything back where they belonged, all the while wondering why her grandfather was collecting evidence of the werewolf's existence. She couldn't figure out what the point of it was — almost everyone already believed anyway.

After turning the light in the study off and shutting the door firmly behind her, Anastasia hurried to her bedroom, where she proceeded to sit in her rocking chair, with a soft blanket wrapped tightly around herself for comfort. Unfortunately, finally taking a minute to rest didn't stop her from dwelling on the crazy events of today and especially the potential consequences.

Her world now felt unreal because she could no longer deny the reality of supernatural creatures and perhaps all things that went bump in the night. While her initial reaction had been to confront her grandparents, she wondered if that was actually a smart idea. What if they wanted to send her home to keep her safe now that she knew the truth? They'd already proven they were willing to go to great lengths to make sure she was out of harm's way. She just wasn't ready to take that chance because leaving Cedar Falls meant saying goodbye to Frost.

Although Anastasia couldn't bear the thought of being without Frost, that didn't stop her from feeling very frustrated with him. In fact, he was as bad as her grandparents. She was certain that he knew about the werewolf because he was smart, observant and apparently more knowledgeable about Cedar Falls Woods than anyone else. Constantly telling her *not* to believe in the werewolf had been such an obvious attempt to cloud her judgment that she felt foolish for not realizing it sooner.

Despite all this, Anastasia sensed that there was another reason for Frost's behavior. Even though she was positive that he wanted to protect her, it was more than that. Could he have been trying to protect the werewolf, too? And if that was true, why? It seemed like a million questions were going through her mind, but Frost was the only one who could give her the answers she was seeking. She needed to get him alone, face-to-face, so they could have a serious conversation. Unfortunately, with Frost no longer coming to her window at night as well as his hectic work schedule, the next chance they would have to talk was tomorrow night, when he picked her up from work.

Getting up and walking to the window, Anastasia pulled the curtains aside to look out. Everything was still and silent, and with the snow-covered trees and ground glistening in the moon's glow, it seemed like just another ordinary night. However, she knew what was really out there, lurking in the woods as both man and beast.

"And I thought *I* used to lead a wild life," Anastasia muttered, her eyes locked on the dense trees that rose high into the starry night sky.

❊ ❊ ❊

It was after seven o'clock on a Friday evening as Anastasia worked alone in the library. She wasn't meant to be by herself, but her co-worker had called in at the last minute, saying she refused to work after dark as long as the beast was on the loose. Anastasia knew that her grandparents wouldn't be happy with this situation; however, she saw no other alternative since she couldn't close the library early nor ask her grandmother, who was at another impromptu town meeting, to fill in for the absent co-worker. Anastasia wasn't that concerned, though. After all, it wasn't like a werewolf could open a door. She almost laughed at the thought.

Placing a stray book upon the shelf, Anastasia realized that there was nothing else to do. The library was meticulously clean and organized, probably due to the fact that no one had entered for over two hours, and she'd long ago finished all her assigned tasks. With the opportunity at hand, Anastasia could no longer resist the urge to hurry toward the library's main computer and turn it on. This was the computer which held a comprehensive database of articles entitled The Cedar

Falls Archives, and Anastasia was dying to access it.

Typing the password she'd once seen her grandmother use, Anastasia quickly found the database and then searched *Cedar Falls Werewolf*. Ever since she began taking the myth seriously, she'd kept mentally replaying two conversations she'd overheard. Both the girl in the lunchroom at school and the medical assistant had said a werewolf attack occurred seventeen years ago. If this was true, the story must have been all over the Cedar Falls press, regardless of how small and poorly funded their printing operations were.

The database was slow, with the search taking almost a minute to complete; however, once it was done, Anastasia was left with an abundance of articles. In anticipation, she began skimming through them, but she was soon disappointed to learn that they offered no information about the werewolf. It was like Cedar Falls wanted to keep it their dirty little secret.

Frustrated, Anastasia was seconds away from abandoning the search when one particular article caught her attention. Dated seventeen years ago, the article was about a large female wolf who had been captured and killed in Cedar Falls Woods. According to the journalist, the wolf was hunted solely because of her size, with no rogue-like behavior having ever been reported. As the accompanying image finished loading, Anastasia gasped; the wolf wasn't just large – she was huge! Even more shocking was the wolf's eyes because, despite being dead, they were still open, vibrantly blue and looked exactly like Frost's. In an instant, she knew that this wolf was actually a werewolf, even if the publisher was too scared to state the whole truth.

With a racing heart, Anastasia shakily stood up and began searching for a book that someone had returned earlier today. She soon spotted the spine of the book, which read *A Guide to Wolves*, and then pulled it from the shelf. Trying to stay calm and as rational as possible, she opened the book and read feverishly.

Immediately, the book instilled in Anastasia the significance of the wolf. They were strong, brave and territorial animals who were at the top of the food chain, with no predators other than humans. Wolves truly were the rulers of the woods and a symbol of knowledge and power.

Just like Frost, Anastasia thought with a chill, while remembering the time he'd somehow known that they were being stalked by a cougar. The way he'd handled the situation displayed strength, bravery and territorial traits, and that cougar was definitely submissive to Frost. There had been nothing normal about that encounter, and her suspicions were heightened by Frost's mysterious claim that he had a great affinity with nature.

Gulping, Anastasia continued to read, discovering that several case studies had proven wolves to have excellent memories. *Frost has an unhuman-like memory*, she recalled. *There's no way he could've remembered being an abandoned baby in the woods. That is, unless he's not human...*

Anastasia could hardly believe the thoughts that she was having, but it was all too coincidental. The more she read, the more connections she made between wolves and Frost. Wolves were warm-blooded, with temperatures naturally rising to 102 degrees; Frost was always hot, and he would never give her a real explanation for this oddity. As for the ability to withstand the cold, he'd insisted on staying on the other side of her window, despite the freezing weather, and he actually seemed to enjoy it! Even his night vision was unlike an ordinary humans'. He saw too well in the dark and could navigate through the woods in the harshest of conditions. These traits also belonged to wolves.

Then there were the little things, like how his intense eyes glowed in the dark, exactly like an animals'. The way he'd reacted when hearing people talk about the Cedar Falls werewolf was also unusual, especially for someone who had proven himself to be unafraid of dangerous creatures. He'd been scared and tense, as if fearing the exposure of a secret. Additionally, the way that Frost had abruptly stopped coming to her window at night when the werewolf hunt increased was beyond uncanny.

Everything Anastasia had once found alluring about Frost now frightened her. She'd been too infatuated with him to see that his behavior and traits crossed the line of unique and entered abnormal at best. However, despite all of this, she couldn't forget how Frost was always there for her, saving her both mentally and physically. He was loving, gentle and most definitely incapable of the accusations which had been hurled at the werewolf. Better yet, there was a strong possibility that Anastasia was completely wrong about Frost. Maybe she was sick with more than a cold; maybe she was starting to hallucinate.

"Anastasia."

Gasping, Anastasia looked up to see Frost standing at the library's entrance. She hadn't heard him come in, and she'd temporarily forgotten that they'd made arrangements for him to pick her up after work. Was it already that late? Anastasia looked at the clock to confirm that she should've begun closing up ten minutes ago.

"Hey, Frost," Anastasia replied in a strained voice, while shoving the book onto the shelf. "I'm, um, not quite ready yet."

"Take your time."

Working quickly, Anastasia turned off all the computers and then retrieved her coat. The whole time, Frost had stood there, silent, still and watching her. This gave Anastasia a creepy feeling, but it was more than just that. Frost appeared unhappy and stressed. Normally, she would've begged him to tell her what was wrong; however, she now wondered if she really wanted to know.

"I'm ready," Anastasia said, before switching off the lights and following Frost outside.

After locking the library door, she entered Frost's SUV. Apart from a few casual niceties, they didn't speak during the drive to her house. Anastasia was positive that something was very wrong. Did Frost somehow know that she suspected him of being the werewolf? It didn't seem possible, but who knew what type of special skills he possessed.

Finally, Frost brought his SUV to a stop outside her house and then sat there, as silent and reserved as ever. He looked as if he wanted to speak but couldn't find the right words. Anastasia knew that look very well; she'd seen it upon her mother's face many of times.

"Can I come in?" Frost blurted out.

Anastasia was taken aback since Frost had never shown any interest in entering her house. Before tonight, if he'd made the same request, she would've assertively answered *yes*. However, she was now uncertain, and she could tell that Frost sensed this hesitation.

"I know your grandparents are out," Frost continued, "and we really need to talk – tonight."

"Okay," Anastasia hardly whispered as she numbly unbuckled her seatbelt and exited the SUV.

As she unlocked the front door and held it open for Frost, she wondered if she was making a big mistake. What if Frost wanted to eat her? That's what werewolves did, right?

"Can we go to your room?" Frost asked, after Anastasia had gestured toward the couch in the living room.

"Um, sure," she replied, while slowly leading him there.

Once in Anastasia's room, Frost began pacing like a caged animal. She couldn't help but see the irony in this; however, she was more concerned with how distressed he appeared. Although Anastasia now felt a little wary around Frost, she still cared about him a lot.

Suddenly, Frost stopped pacing and grabbed hold of Anastasia's hands. "I'm leaving," he said in a sorrowful tone.

"What?" Anastasia was hardly able to choke out. She would've been less shocked if he'd admitted to being the Cedar Falls werewolf, because she'd never once thought that he'd ever leave her. "Why?" she demanded, when Frost failed to offer an explanation or even respond.

"I...I can't tell you."

"You can't or won't?" Anastasia snapped as she tore her hands from Frost's grasp; his touch was getting too hot for her to handle, anyway.

"Please try to understand, Anastasia. I'm doing this to protect you."

"Protect me from what?" she challenged.

Frost opened his mouth to answer, but no words came out. Instead, he cast her an apologetic look and said, "You have to trust me."

As Anastasia looked at Frost, anger and upset swelled within her. This caused her to recall a certain chapter from the book about wolves. It had said that wolves used a combination of instincts and emotions to guide their behavior. Naturally social animals, they were capable of displaying love, hate, loyalty, and fear. These emotions were so strong that even mild-tempered wolves could become aggressive and unpredictable.

Powerful emotions can change a wolf, Anastasia summarized, her mind racing with thoughts. *Maybe that's why Frost's so afraid to be passionate with me. Could a real kiss actually transform him into a werewolf, regardless of whether or not there's a full moon?*

Unable to suppress her curiosity any longer, Anastasia stepped toward Frost, put her hand behind his neck and then brought his face close to hers. She looked into those beautiful eyes for a moment before locking her lips with his.

Frost was receptive to her affection, but only for a few seconds. As he tried to pull away, Anastasia wrapped both arms tightly around his shoulders and pressed her body against him. Frost's will to resist dwindled until he was kissing her passionately. His touch and movements were seductive, even as they stumbled toward the bed. Against Frost's increasingly hot body, Anastasia felt herself melting.

Then everything started to change.

Anastasia let out a cry of pain as claws dug into her back, but her wail was overpowered by the sound of Frost's bones snapping as they began to take on a different form. Almost as shocking was the way his warm, soft embrace turned into the eerie sensation of his sprouting fur pricking at her skin. Frost howled as he finally let go of Anastasia and fell to the floor, his clothing ripping as he completed the transformation. Before she knew what was happening, a large white werewolf rose to his feet right in front of her.

At the exact same eye level, Anastasia and Frost stared at each other for what seemed like several moments. Breathless and in awe, she noted how his fur was whiter than the purest snow and the way his eyes, which were larger than ever, shone so much brighter. His stature was powerful and imposing, but he appeared tame and in control. Anastasia instantly knew that she had nothing to fear.

Frost's the beautiful werewolf from four nights ago, she realized, *and unlike my other dream, it had all been real. I can't believe I was so blind.*

Suddenly, Frost bounded toward Anastasia's open bedroom door, causing a strong panic to rise within her chest. He couldn't leave her, especially now. There were too many unanswered questions, and even more important than that, they needed one another.

"Frost, please!" Anastasia cried desperately, before it was too late.

Frost hesitated at the door and then looked back at Anastasia, his eyes filled with sadness. Slowly, she approached him until they were face-to-face once again. Frost's fur flattened to his body, and his head and tail lowered, clearly indicating that he was ashamed.

Carefully, Anastasia reached out to touch Frost's head. She wanted to offer him comfort and let him know that somehow, it would be okay. However, he backed away, as if he'd never experienced affection while in werewolf form. Anastasia wouldn't give up that easily, though. She tried again and was soon stroking his soft, fine fur.

I'm petting my boyfriend's fur, Anastasia thought slowly. *This is surreal.*

Anastasia's touch must have had a soothing effect on Frost because within a couple of minutes, he began to transform back into his human self, starting with his claws slowly morphing into fingers and then his fur receding into his skin. It was like watching a nightmare unfold, but this was real, and Anastasia found herself stepping backwards slightly, overcome with a mixture of fascination and unease. However, her attention was quickly drawn away from the oddity of interspecies shape-shifting as she realized that Frost was naked. As he panted over the exertion of transforming, she could see sweat shimmering on his defined muscles and the heat rising from his excessively hot body.

Damn, Anastasia thought, politely averting her eyes from

Frost and onto a nearby mirror.

Quickly, Frost put his clothing back on, but since it was ripped at the seams, it merely hung like rags. Obviously embarrassed, he muttered, "I always keep spare clothing in the car."

"How?" Anastasia demanded abruptly. "How is this possible?"

Taking her hand, Frost led Anastasia to the bed. He was silent for several moments, as if trying to find the courage to be truthful with her. Then he began to speak in a very serious tone.

"I can't give you the answers you're looking for because I don't know how or why this has happened to me. Somehow, I always felt different, but it wasn't until turning thirteen that I discovered just how truly different I was." He paused briefly to swallow hard. "I remember the first time I became a werewolf so vividly. It was an early spring night and as usual, I was hiking in the woods. Then all of a sudden, it hit me – a pain so intense that I thought I was dying. The next thing I knew, I was running through the woods on all fours and howling at the full moon. I panicked like hell and spent that whole night fleeing, as if I could somehow outrun the curse. I did return to my human form, but not until the following morning. When I came home, dressed in torn clothing, my parents were frantic and demanded to know what had happened, but of course, I couldn't tell them. I couldn't tell anyone."

"Am I really the only person who..." Anastasia began.

"Who knows that I'm a furry freak?" Frost finished for her. "Yes."

"Why didn't you tell me sooner? I could've helped you."

"I wanted to tell you, but I didn't know how. I came to your window on Monday night, and when I saw your grandfather and his hunter friends, I got so angry that I shape-shifted. Then I saw you out there, and I wanted to show you the real me, but you ran away. I was the one who took you home when you were hurt."

"I made myself believe it was a dream," Anastasia said, while hugging him tightly. "Frost, I'm so sorry."

"No, *I'm* sorry," Frost protested. "I've been seen too many times, and I really lost control with Pete. I swear I never meant to hurt him."

"I know," Anastasia said, finally understanding the look Frost and Pete had shared the night of the town meeting. Pete must have seen the similarity between Frost's eyes and the werewolf's, but he probably couldn't bring himself to believe it. "Everything's going to be alright."

"No, it's not," Frost argued. "I'm turning into a werewolf almost every night now, and I'm not exactly sure why. I need to leave, Anastasia, before I'm killed."

"Then I'm coming, too," Anastasia stated as she jumped up from the bed and prepared to pack her bags.

"You know I can't let you do that," Frost said, while putting back the clothing she'd taken from her drawers.

"Don't try to stop me," she threatened.

Gently, Frost reached for Anastasia's arm and pulled her in close. He looked into her eyes, his own almost brimming with tears. "I love you, Anastasia," he said softly, "and I'd rather die than let any harm come to you."

Anastasia's heartbeat quickened as she placed both hands upon his face and kissed him gently. Every inch of her body tingled, and with each passing second, her desire for him only burned stronger. However, she knew that if the kiss turned passionate, he'd turn into a werewolf, so she reluctantly stopped.

"I love you, too," Anastasia whispered. "For the longest

time, I've felt nothing but pain and isolation. You've changed that. You've changed me."

"I'm a werewolf," Frost muttered sadly. "Are you sure you can handle that?"

"Just be with me, Frost. I don't care about anything else."

As he hugged her, Anastasia could tell that there was something bothering him, something more than his dire need to escape from Cedar Falls. "What's wrong?" she asked with concern.

At first, Frost hesitated, but after a comforting nod from Anastasia, he began to open up. "There's a slight chance that my biological parents, who I can only assume are werewolves, too, may still be alive. Two years ago, I came across a cabin deep in the woods, and although it was empty, there was a very faint scent that was familiar. I think it was from my father."

"If your parents are alive, why haven't they found you yet?" Anastasia pried.

"No one looks for what they don't want to find," Frost replied. He then shook his head, as if trying to erase his thoughts. "I shouldn't have mentioned it. Forget it."

"No," Anastasia protested. "We have to find your parents. How would you feel if they were killed and you didn't even try to warn them about the hunt?"

"They obviously didn't care when they left me to die in the woods."

"You're so much better than this, Frost. Besides, don't you want to know why they left you? Maybe you can finally get all the answers you've been looking for." She paused briefly before thoughtfully adding, "Perhaps it's the anger toward your parents which is making you shape-shift so often. You need to confront them to finally let go of your rage. Control your emotions, control your transformations.

It's worth a shot, isn't it?"

"Of course it is," Frost replied, "but the scent is so weak, and what if they aren't even in Cedar Falls Woods anymore?"

"And what if they are?"

Frost sighed. "Fine. I'll go look for them, but you should stay here until your cold gets better. I'll come back for you, I promise."

"You're not going alone," Anastasia interjected. "Anything could happen, and I need to know that you're safe."

"There's no arguing with you, huh?" Frost asked, while taking Anastasia's hands in his own.

"It's a lost cause," she concurred.

Frost smirked but then quickly turned serious. "We'll leave before dawn, taking a circular route through the woods so more ground can be covered. At dusk, we should reach the old cabin. That's roughly the half-way point and where we'll spend the night. Come morning, we will continue on this course until arriving back here, regardless of whether we've found my parents or not. It'll be dark then, and driving to Hartfield unseen shouldn't be a problem. That's where we'll make our new home." He paused. "Are you sure this is what you want?"

"Yes," Anastasia said assertively. "Now go home and pack."

Before leaving, Frost gave Anastasia a very warm hug and a soft kiss. "See you tomorrow and every day after that," he whispered in her ear.

Then he was gone.

Hurriedly, Anastasia packed only what she thought she would need, although she wasn't exactly sure what that was. She'd done a lot of crazy things in her life, but running away with her werewolf boyfriend definitely topped the list tenfold. Was she really going through with this? Anastasia knew that the answer was yes the moment she recalled the way Frost held and kissed her. She'd never been loved like this before, and she refused to ever be without him.

Part Seven

The Deep, Dark Woods

Dear Grandma and Grandpa,

I'm leaving Cedar Falls and returning to Toronto. Frost is taking me to the train station, so by the time you read this letter, I will already be gone — there's no point in trying to stop me. I've talked to my mother about this decision, and she's agreed that it's in everyone's best interest for me to come home. I will send for the rest of my belongings at a later date.

I want to thank you for opening your hearts and home to me. Your support and love has meant so much, and I've learned a lot about myself in these past few weeks. I couldn't possibly begin to express my gratitude for everything you've done — I'll never forget it.

Love always,
Anastasia

Anastasia didn't hesitate as she positioned the handwritten note on the kitchen table – a location where her grandparents would surely find it when they woke up. She'd truly meant those words, especially for her grandmother; adding her grandfather's name was a mere nicety since they hadn't been on good terms for some time now. Nevertheless, she hoped that they wouldn't be too hurt by her quick departure. She knew that it was very rude, but it was just something that she had to do for her and Frost.

Her cell phone vibrated, alerting her of an incoming text message. It was from Frost, stating that he was waiting for her at the bottom of the driveway. Anastasia took a deep breath, readjusted her overstuffed backpack and then hurried out of the house, making sure to close the door gently behind her. The feeling was bittersweet.

Outside the temperature was chilly, but unlike the past few days, it wasn't unbearable. Anastasia was more than a little grateful for the slightly milder weather because she knew that she'd be facing the elements for the next two days. The thought alone made her shiver, or maybe it was her worsening cold.

In the early morning darkness, Anastasia made her way toward Frost's SUV, where she saw his tall, muscular silhouette standing near the passenger side. A mixture of nervousness and excitement instantly rose within her as he greeted her with a quick kiss and then opened the door. When they were both inside, an awkward silence filled the SUV. They were entering a new stage in their relationship, and they knew that everything was about to change.

"Are you sure this is what you want?" Frost finally broke the silence. "There's still time to back out."

"Just drive, Frost," Anastasia replied, her mind firmly made up.

Looking at Anastasia, Frost smiled, revealing teeth so white that it seemed to light up his face. How the hell hadn't she noticed that before? What she did immediately observe, however, was the change in Frost's expression as he continued to stare at her – he now appeared very concerned.

"What?" she asked self-consciously.

"Do you feel alright?" Frost asked. "You don't look good and..."

"I didn't have time to apply make-up, and I *was* going to wear my stilettos but I was concerned about practicality."

"Anastasia, I'm not going to joke about this. I'm worried about you. Has your cold gotten worse?"

"No," Anastasia lied, unwilling to tell Frost about the multiple symptoms which had left her feeling uncomfortable and even a little weak. He'd just insist that she stay home, and that's not what she wanted. Instead, she quickly changed the topic. "So, what did you tell your parents?"

"There was a last minute school trip," Frost answered with a sigh, while starting to drive away. "I'll have to tell them the truth eventually – well, as much of it as I can."

Sensing Frost's sadness, Anastasia spoke in a reassuring tone. "You know, we will return to Cedar Falls. This werewolf craze will pass, and you'll find a way to control your transformations."

Frost was quiet for a moment, as if thinking about Anastasia's words. "You're always optimistic," he finally commented with admiration. "That's one of the many reasons why I love you so much."

Anastasia couldn't help but snort. "Me, optimistic? You must be thinking about someone else."

"Maybe I see you better than you see yourself."

"Or maybe you just make me feel like everything will be okay," Anastasia answered quickly.

Frost smirked before muttering, "Maybe."

Making a sharp left turn, Frost drove onto a narrow, unmaintained road. Even though he proceeded slowly, the SUV bumped roughly over drifted snow that was now frozen. Minutes later, they reached a dead end. Frost parked there, his SUV partially concealed by branches which hung low due to the amount of snow upon them.

"It's now or never," Frost told Anastasia, his eyes

revealing a hint of concern, despite him appearing firm and determined otherwise.

Anastasia nodded before grabbing her backpack and exiting the SUV. Frost copied her actions, stopping only to retrieve a small sign and place it behind the windshield. After reading the sign, which bore the words, *Gone Hunting*, Anastasia cast Frost a skeptical look.

"It's unlikely that anyone will find our SUV," Frost explained, "but if they do, consider the sign as insurance. No one will ask questions if they think we're after the werewolf."

Taking her hand, Frost led Anastasia into the woods. Even though she'd been surrounded by trees for the last several weeks, it somehow felt like she'd discovered a new world. The light was dim, and any which way she turned, there were shadows of tall, leaning trees that appeared to guide them deeper into the woods. Even the air was fresher, causing Anastasia to inhale at a slower pace. She was beginning to feel like she was in a fairy tale, and she wanted nothing more than to fall into all its romance and adventure.

"I feel more at home out here than anywhere else," Frost said whimsically. "It's where I belong."

"Is that a werewolf thing?" Anastasia asked hesitantly, not wanting to offend Frost despite her desire to know everything about his supernatural secret.

"Could be," Frost replied with a nonchalant shrug, "but it's probably more of a Frost thing. I'm a man first and a werewolf second. It's always been that way and nothing's going to change." He was silent for a moment before adding, "Tell me the truth. Does all of this freak you out? Do *I* freak you out?"

"Actually, no," Anastasia confessed. "Call it shock or denial, if you want, but either way, I'm oddly comforted by the fact that there's more to life than meets the eye."

"You may say that now, but once you see the real me..."

"I already have," Anastasia interrupted, stepping in front of Frost so she could look him in the eyes, "and I like *everything* that I see."

Frost gave Anastasia a smile and then quickly kissed her. "You're one of a kind, Anastasia, and you can trust me on that because I know a thing or two about rarities."

To conceal her blushing cheeks, Anastasia looked away and resumed walking. "So, how exactly will this work?" she began to ask. "I assume we're not just calling out their names – not that we know them in the first place."

"Even as a human, I can hear, smell and see things that others can't. I've learned to control the intensity of these senses while in my current state, but when I turn into a werewolf, they take over. It's like the ultimate rush, as if the world and every little thing around you is suddenly coming to life. These are the senses that will help me find my parents."

"It sounds kind of magical," Anastasia noted aloud.

"Sometimes it is," Frost admitted. "Other times it feels like a curse."

"There's still one thing I don't understand," Anastasia said. "On the night Chloe was attacked, there was a full moon, but you weren't a werewolf."

"Over the years, I've discovered that many of the werewolf myths we know from books and movies are actually true, but unlike popular belief, we're not slaves to the full moon. It only has power during that first transformation, as if it triggers something inside of you and unleashes the wolf." Frost sighed before adding, "I wish my transformations really were controlled by the moon. It would make my life a lot easier."

Now silent, Anastasia and Frost trekked onwards. As the sun rose higher in the sky, an orange-like glow was cast upon the woods. Unfortunately, this comforting light was soon left behind. Their surroundings had once again darkened due to the trees which had grown taller, fuller and denser. This caused Anastasia to shiver and realize that even fairy tales had sinister moments.

Abruptly, Frost stopped walking to examine the area. "This is the perfect place," he concluded, while beginning to undress and place the clothing into his backpack. "The snow is compact and icy because of the lack of sunlight – it'll be harder for anyone to track us from here."

"Um, Frost, what are you doing?" Anastasia asked, even though she suspected that she already knew the answer.

"How else did you expect to cover so much ground in so little time?" he asked with a devilish smile, right before wrapping Anastasia in his arms and kissing her with a deep, almost hunger-like desire.

It didn't take long for the transformation to commence, followed by a howl that indicated Frost had become a full-fledged werewolf. This process now filled Anastasia with fascination and even excitement. She could only imagine what it was like to shape-shift into a whole other identity – it must feel surreal and very empowering.

Frost proceeded to lower himself to the ground and then look at Anastasia, as if waiting for her to do something. She stared back at him for several moments, wondering what he expected from her. When Frost let out a small yelp, in a supposed attempt to communicate with her, and tossed his head sideways to glance at his back, Anastasia finally realized what he wanted.

Slowly, Anastasia approached Frost. He let out another yelp, while twitching his back paw. Hoping that she was reading his body language correctly, Anastasia gently stepped onto Frost's massive paw. With one swift movement, he lifted her onto his back. The next thing Anastasia knew, he had risen, picked up his backpack in those powerful jaws and was going forward at an incredibly fast pace.

Anastasia gasped as she watched the woods become nothing more than a dark blur. Her heart thudded within her chest, and she clung onto Frost's fur until her hands felt numb. Nonetheless, she'd never felt so alive. It was like he wanted to share with her the greatest aspect of being a werewolf, and she couldn't help but experience a sense of power from being situated so high upon him. Together, Anastasia felt like she and Frost could accomplish anything. They truly were the rulers of the woods.

After six long hours of running through the woods, with only a few minor breaks in between, Frost came to a stop beside a pile of snow-covered boulders. He then bent down, clearly indicating that Anastasia should get off. She was grateful for the chance to stretch her very stiff legs, and as she did so, she realized that it now felt odd *not* to be charging through the woods with the cool wind whipping at her partially exposed face. It was like Anastasia had also been a werewolf for the past few hours and was now slowly returning to the human race. She couldn't fathom how Frost ever adjusted to such a jarring change, especially since it was more than just a feeling for him.

Expecting Frost to shape-shift back into his human self, Anastasia waited patiently for several moments. However, as he continued to lie on the ground, his heavy panting finally lessening and his stomach growling with hunger, she came to the conclusion that she'd be having lunch with a werewolf today.

After retrieving their lunches from her backpack, Anastasia sat upon the large but low-lying boulder where

Frost was resting. As she leaned against him, appreciating the way his heat penetrated her many layers of clothing, she unwrapped the sandwich and energy bar which she'd brought for him. Hand-feeding Frost, she watched in amazement as he ate both items with only one bite. Anastasia then handed him an apple, before forcing herself to eat even though her cold had left her with little appetite.

"Are werewolves even supposed to eat this stuff?" Anastasia asked as she reluctantly nibbled at her energy bar. "Shouldn't you be hunting deer or something?"

Looking at Frost, Anastasia believed that he understood every word she said. Although she hadn't spoken to him while they searched for his parents, she'd only done so because she thought that she'd be a distraction. If they were going to find his parents, Anastasia knew that Frost's complete concentration had to be on his scent and hearing senses.

Suddenly and almost symbolically, a raven flew overhead, making his way skillfully and speedily around the tree branches which seemed to be sticking out everywhere. The raven let out a single but loud, *Caw* before disappearing from their sight. As Anastasia watched Frost begin to salivate, she confirmed that a lunch made for a human would definitely not be enough for a werewolf.

"Go hunt," Anastasia encouraged him, noting the way his stomach continued to growl. "Please, you need to keep strong."

Defiantly, Frost shook his massive head and then stared at Anastasia's half-finished lunch. For a second, she thought that he was going to eat it, but instead, he used his snout to push it toward her. From the look in his eyes, Anastasia knew that he was strictly telling *her* to eat.

While she finished her lunch, Anastasia wondered if his

refusal to hunt was because of her. He probably thought it would gross her out and make her see the beast instead of the man. Of course, Anastasia would never actually think that way, but it made her nervous that Frost wasn't being his true werewolf self.

Deciding to deal with this issue at a later date, Anastasia focused on a more dire concern and the very reason why they were out here in the first place – had Frost come any closer to finding his parents? Although it was difficult for Anastasia to pinpoint anything while traveling at such a fast pace, it had appeared that the woods were empty. For the most part, Anastasia was happy about that since running into werewolf hunters was a fear she wasn't even able to express aloud. However, it also made her ponder just how isolated and deep in the woods they really were.

"What's the verdict so far?" Anastasia finally asked, nervous to hear the answer. "Did you find any evidence of your parents' whereabouts?"

Frost shook his head for the second time that day. From the way his eyes and ears lowered, Anastasia knew that he was very distraught. She wished there was more that she could do to help, but the problem was that she had no idea of how to go about doing such a thing. Although Anastasia hated to admit it, this undertaking was clearly more difficult than she'd originally thought.

"The day's not over yet," Anastasia said, while placing her hand upon Frost's paw in a comforting manner. It was a sweet and simple gesture, but it was the best that she could do at this moment in time. "There are so many areas where we haven't looked," she continued, "and I know we'll come across them if they're still in..."

Anastasia was interrupted as Frost let out a loud sneeze that shook his entire body. Concerned, she studied him, taking particular notice of how he lay limply upon the ground. At first she'd thought he was merely tired due to all that running, but now she worried that it was something more.

"I hope I haven't given you my cold," Anastasia said, right before he sneezed again. "Frost, I think you'll need to take it easy," she added quickly, realizing that she would also benefit from more rest.

In response, Frost got up and encouraged Anastasia to do the same by gently pushing her with his snout. Using their goal as a motivating factor, she stood up, retrieved both their backpacks and then hoisted herself upon Frost. A split second later, they were off once again, speeding through the woods in a desperate search.

Within only a few minutes, Anastasia could tell that something had changed. It felt like Frost's balance was slightly off, and even scarier than that, his breathing sounded nasally and somewhat labored. Fearing that she would fall off as his movements became increasingly jerky, Anastasia tightened her grasp on him. She now questioned if they'd actually be able to make it through the remainder of the day.

CRACK...

The sound of ice breaking around Anastasia and Frost was so sharp and sudden that it seemed to penetrate into her very soul, ensuring that she wouldn't soon forget the terrifying noise. Then the next thing Anastasia knew, they were completely submerged in water so cold that it must have been only a degree or two above freezing. As she felt the pressure of the swiftly moving water, a strong panic seized Anastasia, leaving her immobilized. It was this current which dragged them deeper into the dark, unforgiving river.

Frost fought against the flow of the river, but even with his powerful limbs, he was merely treading water instead of propelling them upwards. Continuously, Anastasia smashed against him and the relentless current. Her grasp on Frost was quickly weakening, and her lungs ached for air since she'd never had an opportunity to take a deep breath before plunging into the water. With the utmost urgency, Anastasia began kicking her legs and, despite the fact that her attempts were done in vain, she refused to stop trying. However, she knew that the course of the river was too powerful for her, and if Frost couldn't muster up more strength right now, they would surely be swept under the ice and then drown.

Please, Frost, Anastasia thought desperately, *you have to do this.*

As if somehow gaining strength from Anastasia's silent plea, Frost kicked harder and faster than he likely thought possible. Slowly, they inched upwards. A few moments later, he broke the surface, allowing them both to take a much needed gasp of air. Not wasting any time, Frost grabbed onto the edge of the broken ice and began ascending from the river. That's when the familiar sound of cracking ice filled their ears. Forced back into the water, Frost kept reaching for the edge, but every time he tried to pull them out, it would break. Their weight was too much for the ice to withstand, and it looked like there was no way out.

By now, Anastasia was so cold that her whole body was almost numb. Making the situation worse were her clothing and the backpacks, which had become excessively heavy and were pulling her downwards. The urge to free herself of these items overwhelmed Anastasia, yet she was helpless to do anything about it since she could hardly even move. Her grip on Frost, as well as the fleeting moments when he surfaced in failed attempts to escape, were the only things keeping her alive.

Although Frost must have also been exhausted, it was

apparent that he was far from ready to give up. With a powerful lunge, he surfaced again, but this time he clung onto the ice, continuously moving forward a millisecond before it broke. Frost's quick movements made it impossible for Anastasia to maintain her grasp on him any longer, and when he finally pulled himself out to relative safety, she wasn't with him.

From under the water, Anastasia looked up to see Frost peering down at her. Despite her heavy eyes and blurred vision, the expression of panic on his face was crystal clear. Acting fast, he plunged his front leg into the water, but she was too deep for him to reach. Ice chips splattered into the water above, causing Frost to retreat slightly so he wouldn't fall in.

In a final attempt to save herself, Anastasia tried to tread water. Unfortunately, it was useless. She could no longer feel her body and even though her mind willed her to keep fighting, it was just too much for her. The current took Anastasia deeper until darkness surrounded her, but somehow she'd found inner peace. She knew that she was dying, and as she closed her eyes one last time, her mind flashed with images of her grandparents, Chloe, her mother, and most vividly, Frost.

❊ ❊ ❊

The delicious aroma of freshly cooked stew filled the air, slowly easing Anastasia back to consciousness. Gently, her eyes fluttered open to reveal that she was in an old, abandoned log cabin. Although it was a small one room place, the cabin was lined with several long shelves which contained a variety of jars, tools and pots and pans, all on display and neatly categorized. It was an impressive collection that had clearly helped to sustain a family some time ago.

As Anastasia continued to scan the cabin, noting the dust-covered homemade furniture and numerous strange knickknacks, her focus turned to an old-fashioned fireplace, which was lit and being used to cook the contents of a medium-sized black pot. Frost, in his human form, stood in front of the fireplace, stirring the stew in a tense manner. The whole situation felt so dream-like that Anastasia momentarily wondered if she had indeed died.

Before Anastasia could call out to Frost, he turned around as if somehow sensing that she'd awakened. Without saying a word, he hurried to her side and then wrapped his arms around her. Frost's grip on Anastasia was so strong and passionate that he didn't need to speak; she knew that he couldn't be more grateful and relieved that she had survived. For several minutes they stayed that way, lying in the bed which Anastasia had somehow found herself in.

"I'm so sorry," Frost finally spoke, breaking the embrace only so he could look her in the eyes. "I should've heard the water running beneath the ice. I should've known that we were walking on top of the Great Rapids." His voice cracked with overwhelming emotion as he added slowly and angrily, "I should've never taken you out here."

"There's no way I can be alive," Anastasia muttered, even though she hardly felt like she was living. Every inch of her body burned from recovering frostbite and her cold symptoms had only worsened.

Reaching for her hand, Frost continued to speak in an angry tone. "I went back into the water and wouldn't leave until you were with me. From the first day I met you, I promised myself that I wouldn't allow any harm to come to you, either by my own paws or any other force. I've let you down, Anastasia, and now you have to return home."

"No," Anastasia protested. "You don't have the right to make decisions for me. I'm here because I chose to be."

"Finding my parents isn't worth losing you," Frost practically interrupted. "You're my only priority."

"Shut up, Frost. This isn't your fault," Anastasia began to interject. However, she couldn't finish her sentence as she began to cough harshly. The coughing fit passed, but she was left with an even sorer throat which she tried to ease by gently massaging her neck. Unfortunately, it didn't help in the least.

Appearing concerned, Frost quickly stood up and retrieved a bowl which sat upon a small table beside the fire. Using an old bronze ladle, he filled the bowl with stew and then returned to Anastasia's side. Handing her the bowl and a spoon which matched the ladle, he cast her a stern look.

"Eat," Frost instructed. "It's just rabbit and water, but it'll make you feel better."

"Thanks," Anastasia said, before sitting up with some difficulty and then taking the bowl and spoon. As she ate the stew, a warm sensation filled her body. With a sudden hunger, she hastily finished her meal. "You hunted," she commented, smiling at Frost as he watched over her. "It's delicious."

"Then I guess I should eat, too," Frost said, smiling back at her. It was like he was saying he understood that she accepted him, both as a man and a werewolf.

"You shouldn't have started that fire," Anastasia pointed out, while Frost retrieved stew for himself and began to eat. "Someone might see the smoke."

"I found matches, so it kind of seemed like fate. Besides, I needed to dry our clothes and backpacks somehow."

Anastasia looked down at herself, finally realizing that she was wearing nothing other than her key pendant necklace and a long plaid shirt which belonged to Frost. She blushed, while thinking about the way she'd ended up in his clothing. Although Anastasia had never been self-conscious about her body, the situation left her feeling a little uncomfortable.

"So, you think this is your parents' old cabin," Anastasia stated, wanting to change the topic.

"You should get more sleep," Frost advised, blatantly ignoring her comment likely because the subject was too painful. "I'm still concerned about you."

Anastasia looked out the small window to see that it was dark outside. However, it was impossible to tell if night really had fallen or if they were so deep in the woods that sunlight couldn't penetrate through the surrounding trees. Regardless, Anastasia wondered how long she'd been unconscious.

"I'll put this outside to cool," Frost said, proceeding to pour the remainder of the rabbit stew into a smaller pot which had a lid. "We can have it for breakfast."

As Frost passed by Anastasia, he suddenly swayed unsteadily. She hurried to his side, but by that time he had regained his balance. As Anastasia studied Frost, she noticed the beads of sweat that had formed upon his forehead and also the very pale color of his skin. Then, as quickly as his unsteadiness had passed, the sweating and paleness disappeared.

"Frost, what's wrong with you?" Anastasia asked with wide, terrified eyes.

"Please, go back to bed. I'll be there in a minute."

Obediently, Anastasia returned to bed, where she waited anxiously for him. When Frost re-entered the cabin, he said nothing and instead retrieved logs from a woodpile that had likely been stacked by his parents. He then placed them in the fire, creating sparks that looked similar to little red fireflies.

"Why are you acting so strange?" Anastasia demanded,

unable to take the silence any longer.

After a deep sigh that seemed to release his pent-up anger, Frost sat gently next to Anastasia. "This may have been all for nothing," he began. "I never get sick, but somehow I've caught your cold. I thought I could carry on, but that's obviously not the case. My senses are blocked – I can't hear, smell or track like I usually do. I'm useless out here."

"You could never be useless," Anastasia whispered, while placing her hand against his cheek.

"You're the only one who seems to believe that," Frost whispered back.

Lightly kissing his lips so she wouldn't turn him into a werewolf, Anastasia guided Frost to lie down on the bed with her. He seemed to relax as they held each other tightly, with Anastasia resting her head upon his chest to hear his heartbeat. Despite everything that had happened today – including almost dying – it now felt like she was in paradise. From the crackling fire which produced a romantic glow to merely lying in bed with Frost, Anastasia knew that she could easily spend forever in this little cabin.

Sitting up, Frost began to wrap the old quilt around them, but then he stopped to look at her closely. "Is this alright?" he asked seriously.

"Yes," Anastasia answered, a little uncertain about what he meant.

"Good," Frost said, before settling in for the night. "There's only one bed, but I don't want you to think I'd ever take advantage of you – at any point during the day."

Anastasia instantly understood that he wasn't just talking about sharing a bed but also the fact that he'd undressed her to prevent hypothermia. He was such a gentleman, even when she kind of wished he wouldn't be. Werewolf or not, Anastasia could now say with the utmost certainty that she'd never met a guy like Frost before.

"I know," Anastasia replied, before wriggling in bed until she found the perfect spot in his arms. "Hey, Frost," she began to ask a few moments later, "have you ever met another werewolf? I mean, you must've traveled these woods hundreds of times since your thirteenth birthday. Maybe there are others out there, if not in Cedar Falls Woods, then somewhere."

"If there is, I haven't found them. I've spent countless hours researching werewolves, but all I've uncovered are fairy tales and reports supported by intangible evidence. Werewolves aren't supposed to exist, so I don't know what I expected to find. However, my efforts did lead me to a German newspaper archive from the late eighteen hundreds. I've never read about that many werewolf sightings coming from one area – it really struck me as weird."

"Maybe you're on to something," Anastasia pointed out.

"Probably not," Frost replied with a sigh. "The articles sounded sensationalized, and we know how people see what they want to, especially when the idea has already been put into their heads." He paused to smile at Anastasia and smooth her hair lovingly. "You really should get more sleep."

"Yes, doctor," Anastasia teased, before kissing him goodnight and then closing her eyes.

It was impossible for Anastasia to know how long she'd been asleep when she awoke to the sound of a howling wolf. For a fleeting moment, she thought that Frost had left the cabin to run in the woods. However, as Anastasia turned to her right, she realized that he was still sleeping beside her. She sat up, listening as the howling continued. It was quieter than before, and soon it disappeared completely.

"Did you hear that?" Anastasia whispered to Frost. When

she didn't receive a reply, she tugged on his arm. "Frost, wake up," she hissed in vain.

A chill swept through Anastasia's body, likely from a combination of her cold and fear. Even the fire was starting to die, creating a very creepy atmosphere. Shivering, Anastasia lay back down in bed. Although the howling had ceased several minutes ago, the wolf's sad, desperate call kept replaying in her mind.

Part Eight

Heart of the Beast

As Frost lay sound asleep, Anastasia crept out of the warm, comfortable bed, careful not to make any noise. She'd been awake for over an hour, and although she should've been relishing in the fact that she was lying next to Frost, she was too preoccupied with thoughts of the wolf howls which had haunted her dreams. This time, however, Anastasia knew that those howls weren't just a figment of her imagination; they'd been real and not too far away. All she needed now was to follow the wolf's tracks because there was a good chance that it would lead to Frost's biological parents.

After putting on her winter clothing and then walking toward the door, Anastasia stopped to cast Frost a quick glance. She wanted him to come with her, but he obviously needed more rest. Besides, her plan required immediate action; she'd have to find the tracks before any snow could conceal them. Once she had found the prints, she'd go back to the cabin and awaken Frost. From there, they'd continue on together. It seemed like a foolproof plan, and Anastasia couldn't be happier about actually being an asset to their mission.

Everything was eerily silent and still as Anastasia exited the cabin and made her way throughout the woods. Dawn must have broken some time ago, even though the dark, bleak atmosphere of this tree-laden place made that hard to believe.

The only sounds came from Anastasia's nasally breathing and heavy footsteps, but to her, the thudding inside her head was the noisiest of them all. Not surprisingly, she was getting sicker, and the day's bitterly cold temperature definitely wouldn't be helping her to feel better anytime soon. Nevertheless, Anastasia trudged onwards, constantly keeping her eyes on the snow.

An hour passed, or maybe it was two; either way, the only thing Anastasia could be certain of was that she hadn't come across any tracks. Finally looking up to stretch her very stiff neck, she gulped as she studied her surroundings. She'd entered a clearing, and as a large cloud moved slowly past the sun, the brightness caused her to squint in response. Anastasia hadn't meant to search this far afield, and she silently cursed herself for being so foolish.

Immediately rectifying her mistake, Anastasia turned around and began to follow her own footprints. She tried to hurry, but exhaustion and an ache that penetrated her very bones kept her at a walking pace. Anastasia was weak, and even though she should've been freezing by now, she actually felt hot; so hot, in fact, that she contemplated removing her scarf and gloves.

It's like an inferno, Anastasia thought in a disoriented manner as she started to break out in a feverish sweat. Suddenly, a strong dizzy spell swept over her, causing the woods to spin wildly with seemingly no stop in sight. Anastasia stumbled to the ground, where she closed her eyes and waited for the dizziness to end. It did cease, but she was left feeling weaker and sweatier than before.

"Damn," Anastasia muttered aloud, before slowly standing up to discover that she'd regained her balance. "I guess I should've eaten breakfast this morning." She let out a forced laugh, despite not finding any of this funny. Anastasia knew that she was sick, but she'd been reluctant to admit it because that meant delaying their search for Frost's parents. Unfortunately, her worsening condition could no longer be ignored.

"Frost!" Anastasia called as loudly as her sore throat would allow. "Frost, I need you!" She'd begun walking again, but her steps were that much smaller and slower, causing her to doubt that she'd make it back to the cabin by herself. Anastasia just hoped that Frost could somehow hear her distressed calls.

The sound of paws thudding heavily upon the frozen ground, in an attempt to reach Anastasia as quickly as possible, filled her with relief and even joy. Frost had heard her cries and was coming to save her. She imagined being at the cabin in no time, resting in the soft bed while he nursed her back to health.

"Frost!" Anastasia shouted, wanting to urge him forward faster. "I'm here, Frost!"

Anastasia's plea caused the opposite of her desired effect as the thudding stopped abruptly. Confused and upset, she stood still and listened, but she heard nothing other than her rapid heartbeat. It felt as if everything else in the woods had died, leaving Anastasia completely alone.

Growl...

Or maybe Anastasia wasn't as alone as she'd thought. That growl had come from somewhere in the vicinity, yet as she turned around to carefully scan the area, she saw nothing and no one. Shakily, Anastasia waited for something to happen, but the woods remained deathly quiet and seemingly devoid of any life.

"Frost?" Anastasia called out weakly, even though she knew that he'd never growl at her, especially in such a menacing tone.

Suddenly, in the distance appeared a figure so white that it was impossible to identify who – or what – it was. As if emerging from the snowy ground, it proceeded forward at a steady pace, creating a loud, scary thump with each and every step. Although Anastasia still couldn't tell what she was about to face, she knew with complete certainty that the figure coming toward her was sinister. Its mere presence seemed to cast a forbidding shadow over the clearing, and she'd never experienced such a strong sense of impending doom.

Slowly, the figure started to come into view, and as it drew closer, terrifying features were revealed. It was a wolf who looked very similar to Frost when he was in his shape-shifted form. He had a large, imposing stature and was covered in white fur which appeared matted and somewhat dirty. Hunched, the wolf moved stealthily, as if constantly on edge and ready to fight at any given moment. In an instant, Anastasia knew that he was a werewolf.

"What the hell?" Anastasia whispered in a stone-cold tone. This wasn't at all what she'd expected to find, and now she wished that she'd never looked in the first place. If this was indeed a relative of Frost's, she didn't want to meet the rest of his family.

Turning around, Anastasia ran as fast as she could; unfortunately, that wasn't very quick. Still weak, exhausted and slightly dizzy, she knew that successfully fleeing from the werewolf was highly unlikely, but that didn't mean she wouldn't try. As he began to chase her, the familiar sound of his paws thumping upon the ground became louder, causing an almost earthquake-like effect. The werewolf was close – too close.

Seconds later, a sharp pain shot throughout Anastasia's body. The werewolf had pounced on her from behind, bringing them both hurtling toward the ground. As if by mere luck, Anastasia avoided being crushed by him, but she knew that she was still in great danger. Fueled by the intense rush of adrenaline that was coursing through her veins, she tried to get up and run. However, the werewolf obviously had other ideas as he leapt on top of Anastasia and pinned her shoulders down. Under the strength of the beast, she screamed in agony and fear.

Anastasia's cries were soon overpowered as a ferocious growl sounded nearby. Then the next thing she knew, someone tackled the werewolf hard and fast, releasing her from under his paws in the process. Gasping, Anastasia tried to get out of the way, but the best she could do was shuffle backwards by a few feet. With a combination of terror and astonishment, she watched as Frost, in his shape-shifted form, fought the rogue werewolf. He must have heard her plea for help after all.

From the way the two werewolves were rolling on the ground, in an attempt to force the other into submission, it was impossible to tell who was the strongest. Simultaneously, they snapped and snarled, while swiping their massive paws at each other's faces. As the rogue werewolf bit Frost's shoulder, causing him to yelp in pain, Anastasia winced and looked away. Once again, she felt the emotional pang of being useless to help Frost.

"Please stop!" Anastasia begged in desperation.

The werewolves paid no attention to her and instead began to fight more vigorously. Even their growls were deeper and filled with urgency, as if each werewolf was saying that he'd be the last one standing. From multiple bite wounds and scratches, blood flowed quickly, staining their fur horrific shades of red. It was clear that this was a battle to the death, and if the rogue werewolf won, Anastasia would be his next conquest – and meal.

Like watching a nightmare unfold right in front of her eyes, the werewolves rose on their hind legs and bit one another viciously. As the fighting intensified, the rogue werewolf struck Frost, causing him to be tossed like an overstuffed plush animal before landing on his back with a sickening thud. Wasting no time, he pounced on Frost, as if ready to deliver one final, fatal blow.

That's when the oddest thing happened. Seemingly losing all interest in fighting, the rogue werewolf brought his face close to Frost's and studied him carefully. Obviously taken aback, Frost made no attempt to attack. They stayed that way for several moments until the rogue werewolf let out a low, sorrowful moan and then hurried away.

Quickly, Frost leapt up from the ground. He appeared steady and alert, as if he'd already recovered from last night's illness – possibly due to a resilient werewolf gene or something of that nature, Anastasia could only guess. However, as strong and determined as he looked, it was clear from the heavy blood flow that he was badly hurt.

Frost motioned for Anastasia to climb upon him. Weak, and also concerned that she'd unintentionally increase his pain, she slowly lifted herself up. Then he took off, running so fast that Anastasia barely had time to wrap her arms around his body. While struggling to stay on top of him, she realized that she had another thing to worry about; Frost was following the rogue werewolf's tracks.

"What are you doing?" Anastasia yelled, afraid that Frost had gone insane. "He wants to kill us! Turn around *now*!"

Apparently unwilling to acknowledge Anastasia's request to get the hell out of there, Frost continued to race forward. She was infuriated by how easy it was for him to put them both in danger just to win a fight. It was so selfish, not to mention foolish. It was also a part of Frost that she'd never seen before. The memory of him vowing to always protect her filled her mind. Had that only been a lie?

All too soon, Frost and Anastasia left the clearing and entered an area of the woods which kept getting darker because of the numerous trees. It felt like night had fallen early, and the haunting caw of an unseen raven made the atmosphere that much more sinister and unnerving. This was by far the creepiest part of Cedar Falls Woods that Anastasia had ever seen.

"I want to leave," Anastasia said angrily as Frost moved skillfully in between the trees. "I mean it, Frost. You're acting like a complete ass." Her rant was nowhere near finished, yet she found herself at a loss for words as her eyes settled upon something very unusual.

There, less than fifty feet away, was a tiny log cabin made for one. Located after several bends in the woods and well-concealed with no visible windows, it was evident that the person who had built it wanted to be left alone. However, Frost was obviously not going to steer clear as he swiftly approached the moss-covered cabin.

Coming to an abrupt halt, Frost motioned for Anastasia to climb down from his back. After reluctantly doing so, the first thing she noticed was a thick, heavy-looking door which had three rusty locks. These locks were pointless, though, as the door was already slightly ajar and creaking gently despite the lack of wind. Even more disturbing than this cabin — which definitely looked like it was haunted — was the large werewolf prints that led inside.

As Frost cast Anastasia a serious glance, she understood that he wanted her to stay there. Well, that was one instruction that she wouldn't be following. Against her wishes, he'd dragged them both into this second encounter with the rogue werewolf, and now he was telling her to wait outside? Frost needed to learn the hard way that they were in this together, and Anastasia wasn't afraid to show him what she was made of.

With a powerful lunge, Frost burst into the cabin. Anastasia was right behind him, and as her eyes slowly adjusted to the darkness, she realized that the interior of the cabin was creepier than the exterior. It was so dreary and musty-smelling that it felt inhospitable at best. As Anastasia stepped beside Frost to get a better look, a startling vision was revealed. In the middle of the cabin, sitting deathly still in an old rocking chair, was a man. His back was to Anastasia and Frost as he stared at an unlit fireplace.

"You shouldn't have followed me, Russell," the man spoke in a deep, harsh voice.

The man's words were few and simple, yet even Anastasia felt the significance of what he'd said. Who was he, and more importantly, why was he calling Frost by that name? As she glanced at a serious-looking Frost, who had returned to his human self, she realized that he knew more about this man than she did.

Standing up, the man revealed himself to be tall and evidently very thin due to the way his red and black plaid jacket and old jeans clung to his body. Like Frost, the darkness enhanced the hue and brightness of his eyes, but that's where the similarities ended. His hair was as white as snow, and he had a long, deep scar running across his left cheek. Likely in his mid-fifties, the man had a sour expression upon his face and a tense, defensive body language. A mere glimpse in his direction made it clear that he'd suffered a very hard life.

After retrieving an outfit identical to the one he was wearing, along with a pair of black leather boots, the man handed them to Frost. "You'll have to shake off the dust," he advised, "but it's a hell of a lot better than your birthday suit."

"Who are you?" Anastasia asked as Frost silently snatched the clothing and put it on.

The man remained as quiet as Frost, while picking up two old steel buckets that sat next to the fireplace. He then stepped outside and returned a moment later, after having filled them both with snow. He proceeded to start a fire with sticks from a nearby woodpile, before placing one of the buckets over the growing flames.

"You can dress those wounds, but then you must leave," he said, although his own cuts had gone untreated.

Without warning, Frost slammed the man against the wall, causing the bucket and its stand to sway dangerously. For the second time that day, the man looked like he wanted to retaliate, but he didn't. Somehow, Frost had a power over him which had nothing to do with strength.

"Is that what I'm worth to you – some old clothing and hot rags?" Frost demanded quickly and harshly. He then forced a laugh, even though he was still obviously seething. "I guess I should consider myself lucky. At least you're not sending me into the woods to die – *again*."

Instantaneously, Anastasia's mouth dropped wide open. Frost's desperate and seemingly irrational desire to chase after the rogue werewolf suddenly made sense. This man was the one he'd hated his whole life; this was his father.

"Why so quiet?" Frost taunted the man, who was refusing to make eye contact with him. "It's been seventeen years. I would've thought you'd have something to say."

"Please, Frost," Anastasia started to reason with him, "this isn't why we're here." She could sense that Frost's anger toward his father was more intense than he'd expected. Yet, she also knew that this wasn't the encounter he had planned for them. If Frost couldn't control his emotions right now, he might find himself completing the very job that the werewolf hunters had set out to do.

"I didn't want you to spend your life hating me," Frost's father finally said, almost looking sad at the thought.

"Don't flatter yourself," Frost replied with a sneer. "I've managed just fine without you."

"I'm glad, Russell, I truly am."

With growing anger, Frost slammed his father harder against the wall. "Stop calling me that!" he cried, his once beautiful eyes now full of hatred.

Anastasia couldn't stand to see Frost this way, and she knew that she had to intervene immediately. Stepping forward, she tried to pry them apart with the little strength that she had left. Unsuccessful, she cast Frost a desperate look.

Grunting, Frost released his grasp on his father, but it was clear that he wasn't finished with him yet. "You owe me," he said in a stone-cold tone. "My girlfriend's sick, and we need a place to stay. We *are* going to remain here until she recovers."

Frost's father studied Anastasia, likely noting the perspiration that she felt all over her face. "She can rest there," he instructed, while pointing at a small, very low-lying bed. "And for goodness sake, get her out of that coat. She'll sweat to death at this rate."

"Where are you going?" Frost demanded as his father stepped into a pair of rubber boots which were placed beside the cabins only exit.

"To gather birch bark," he replied. "It's an old remedy for ailments, including fevers."

"I won't allow her to take it," Frost stated.

"So, she suffers because of you?" he asked rhetorically, while bearing a disgusted expression. "You really are my son." With that said, he left the cabin, shutting the door harshly behind him.

A heavy silence filled the air, which Anastasia finally broke by asking Frost gently, "How did you know it was him?"

"His eyes, his scent," Frost responded slowly, as if reliving the moment, "but mostly the shocked expression upon his face when he realized who *I* was."

"Are you okay?" Anastasia inquired sympathetically.

"I should be the one asking you that," Frost replied, beginning to work quickly to prepare the bed. "Damn," he muttered a second later. "It looks like no one's slept here for years. I wonder if this is even his place. I wouldn't put it past the bastard. He probably killed the real owner."

"Why are you so angry?" Anastasia demanded, trying to stop him from making the bed so he'd take a moment to actually open up to her. "This is what we wanted."

"This isn't what I wanted!" Frost cried in frustration. "We were supposed to get the hell out of Cedar Falls and live a normal life together." He let out a short laugh, almost as if he was mocking himself. "It sounded romantic at the time, but now I see the foolishness of it all."

Anastasia hugged Frost, refusing to let him go even as he tried to retreat in shame. "We were desperate," she said softly, "and nothing's over yet."

"You almost died, Anastasia – *twice*," Frost said solemnly as he guided her toward the bed. "I swear I won't allow that to happen again. Now please get some sleep."

Thankful to have the opportunity to rest, Anastasia readily crawled into the bed which felt like it was made from bird feathers and downy. She was starting to feel dizzy again, and it helped to close her eyes and breathe deeply. Although their journey was far from over, she needed to take this time for herself – everything else would have to wait until tomorrow or whenever she had recovered.

Slowly the minutes ticked by, and despite being physically and emotionally exhausted, Anastasia couldn't sleep. Finally giving up trying, she opened her eyes and turned on her side to watch Frost. He looked both angry and sad, while sitting in front of the fire and carefully dressing his wounds.

"Let me help you," Anastasia offered as she sat up in bed.

With a surprised expression, Frost faced her. "You're meant to be asleep," he scolded gently.

"I can't – at least not without you."

Casting Anastasia a slight smile, Frost wrung out the last rag and tied it around his upper arm before joining her on the bed. He didn't say a word as he wrapped his right, uninjured arm around her and pulled her in close. With a long, overwhelmed sigh, Frost held onto Anastasia tightly, as if she was his sole lifeline.

Their moment of silence was interrupted as Frost's father entered the cabin, bringing with him several long strips of birch bark in one hand and a dead rabbit in the other. Before tossing the items onto a small table, he practically glared at Anastasia and Frost, apparently greatly offended by their affection.

"Fetch me a bucket of water," he instructed Frost, while retrieving a pocketknife that sat upon the mantle. "The Great Rapids is less than five hundred meters away. I trust you'll be able to find it." With that said, he turned his back on Frost and began cutting the birch bark into thin strips.

After rising slowly from the bed, Frost picked up one of the buckets which was still filled with fresh snow. He then approached his father from behind and placed the bucket on the table with a heavy thud. "There's no need for me to leave this cabin," Frost said in a cold, steady tone, "and don't think for a second that I'd allow you to be alone with her."

Clutching the open pocketknife, Frost's father turned to

face him. At first, he appeared threatening, as if he wanted to teach Frost a lesson for being disrespectful. However, his expression soon softened as he responded calmly, "You better get that on the fire then."

Once Frost had added more sticks to the fire and placed the bucket over the increasing flames, they all sat silently, watching as the snow gradually began to melt. When it reached a boiling point, Frost's father carefully filled an old beer stein with the water, using a large wooden spoon to do so. He proceeded to add the thin strips of bark and allowed it to steep briefly before handing the stein to Anastasia.

With a smile, Anastasia took the birch bark tea. "Thank you..." she said, prying for his name.

"Symon."

"I'm Anastasia," she responded, before sipping the tea which was much more tolerable than she would've thought and actually kind of sweet. As she drank the rest of the liquid, a warm sensation spread throughout her body. She hoped that was a good sign.

"That's a beautiful name," Symon commented, his eyes lingering on her for a few moments too long.

The awkwardness reached a peak as Symon's stare covered every inch of her body that wasn't concealed by a sheet. Although Anastasia was used to this type of attention from men, it felt a little disconcerting coming from her boyfriend's father, especially while she sat in bed. Yet, his gaze on her wasn't completely lustful; he almost looked nostalgic and sad.

"Well, my name's Frost — not Russell," Frost said in an annoyed tone, joining the conversation a little late. Defensively, he stepped in between Symon and Anastasia, as if marking his territory.

"I prefer Russell," Symon remarked, looking down on Frost who was an inch or two shorter than him.

"I didn't know I had a choice," Frost snapped.

"That's not necessarily a bad thing," Symon pointed out with a furrowed brow. "It only takes one wrong decision to ruin your life."

"Cut the bullshit, Symon, and tell me something that I actually want to hear – where is she?"

Avoiding Frost's glare, Symon replied, "I don't know who you're talking about."

"Where–is–my–mother?" Frost demanded, prolonging each word as if Symon was stupid.

Even though Frost appeared to be mocking his father, Anastasia could see how vulnerable he was at this moment. Notably, Frost had folded his arms over his chest like he was desperately trying to protect his heart. She knew that he'd wanted to ask that question for a very long time.

"She's not here," Symon answered gruffly.

"Where can I find her?" Frost continued to demand. When Symon failed to answer, he raised his voice. "I have a right to know – tell me."

Suddenly, Symon turned his back on Anastasia and Frost and then slammed one fist against the wall, causing them both to jump in surprise. He remained in that position, shifting only to place his head against the wall as if he'd somehow been defeated. After pausing for a long time, likely to calm himself down, Symon faced them once again.

"She's dead," he said in an eerily cold tone.

Symon's shocking words left Anastasia immobilized. She wanted to comfort Frost, but her overwhelming sympathy for him made it impossible to even look at his face; she knew that he'd be completely heartbroken.

"What...what did you say?" Frost stuttered.

"She died a long time ago. The details don't matter now."

"Yeah, I think they do," Frost interjected harshly. "What

happened to her?"

"Hunters," Symon answered, spitting out the word as if it was poison. Sighing deeply, he continued. "It was a night like so many others. The full moon was high in the cloudless sky as we ran throughout the woods, wild and free. That's when we heard them – hunters, coming at us from every direction. We tried to escape, but they were too fast on their snowmobiles. Looking back, I realize just how outnumbered we were. Although I beat the odds, your mother, Erin, didn't. I wish I'd been the one who was shot by the silver bullet that night, because she was the last werewolf who deserved to die like that."

Anastasia stifled a gasp as she drew a horrific connection between Symon's story and the newspaper article she'd recently read. It had been about a rogue wolf who was killed in Cedar Falls Woods exactly seventeen years ago; only, she wasn't just any wolf – she was Frost's mother. Anastasia tried to suppress the disturbing thought, but the newspaper's supplementary photograph of Frost's dead werewolf mother kept circulating in her mind.

"What kind of man leaves his wife and son to die?" Frost seethed, coming face-to-face with his father.

"You and Erin were my everything!" Symon cried, losing all of the control he'd seemingly tried so hard to keep. "There was nothing I could do to bring Erin back, so I became consumed with avenging her death. I stalked the hunters who took her from me and then I killed them – brutally. Their deaths caused another werewolf hunt, though, and I knew that more loss was inevitable. You were in grave danger, Frost, and I thought if I didn't nurture your inner wolf, you'd have a normal life. When I left you in the woods, I knew someone was coming. I was trying to save you, not kill you."

"You abandoned me," Frost replied quickly, as if unwilling

to really listen to what his father was saying. "Nothing will *ever* change that fact."

"I'm sorry, son," Symon said quietly, while lowering his head in shame.

"I'm not your son," Frost remarked bitterly, glaring at Symon as he passed him to get to Anastasia. Once at her side, Frost took the empty beer stein from her. "Please, Anastasia, you need to sleep."

"Frost, I don't think now's the time..." Anastasia began to say, realizing that he was avoiding the confrontation with his father.

"Don't worry about anything other than getting better," Frost interrupted with a whisper, while leaning over to kiss Anastasia's forehead. "I love you."

Acknowledging how very tired she was and that she couldn't help anyone while in her current state, Anastasia lay back down in the bed. Reaching for Frost's hand, she gave it a gentle, loving squeeze. She wanted Frost to understand that she would always be there for him, especially during painful times such as these.

Now closing her eyes, Anastasia allowed her body to sink deeper into the feathery bed which was, ironically, a little too soft to be comfortable. She feared that she wouldn't be able to sleep as the water in the bucket began to boil harshly and Symon scurried in the cabin, likely getting ready to prepare the rabbit. However, her concerns were unfounded as the exertion of today, along with that soothing, sweet tea, soon sent her into slumber.

Illness had always caused Anastasia to have odd dreams, and tonight was no exception. She found herself back at the clearing where she'd first encountered Symon, but in this version of events, Frost had never arrived. Instead, she remained on the frozen ground, terrified as Symon, in his shape-shifted form, loomed over her. As he drew closer, his once distorted appearance became clearer until every feature was distinct. Full of fear, Anastasia turned her head to avoid Symon's intense, glowing eyes which had creepily doubled in size. Then she screamed. Blood covered the ground where she lay, and it was spreading outwards until the whole clearing was saturated red.

A loud bang, which sounded similar to a bullet being shot, awoke Anastasia with a start. Her heart raced, even after she'd realized that it was just a dream, because in reality, things weren't that much better. Finally looking around, she saw nothing that could've caused such a noise. In fact, everything was oddly calm. Symon sat in the rocking chair, while Frost stood beside him, talking quietly as the rabbit stewed over small, crackling flames. Anastasia was about to call out to Frost when she heard what was being discussed.

"Even if it feels right to love her, it's not," Symon warned Frost. "Take Anastasia back to her family, and let her live a normal life without you."

"I'm not looking for fatherly advice," Frost stated coolly. "I came to warn you about the werewolf hunt, and now that I have, there's nothing left to say."

"Don't listen to me because I'm your father," Symon replied in a hurried, distraught tone. "Listen to me because I've been there. Your mother was a regular woman when we met in these woods and fell in love. I would've done anything for Erin, including turning her into a werewolf when she begged me to do so. She had a romanticized idea of what it meant to be a lycanthrope, but I should've known better. I did it because I loved her – she died because I loved her."

Slowly, Frost responded, "I'm not you."

Symon sighed before standing up and heading toward the

door. He'd only taken one step outside when he unexpectedly turned around. "Please come with me, Frost," he practically begged. "Let me make it up to you. We'll take Anastasia to the hospital, where her family can find her. It's the best option for her."

"Goodbye, Symon," Frost said with a serious expression, "and good luck."

As Frost passed by, on route to shut the door after Symon's departure, Anastasia closed her eyes and pretended to be asleep. Although it seemed foolish, she knew that the last thing Frost needed to be worrying about was her, especially after what had just been said. When she carefully opened her eyes a few moments later, she saw a sad-looking Frost holding Symon's clothing and rubber boots. Symon had shape-shifted into a werewolf and would be fleeing for his mere survival right now. In comparison to his life, both past and present, Anastasia realized that she and Frost were by far the fortunate ones.

Part Nine

Deathly

Over the course of three days, Symon's old, tiny cabin became a second home to Anastasia and Frost. It was there, under the careful supervision of Frost, that Anastasia rested in bed and ate rabbit stew until finally, her fever broke and she regained her strength. She'd even grown fond of their secret place in the woods. Most cherished of all were the evenings spent with Frost, simply cuddling in front of the fire that glowed deep hues of yellow and orange. Although she felt safe and comfortable there, Anastasia couldn't forget about the dangers that awaited them outside.

At this moment, somewhere in the woods, Frost was exposed to those very dangers as he hunted for their lunch. He'd promised to bring back a fish, along with a bucket of water since constantly melting snow was tiresome and a strain on their firewood supply. However, as Anastasia grew impatient and yearned for fresh air, she decided that gathered snow would have to suffice.

After putting on her winter clothing and retrieving the bucket, Anastasia stepped outside. She was immediately met with a cold wind that whipped at her face and made the trees bend and creak. Since Anastasia had been cooped up in the cabin for so long, it felt refreshing to be outdoors, but that didn't mean she was going to venture far – she'd never be that foolish again.

Taking only a few steps, Anastasia leaned over and scooped snow into the bucket. She was almost finished when something unusual caught her attention. There, against the pristine white snow, were several muddy werewolf prints which definitely belonged to Frost. Furrowing her brow, Anastasia wondered where the mud had come from, but she couldn't find any explanation for it. Curiosity overcame her as she started to follow the prints which led to the back of the cabin. From there, they went in a straight line, southwards from the cabin, before disappearing down a slope.

Leaving the bucket at the top of the slope, Anastasia carefully proceeded downwards, making sure to dig her heels into the snow to prevent herself from falling. Unfortunately, her efforts were done in vain as she lost her footing and began to slide quickly. Anastasia let out a surprised gasp after landing with a hard thud. It wasn't the fall that had startled her, though; it was the circular, three foot wide hole in the snowy slope which had left her speechless.

With a loud gulp, Anastasia inched forward on all fours. It was like she'd become an animal who was returning to her den, because she knew with no uncertain doubt that this hole was indeed a creature's home. From the size and location, it seemed fitting that the den would belong to a wolf. However, what Anastasia couldn't figure out was why Frost's increasingly muddy prints led inside and, especially, why he hadn't mentioned any of this to her.

As Anastasia slowly crawled into the den, she brushed aside several tree branches that had likely concealed the entrance until recently. Continuing forward, her body now blocked the little light which had streamed in from outside. Yet, the only thing that concerned Anastasia was her nose. Food had been left to decompose somewhere inside, and was that urine she smelled? Suppressing the urge to be sick,

Anastasia quickly backed out of the den.

Anxiously, Anastasia struggled up the slope, grabbed the bucket and then ran as fast as she could toward the cabin. She ignored the extra weight of the bucket and didn't even flinch as it swung wildly, hitting her leg on several occasions. Right now, all that mattered was finding answers.

When Anastasia reached the cabin, she flung the door open and hurried inside. She was disappointed, and also a little scared, to learn that Frost still hadn't come back. Unsure of what to do, Anastasia began to pace nervously. That's when her eyes settled upon the old-looking journal that Frost had been reading faithfully for the last few days. Anastasia picked up the journal, but she didn't open it right away. Instead, she ran her fingers over the faded black leather cover, all the while thinking how odd it was that a man like Symon had chronicled so many of his thoughts and feelings.

Frost had found the journal behind a pile of firewood, as if Symon had meant for it to stay hidden. Most of the entries that Frost had read to her detailed the growing relationship between Erin and Symon; however, there were many times when he'd read silently, while bearing a very serious expression upon his face. Now, more than ever, Anastasia wanted to know exactly what Frost had been keeping from her. Opening the journal, she skimmed through the yellowed pages, stopping only when she came across a disconcerting entry that had obviously been written hastily and with much emotion.

February 24th

It's been three days — three long, agonizing days since Erin's murder. But what does time matter, anyway? Unless I could reverse it, nothing will bring her back to us. Somehow, Russell knows that everything has changed; he just won't stop crying. My heart is broken, and all I see is darkness. As this anger courses through my veins, I know I'm not in control of my actions.

When I last felt like this, it was because I'd turned Erin into a werewolf. During those dreadful twenty four hours of Incubation, I thought I would go insane. And I would have, if it wasn't for the guidance of my old, dear friend, Julia. However, not even all the members of the founding family could help me now. The war has already begun, and there's no going back.

More confused than ever, Anastasia stopped reading. Although Symon's absolute anger was apparent, that's where the clarity ended. Was Julia part of the founding family? Symon certainly seemed to be alluding to that conclusion. Unfortunately, what exactly they had founded was also unclear. Perhaps it was Cedar Falls, but that was just another guess. Furthermore, what the hell was Incubation? Anastasia furrowed her brow for the second time that day, before continuing to the next journal entry.

February 27th

My fangs and claws are marred by the blood of Erin's murderers, but I haven't found solace in my revenge. I only feel a deep, dark hole inside of me, and it grows bigger every day. Hatred and vengeance have become my life, yet who is there left to blame but myself? If Erin had never met me, she'd be alive today. Like all the hunters involved in that fatal chase, I'm also responsible. How can I possibly continue living while knowing what I've done? I brought death to the love of my life, and I can't bear to think what troubles will befall Russell if he stays with me.

March 1ˢᵗ

Hell has been unleashed in Cedar Falls Woods. The hunters are everywhere and more keep arriving daily with faster snowmobiles and bigger rifles. They are after all wolves, and I've seen many innocent ones slaughtered. Although I know I started this war, I no longer have the desire to finish it. All that matters is that Russell is safe with his new family. Erin would understand why I did this, but now, I truly have nothing left in the world.

During these deadly times, I shouldn't be a werewolf; yet, that's all I can be. I'm turning more frequently and for longer periods of time. When I attempt to return to my human form, the transformation is almost impossible. Despite having never experienced this before, I know what's happening, and there's nothing I can do to stop it. The wolf inside of me will take over.

Completely engrossed by Symon's words, Anastasia turned the page, but unfortunately, it was blank. As she quickly flipped through the rest of the journal, she discovered that nothing else had been written. Letting out a short, disappointed sigh, Anastasia closed the journal and was about to return it to the table when she saw something which chilled her to the bone. There, on the back cover, was a muddy paw print.

Anastasia's mind raced as she stared at the print which undoubtedly belonged to Symon. As he'd predicted, the wolf had overpowered his human self, and it was all because of his uncontrollable anger and guilt – two emotions which were capable of destroying a person or even a beast. Anastasia now understood why Frost hadn't shared this part of the journal or his unearthing of Symon's den; he was afraid of the same thing happening to him. Initially, she'd been certain that finding Frost's parents would help him deal with his transformation woes, but regrettably, it had only made everything much worse.

Suddenly, Anastasia heard someone running outside. Whoever it was sounded heavy-footed, like they were in a great hurry. A few seconds later, Frost burst into the cabin, bare-naked and with an expression of complete fear upon his face. Instantly, he placed the palms of his hands against his forehead and paced back and forth, as if willing himself to think. Not saying a single word, the only noises came from Frost's quick steps and his rapid, shallow breathing.

"What is it?" Anastasia demanded with a racing heart, unable to take the suspense which Frost had created.

"I've ruined everything," Frost choked out. "It's all over."

Grabbing Frost by his shoulders, she forced him to stop pacing and instead look at her. "Breathe," she instructed, "and then tell me what's wrong."

Frost took a deep, shaky breath, but it did little to calm him down. "They...they know," he stuttered, almost as if he was in shock. "They saw me shape-shift into a werewolf."

Feeling her knees go weak, Anastasia tightened her grip on Frost. Although this seemed like the worst possible thing that could happen, she knew that she must stay strong, especially since Frost wasn't currently doing a very good job at keeping himself together.

"You need to tell me everything that happened," Anastasia said gently.

"I guess I wasn't really paying attention because my mind was on my father and how much I wished I could forget about him. Before I knew it, I'd reached the Great Rapids and moments after shape-shifting, I saw them – Mike, Leo, Pete, Mr. Fairbanks, and your grandfather. A few shots were fired, but I was too fast. Even though I managed to lead them far away from here, they won't stop until they've found and killed me. We have to leave now."

Anastasia opened her mouth to speak, but no words came out. What could she possibly say, anyway? Her grandfather, along with four men she'd known for practically her whole life, had just tried to murder the guy she loved. However, Anastasia didn't question for a second where her loyalties lay. The hunters were wrong, and if they refused to acknowledge that, she wanted nothing to do with any of them.

"Get your coat," Frost instructed as he put on his father's clothing and boots. "If they find us while we're in the cabin, we won't have any chance of escaping."

"Why are you getting dressed?" Anastasia asked, expecting him to turn into a werewolf at any given moment.

"I have to do this as a human," Frost replied solemnly.

"Are you crazy?" Anastasia shrieked. "We can't outrun them like that!"

"We don't have a choice," Frost said, his voice now filled with regret. "It was difficult to shape-shift at the Great Rapids, and minutes before I reached the cabin, I turned back into a human against my will. I'm trying, Anastasia, but I can't become a werewolf anymore."

Desperately studying Frost, Anastasia wondered what could've caused the sudden change. After all, the original problem they'd set out to cure was completely opposite to his current one. Something significant must have recently happened to Frost, and as Anastasia's eyes fell upon Symon's journal, she finally understood what it was.

"I've read it," Anastasia said abruptly, while pointing directly at the journal, "and that is *not* your fate."

"It's worse than you think," Frost said, lowering his head sadly. "There's a reason why this cabin was so dusty and bare – my father hadn't been living here for years. He stayed in a den, Anastasia. He became a full-time werewolf."

Gently, Anastasia took Frost's hand and placed it against his heart. "I know about the den," she said softly. "It must have been a terrible way to live, but don't you get it, Frost? Seeing you restored his humanity."

Apparently processing Anastasia's words, Frost was silent for a moment. Then, he quickly released himself from her grasp and took a few steps backwards. With a look of determination upon his face, he shut his eyes tightly, as if concentrating very hard on something. Frost remained that way for several minutes, but when he failed to transform into a werewolf, he opened his eyes and let out a frustrated sigh.

"It's okay," Anastasia said, hurrying to put on her coat, gloves and scarf. Since she couldn't force Frost to become a werewolf, their next best option was to run for their lives. "Do you know how to get to Hartfield?" she asked, while quickly dumping the bucket of snow over the already dying fire.

"I'm certain it's only a few miles away," Frost answered with a nod, before opening the door. "We should be able to reach there before nightfall."

Stepping outside, Anastasia waited as Frost took a long last look at the cabin and then shut the door. Reaching for her hand, he began guiding her throughout a seemingly never-ending maze of trees. Perhaps it was only her perception, but the woods felt colder, darker and much more dangerous.

"When we arrive in Hartfield, there's a lot that has to be done," Anastasia said, trying to concentrate on anything other than her surroundings. She'd been formulating a detailed plan after their original one had gone askew, and she was more than a little grateful that Frost had insisted she carry both of their wallets in her coat pocket. After all, they were going to need money. "We have to find a bank machine, motel and grocery store," she continued, ticking off each item in her mind. "And we'll need to get your truck back somehow."

"Let's just get out of these woods first," Frost replied, his eyes darting around nervously as he urged Anastasia to move faster.

Willing herself forward, Anastasia focused on keeping up with Frost's ever-increasing pace. However, her attention was soon drawn to the faint noise of trees rustling from somewhere behind them. Both Anastasia and Frost stopped dead in their tracks and spun around, but no one was there. After several moments of silence and no visible activity, he nudged her onward.

They'd only taken a few dozen steps when the noise came again, this time from the opposite direction. As the sound grew louder, Anastasia and Frost didn't stop to investigate. Instead, they ran as fast as they could, while trying to avoid slipping on the sleek, compact snow.

Still hand-in-hand, Anastasia knew that she and Frost were fleeing from more than one unidentified person or animal – she could now hear three of them, and they were getting closer. Just as unnerving was Anastasia's certainty that they were intentionally being chased from their route to Hartfield. Whoever was after her and Frost wanted them deep in the woods, where they were defenseless and their screams couldn't be heard.

Frost must have also sensed that they were being driven in a specific direction because without any warning, he pulled Anastasia sideways, forcing her to run in between the trees in a disorienting zigzag pattern. As she struggled past the long branches, she realized that they were actually moving slower. These trees were too close together, leaving little room to move and making it easier for their pursuers to pinpoint their location due to the shaking branches.

Thinking fast, Anastasia resisted Frost's lead and instead forced him underneath a large tree. Almost bent double, she scurried toward the base of the tree and climbed up, wincing as pine needles scraped against her cheeks. It was a bold strategy, but when she looked behind herself, she was relieved to find Frost following her. After ascending several feet, Anastasia and Frost stopped and waited, their heavy breathing completely in sync.

It only took a couple of minutes for the trees to start rustling again, and although Anastasia was undeniably scared, she was also prepared to fight. They had the higher ground, and they could use that to their advantage. With unwavering determination, Anastasia peered through the branches, hoping to catch a glimpse of whoever was there. She couldn't see anything other than trees, but that hardly mattered when she heard the fast approaching footsteps. Anastasia now knew that their predators were humans.

Hunters, Frost mouthed to Anastasia, before placing his index finger over his lips to indicate that she should remain quiet.

Anastasia didn't speak or move as the hunter circled the area. Although it sounded like he was the only one there, she was certain that the others wouldn't be too far away. As for right now, this hunter was so close that she could smell his cheap cologne. She knew that there was no reason for him to be lingering around unless he'd found them. Anxiously, Anastasia waited for him to strike, but instead, he began to walk away until she could no longer hear his footsteps.

The minutes passed slowly as Anastasia and Frost stayed in the tree, afraid to leave too soon in case the hunter or any of his friends returned. Sitting there gave Anastasia time to think about the severity of their situation, and it made her heart ache with sadness. Although she never felt sorry for herself when she was with Frost, it was difficult to remain optimistic with the odds never in their favor.

"We can't stay here much longer," Frost finally spoke in a low tone. "There's not a lot of daylight left, and we aren't prepared to spend a night out here."

Casting Frost a nervous, almost reluctant look, Anastasia slowly rose from the tree branch. Her awkward sitting position had left her legs feeling stiff, and as she proceeded downwards, she paid particular attention to where she placed her feet. Images of falling to her death plagued Anastasia's mind, causing her to lose confidence and, ironically, almost slip. Fortunately, Frost's strong hand was there to steady her before she even knew what was happening.

"Thanks," Anastasia said, feeling instantly comforted by his touch.

"I'll always be there to catch you," Frost replied, looking more worried than ever, "but don't put that to the test too much, okay?"

"I promise," Anastasia muttered distractedly, while concentrating on getting out of the tree.

Once they'd safely reached the ground, Frost quickly started in a northwesterly direction. "We need to find an alternative route to Hartfield," he explained. "It's too dangerous to retrace our steps."

Anastasia certainly hoped that Frost was right because walking amongst the cluster of trees was tedious at best, leaving her to feel even more tired, cold and hungry. In such an unforgiving atmosphere, it didn't take long for her to start fearing that they'd be trapped in there forever. Then, just when she thought that she couldn't take it any longer, the woods became lighter. Knowing that she and Frost were nearing a clearing, Anastasia hurried forward with a renewed sense of hope.

"Wait," Frost said urgently, grabbing Anastasia's arm before she could go any further. Without saying another word, he led her from behind the trees and to the edge of a sun-filled gully.

Looking at the ten foot drop, Anastasia gulped. She was about to thank Frost for the second time that day when she noticed something unusual in the middle of the gully. Although it was difficult to decipher, it sort of resembled a person lying in the snow.

"Frost..." Anastasia hardly choked out.

From his horrified expression, it was clear that Frost had also spotted the person. "I think I see a path," he said, beginning to hurry around the gully. "Stay away from the edge," he added needlessly, since Anastasia was already proceeding with great caution.

Coming to a stop, Anastasia knew that they'd arrived at the area where Frost planned on climbing down. Assessing the danger, she peered over his shoulder to find a long, slightly slanted trail which led into the gully. It would be a tough but not impossible descend.

"This might be ugly," Frost warned Anastasia. "You don't have to come."

"Yes, I do," she answered abruptly. "Now hurry up!"

Concentrating on every step, Anastasia followed Frost, making sure to leave ample space between them. As she felt herself slipping, she quickly dug her heels into the snow, which helped to regain her balance. Letting out a sigh of relief, Anastasia continued on the slope until she finally reached the bottom of the gully just moments after Frost. Unfortunately, there wasn't time to celebrate her small achievement. Even though it was hard to believe, someone was in a worse state than her and Frost, and he needed their help immediately.

As Anastasia hurried toward the person, she instantly knew that something wasn't right. He was lying too flat on the ground, and she couldn't see any boots completing his winter ensemble. When she took a closer look, she gasped with a mixture of surprise and fright. A coat and a pair of snow pants had been strategically placed on the snow to give the impression of a fallen person; however, no one was there.

"It's a trap," Frost said in a stone-cold tone. "We need to get out of here."

Before Anastasia and Frost had a chance to leave, four snowmobiles appeared at the top of the gully, their presence announced by the sound of revved-up engines and the angry cries of the hunters who rode them. One after another, they formed a perfect line, quickly making their way toward the gully's only accessible path. Then, like a well-executed military maneuver, they sped downwards at a dangerously fast pace.

Anastasia spun around, prepared to scale the icy walls with nothing but her bare hands, if that meant they would escape. Yet, as she tried to flee, she found herself being held back. In shock, she looked at Frost. He was grasping her arm firmly and refusing to let go, even when she struggled to free herself.

"It's too late," Frost said in an eerily somber tone.

"Only if we don't try," Anastasia argued, flabbergasted by his behavior and willingness to just give up.

"They won't hurt you," Frost promised. "I'm the one they want."

"Please, Frost," Anastasia begged, while glancing at the rapidly advancing hunters. "It's now or never."

"You don't understand," Frost said, releasing Anastasia's arm so he could place both hands on her shoulders and look seriously into her eyes. "If I run now, I'll always be running.

The only way we can have a somewhat normal life is if I confront them and make them see reason – I'm not a threat to anyone."

Anastasia wanted to tell Frost how incredibly stupid his plan was and that it would likely cost them their lives, but there was no point in voicing her concerns now; the hunters had already formed a circle around them and were closing in at a dizzyingly fast pace. The land vibrated under the weight and speed of the snowmobiles, and the smell of fuel was so strong that Anastasia covered her nose. Worst of all, the hunters were getting way too close, causing her to fear that they would soon be brutally crushed by the heavy machines.

Abruptly, the snowmobiles came to a stop when one of the hunters, who was presumably the leader, signaled for them to do so. After dismounting, they removed their helmets, revealing themselves as Leo, Mike, Pete, and Mr. Fairbanks. Quickly, they retrieved their rifles, which were strapped over their shoulders, and pointed them at Anastasia and Frost. In vain, Frost attempted to place himself between Anastasia and the rifles, but regardless of which way he turned, they were both in danger.

"I'm not who you think I am," Frost said, his voice loud and clear. "I've given you no reason to fear me, and this is all very unnecessary."

"You tried to kill my daughter!" Mr. Fairbanks yelled, practically shaking with anger as he proceeded closer. "I want a confession, boy."

"He saved us!" Anastasia cried, moving in front of Frost before Mr. Fairbanks could come any nearer. "What I told you in the hospital was true – it was a cougar that attacked Chloe."

"I can't imagine what crazy lies he's been telling you, but I've seen the monster with my own eyes," Mr. Fairbanks said to Anastasia. "Come with me, while you still can."

Despite Frost's attempt to pull Anastasia behind him once again, she refused to back down. She was determined to convince Mr. Fairbanks to lower his rifle. If he did, maybe the other hunters would, too. Taking a leap of faith, she stepped forward.

"That's a good girl," Mr. Fairbanks encouraged her. "Your grandfather will be so relieved to know that you're safe."

Trying hard to ignore his patronizing tone, Anastasia took another step. "Mr. Fairbanks, you've known me since I was a child. Please, trust my judgement because I would never be with a murderer."

"It's going to be alright," Mr. Fairbanks said in a tone that was too calm for the current situation. "When this is over, you'll be able to get back to your normal life. That's what you want, isn't it, Anastasia?"

Realizing that Mr. Fairbanks hadn't listened to a word she'd said, she stopped and stared at him. His rifle remained in the same shooting position because he obviously had a plan of his own. He, or one of the other hunters, would kill Frost as soon as she was out of harm's way. The thought that she was responsible for Frost's life made her feel sick.

Before Anastasia had the chance to decide what she would do next, Mr. Fairbanks reached out and grabbed her. With a firm grip, he forced her forward and then wrapped one arm securely around the bottom of her neck. Although Mr. Fairbanks wasn't hurting her, Anastasia knew that she'd made a fatal error. The hunters were now completely in control.

"It might be difficult for you to understand, but I *am* saving you," Mr. Fairbanks whispered to Anastasia, his hot breath tickling her ear in a very uncomfortable manner. "There's something you have to do for me, though. I can't shoot a boy – turn him into the werewolf."

Feeling her blood go cold, Anastasia whispered, "Never."

"Then we're all damned," Mr. Fairbanks said sadly, while steadying his rifle and preparing to fire at Frost.

"Frost, run!" Anastasia shouted in terror as she struggled in Mr. Fairbanks' grasp.

Anastasia's cry was overpowered by a loud, ferocious growl, followed by the presence of Symon. The only way he could've gotten there was by jumping from the top of the gully, and as he bounded toward them, it was clear that he was ready to fight. Unfortunately, so were the hunters.

Taking aim, Mike and Leo fired several shots at Symon, but his movements were so fast and erratic that the bullets kept flying by him harmlessly. Bravely standing their ground, both hunters continued their attempt for a clear shot, even up to the moment when Symon pounced on Leo, causing him to fall. Almost simultaneously, Frost sprang into action, taking Mike by surprise and knocking him over as well.

Having been overly preoccupied with watching Symon dodge bullets *and* unsuccessfully trying to free herself from Mr. Fairbanks, Anastasia hadn't seen Frost transform. However, she knew that he'd done it quickly because accepting his inner wolf was the only way any of them were going to survive. Frost had proven this perfectly since they'd now gained some control of the fight; Symon had Leo pinned under his paws, and although Mike was slowly recovering from the blow, his rifle had skidded across the snow.

As Frost circled Mike to prevent him from getting up, it was apparent that he had reservations about what he should do next. Anastasia knew that he didn't want to harm Mike, but did he really have a choice? As for Symon, his intentions were crystal clear as he let out an unearthly howl and then sunk his fangs into Leo's shoulder.

Leo's shrill cry echoed around the gully, causing Anastasia

to shudder with repulsion. However, it was what happened next that really freaked her out. After Symon's bite, Leo's body immediately stiffened, leaving him looking like the world's most realistic statue. As he lay there motionlessly, it was impossible to tell if he was alive or dead.

"Shoot him, Pete!" Mr. Fairbanks yelled, unable to do the task himself as he fought to maintain his hold on Anastasia.

Evidently out of his element and suffering from shock, Pete hadn't moved a muscle since Symon's arrival. However, Mr. Fairbanks harsh command was enough to break his trance, and after quickly regaining his composure, Pete shot at Symon. The bullet must've been close — very close. Nonetheless, Anastasia was certain that it hadn't hit Symon because he was now running furiously toward Pete.

With a powerful lunge, Symon tackled Pete to the ground and then grunted in frustration as he slid sideways on the icy snow. When he'd risen on his paws once again, he leapt for the fallen hunter. In retaliation, Pete grabbed for his rifle, which lay beside him after being knocked out of his hands. Clutching the rifle by the barrel, he swung it against Symon's ribs, creating a sickening thud.

Up until this moment, Frost had lingered over an almost recovered Mike, hesitant and looking as if he couldn't bring himself to bite a human. However, when he'd heard the hit which Symon had sustained, he gave Mike a threatening glare and then rushed to his father's aid.

Growling in a deeper tone, Symon struck Pete across the chest, ripping his coat and quite possibly his flesh. Down but definitely not out, Pete grunted loudly and began turning the rifle around, his fingers inching closer to the trigger. With an effortless swipe, Symon sent the rifle flying onto the snow, where he crushed it into several pieces merely by stepping upon it. Pete's eyes went wide with terror, right before Symon bit him.

Anastasia winced as she watched the violence unfold. She knew that Frost was also affected by the brutality because after arriving at his father's side, he stood over Pete and lowered his head sadly. Suddenly, Anastasia's attention was drawn away from the two werewolves and onto Mike, who was slowly creeping toward his rifle.

"Watch out!" Anastasia cried with urgency, finally getting Frost and Symon to notice Mike's actions.

Immediately, Mike stood up and ran, stopping only when he'd retrieved his rifle. Reaching him before he could shoot, Frost slammed into Mike, causing him to skid across the snow. Yet, even then, the resolute hunter kept his rifle securely in tow. Getting into the fight, Symon went for an attack but had to retreat when Mike fired at him. Obviously not pleased, Symon struck Mike's face and then leapt on top of him.

"You need to stay still and shut up," Mr. Fairbanks warned Anastasia, losing his composure and perhaps his sanity, too, as he gazed upon the increasingly bleak scene.

"Just let us go in peace and this will all stop," Anastasia promised in a shaky tone.

"I said shut up!" Mr. Fairbanks yelled, tightening his arm around her neck.

Choking, Anastasia tried to call to Frost for help, but she could only manage a meek cry. Luckily, that was good enough. Frost's ears twitched and after he'd looked up, an expression of horror appeared on his face. Then, faster than Anastasia had ever seen, he ran to her. Beginning to circle them so Mr. Fairbanks couldn't get a decent shot, Frost snarled viciously. However, this only caused Mr. Fairbanks to fire erratically at him, while strengthening his grip on Anastasia's neck.

As a succession of bullets flew around her, penetrating into the snow, and she fought to take even the smallest of breaths, Anastasia felt panic seize her body. Although she was also suffering from physical and mental exhaustion, she wouldn't give up. Apparently, neither would Frost because with one fierce, anger-fueled attack, he knocked Mr. Fairbanks and Anastasia down.

Now lying on the cold, hard snow, Anastasia's body ached from the impact, but at least she was free from Mr. Fairbanks and able to take a much needed deep breath of air. Almost instantly, Frost was at her side, licking her face with his warm, wet tongue to make sure that she was alright. The dizziness that Anastasia had been experiencing soon passed, as did the pounding in her head; yet, she was filled with a new fear when she saw the frightening scene that was just ten feet away.

There, hunched over a bitten Mike, was Symon. At first, Anastasia had wondered why he was acting so strange, and then she'd seen it – blood, running from his left paw and marring the snow. Symon no longer looked like his usual strong self, and as he panted heavily, it was evident that he was in a great deal of pain. Although Mike's rifle now lay harmlessly in his stiff hand, the damage had already been done, and if he'd used a bullet made of silver, then Symon's condition would only worsen.

"Go to your father," Anastasia said, fully aware that Frost had chosen to remain with her.

Appearing reluctant, Anastasia had to nod reassuringly at Frost before he would leave her. When he finally did, she watched with slight disgust as he caringly licked his father's wound. Symon responded with a pained moan, although Anastasia was certain that Frost's show of affection meant everything to him.

Suddenly, Anastasia heard a groan coming from nearby. Lifting herself onto her knees, she turned around to see Mr. Fairbanks, who had also risen. With a rifle in his hands and an expression of fury upon his face, it was clear that he wouldn't stop until he'd fulfilled his purpose of killing a werewolf – or two.

Before Anastasia had the chance to scream, Mr. Fairbanks fired directly at Frost, who was too concerned about his father to notice what was happening. Symon had been watching, though, and as he jumped right in front of his son, it was obvious that he knew exactly what he was doing. The bullet hit Symon in what could've only been his heart, causing him to immediately fall to the ground and then lie there lifelessly.

In shock and dismay, Frost stared at his father and whimpered. Then slowly, as he raised his head, the sorrowful moan turned into a growl that seemed to come from the very depths of his soul. With his lips curled back to reveal sharp fangs, Frost glared at Mr. Fairbanks before charging toward him.

Standing firm, Mr. Fairbanks shot at Frost. When no bullet was released, he fired again only to confirm that the rifle was out of ammunition. Mr. Fairbanks appeared terrified, but he remained stationary since running for his life wasn't feasible. Vicious and relentless, Frost pounced on him, clawed his coat open and then pierced his fangs into his chest. Never having the chance to fight back, Mr. Fairbanks merely moaned before turning stiff like the other hunters.

Fumbling backwards, Frost gaped at Mr. Fairbanks, obviously greatly distressed by what he'd done. After a long, tense moment, he cautiously neared him once again. With his nose, Frost gently nudged Mr. Fairbanks, as if he could somehow wish him back to life. Of course, it didn't work.

A low whimper, which was hardly audible, caused Anastasia to turn away from the heartbreaking scene, only to be met with another. She was shocked to discover that Symon was still alive and, unfortunately, suffering immensely. Frost heard him, too, and in a flash, he was at his father's side. Appearing almost angry, he took hold of Symon by the scruff of the neck and attempted to pull him up. Yet, despite Frost's continual effort, he couldn't get him to stand up.

"Frost, stop it," Anastasia said quietly, while placing her hand upon his back.

Refusing to give up, Frost released his father and instead snarled, as if commanding him to get up or else. In response, Symon looked at him, his eyes tell-tale signs that he was slipping away. However, he managed to gather enough strength to raise his head slightly and rub his snout lovingly against Frost's cheek. Then, with a soft sigh, Symon took his last breath.

As he held his father, who remained in his shape-shifted form even in death, Frost returned to his human self and wept. Desperate to offer any kind of comfort, Anastasia retrieved Frost's ripped top and jeans and began to dress him. She then hugged him tightly until she felt tears swelling in the corner of her eyes. This was all so unfair, and she had no idea how she'd ever be able to help him through the pain.

The familiar sound of an approaching snowmobile caused Anastasia and Frost to stand up anxiously, moments before the rider came to a stop in front of them. Dismounting and then removing his helmet, Anastasia's grandfather scanned the area. From the fallen hunters and werewolf, to the frazzled state of Anastasia and Frost, he was clearly overcome with shock and sadness.

"There was more than one werewolf," Mr. Lockhart muttered to himself, as if trying to make sense of the situation.

"How could you send a team of hunters after us?" Anastasia yelled, shoving her grandfather backwards. "Do you really hate us that much?"

Grabbing Anastasia by her shoulders, he forced her to look into his wide, tear-brimmed eyes. "When I realized Frost was the werewolf and that you were with him, the hunt was over for me. I knew I'd never be able to convince Leo, Mike, Pete, and Fairbanks to stop, so I did the next best thing – I told them to go on without me while I gathered the closest groups of hunters to aid us in the fight. In actuality, I stopped the hunters by telling them that the werewolf had already been killed. Thankfully, they believed me because if they hadn't, Frost wouldn't be alive."

Uncertain of what to say, Anastasia remained quiet. Although her grandfather had done the right thing in the end, he'd also caused them a lot of turmoil along the way. Did he really expect her to just forgive and forget? While she knew that she'd eventually forgive him, it most definitely wouldn't be today.

"How did you find us?" Frost demanded cynically.

"The gunshots," Mr. Lockhart replied, his attention turning to the hunters once again. "Are they dead?"

"No," Frost replied, startling Anastasia in the process. "They're in a state referred to as Incubation. When twenty four hours have passed, they'll awaken as werewolves. I'm afraid the same can't be said for my biological father – his wounds were lethal, but you already knew that."

"I'm sorry things had to turn out like this," Mr. Lockhart began to say.

"None of this *had* to happen," Frost interrupted angrily. "You and the other hunters chose to exact revenge because of fear and paranoia. I didn't deserve this, yet I have to live with the consequences of your hateful actions."

"I did it for Anastasia and my wife – to protect them."

"You've done an outstanding job," Frost said sarcastically, while wrapping his arms around a cold, shaken-up Anastasia.

"I can right some of my wrongs by giving you the opportunity to get your life back," Mr. Lockhart offered. "I'll take care of these men, and as for everyone else, your father's body is proof that the wolf has been killed. You can return to Cedar Falls with your secret intact."

"You're sick and deluded," Frost said, while pointing his finger accusingly at Mr. Lockhart. "I won't allow my father to become some spectacle, and even if I did, that would only make the hunt worse. People will think there are more werewolves."

"History proves otherwise," Mr. Lockhart interjected. "One normal, albeit large, wolf stalked these woods and now he's dead. The story isn't all that interesting. Besides, the town wants to believe that they're safe, and with this proof, there's no reason for them to live in fear any longer."

Despite the fact that her grandfather's words had merit, Anastasia cringed at his insensitivity. Feeling defeated, she turned to Frost and said, "I don't think we have much of a choice. We're seventeen – how long can we really be on the run?"

Frost hesitated before looking straight at Mr. Lockhart. "Fine," he said through clenched teeth. "You can have my father's body *after* you've given me a chance to save these men."

"They need to be killed now," Mr. Lockhart argued, visibly upset. "There isn't another option."

"Let me worry about that," Frost said sharply. "In the meantime, no one else dies."

There was a long, tense pause which Anastasia's

grandfather broke with a heavy sigh. "You have twenty four hours," he replied, finally accepting Frost's proposal. "What can I do to help?"

"We can't leave four hunters and a werewolf out here – they'll have to be taken to my father's cabin. Once that's done, Anastasia and I will return to Cedar Falls, so you'll be standing guard over the cabin while we're gone. Also, we'll need a car, and I'm assuming you guys didn't travel from Cedar Falls on your snowmobiles."

"No, we parked at the end of rural road number fifteen in Hartfield, at the edge of the woods."

"We'll find our way," Frost said with a confident nod, taking a step toward one of the snowmobiles.

"You better have a damn good plan," Mr. Lockhart warned, momentarily stopping him, "because I won't allow Cedar Falls to get any more werewolves."

"Neither will I," Frost promised. He began to rummage through one of the hunter's camouflaged-patterned packs, finding coils of rope and a change of clothes which were almost his size.

Working together, Anastasia, Frost and Mr. Lockhart secured each hunter to the snowmobiles, tying them tightly so they wouldn't fall off while traveling to the cabin. It was a difficult task, especially as night fell upon them, and Anastasia couldn't stop herself from wondering if their plan would work – although she wasn't entirely certain what their plan entailed. When they were finally ready to begin their trek, Anastasia's grandfather abruptly pulled her aside, causing Frost to look on in concern.

"Your mother's here," he said solemnly. "When we called to see if you'd arrived home safely, the truth came out – well, most of it. Kendall's been worried sick for days, and she still doesn't know if you're okay. Please, Anastasia, I can take you home."

Processing her grandfather's words, Anastasia stared at him dumbfounded. She'd always thought that her mother wouldn't return to Cedar Falls for anything or anyone; now she knew how completely wrong she'd been. "I'll let Mom know I'm fine as soon as I can," Anastasia hurried to say. "I'm not going home, though – at least not yet."

Her grandfather opened his mouth, likely to protest her decision, but he was interrupted by Frost, who was already seated on a snowmobile and ready to leave.

"Time's running out," Frost called to them in an urgent tone. "Are you with me or not?"

I'm with you, Frost, Anastasia thought, while taking another look at the soiled land. She found it hard to believe that a fight, which had only lasted mere minutes, could inflict so much damage. In those fleeting moments, everything really had changed, and she knew that none of them would ever be the same again. Yet, for all its tragedy, this battle between man and beast had given Anastasia a new appreciation for her life and the people who were still in it.

❋ ❋ ❋

Part Ten

Wolfsbane

The car's headlights illuminated the deserted, tree-lined road, creating an eerie, foreboding sensation as Anastasia and Frost sped from Hartfield to Cedar Falls. Looking at the neon green digits on the clock revealed that it was almost seven a.m. They'd spent too much time – all night and a few hours of the early morning – transporting Symon and the hunters to the cabin. With no direct access that could accommodate snowmobiles, locating a path to the cabin proved far more challenging than they'd originally predicated. Now, Anastasia and Frost had less than eleven hours before dusk would fall, turning the hunters into werewolves forever.

As if the task ahead of them wasn't hard enough, Anastasia and Frost were sleep-deprived and functioning on adrenaline. After securing Symon and the hunters in the cabin, they'd driven a snowmobile through the woods, searching until they found the men's vehicles and hitched trailers parked at the edge of Hartfield. Taking her grandfather's car, they'd only made one stop for fast-food before beginning the next part of their journey. This had left Anastasia and Frost with little chance to talk – until now.

"You seem so certain about what we're doing," Anastasia said, referring to the look of concentration which hadn't faded from Frost's face since leaving the woods. She, on the other hand, had never felt so confused, anxious and overwhelmed in her entire life.

"I don't know what I'm doing," Frost confessed, not taking his eyes off the road. "I'm just hoping that I do."

"Translation, please?"

"I'd never heard of Incubation before, and any knowledge I have on the subject came from reading my father's journal. His references were vague, though, and he appeared to be more interested in finding a cure than the process of turning a human into a werewolf. I'm taking guesses here, Anastasia, but I think there's someone out there who has real answers."

"Julia," Anastasia muttered. "Do you know who she is or, better yet, how we can find her?"

"Not exactly," Frost admitted, pausing briefly before continuing in an uncomfortable tone. "Kate's ancestors founded Cedar Falls. She's the one we have to ask."

Anastasia's mind instantly returned to the moment when Kate had made the claim that Cedar Falls was *her* town. Now that she knew the truth, Kate's haughtiness actually made sense. Nevertheless, Anastasia felt her heart sink because there was little to no chance that she would help them.

"Are you sure there isn't another way to find her?" Anastasia practically begged. "We could try the phonebook or something, *anything*, else."

Firmly, Frost shook his head. "You know how small Cedar Falls is, so there has to be a reason why I've never met Julia. Finding her is going to be tough, and if she really is Kate's ancestor, then we have no other choice. I just pray that Julia's still alive and able to tell us how to stop the transformation."

With the snow-covered roads becoming increasingly slippery, Frost returned his full attention to driving. As silence filled the car, Anastasia finally had the chance to rest her head against the cool window. She took a deep breath and then closed her eyes, praying for even a few moments of sleep. Unfortunately, images of the fight and, more prominently, Frost's dead father kept circulating in her mind. Realizing that a peaceful slumber wouldn't be an option anytime soon, Anastasia sighed and turned her gaze toward the horizon, where the sun was slowly starting to rise.

Shortly before nine a.m., Anastasia and Frost arrived in Cedar Falls. It felt strange being back in what appeared to be a normal town, especially after experiencing such surreal events in the woods. Adding to her unease was the possibility of seeing her mother. If they ran into each other, Anastasia had no idea what she could say to make up for all the stress and worry her disappearance had caused. This latest incident might even be worse than her arrest – at least then her mother had known her whereabouts.

Anastasia's obsessive thoughts were interrupted as Kate's ever pristine house came into view. With the curtains drawn and no cars visible, it appeared as if the McKinleys weren't home. However, that didn't hinder Frost from pulling into her driveway and coming to a stop. Although Anastasia had several reservations about being there, Frost was clearly unwilling to let anything stop him.

"I think it'd be best if you waited in the car," Frost suggested tactfully. "Kate might be more willing to talk if I'm the one asking the questions."

"My thoughts exactly," Anastasia said, before he gave her a quick kiss and then exited the car.

As Frost approached the large, wreath-bearing door, Anastasia rolled down the passenger side window slightly and then crouched at the bottom of her seat. If Kate was home, she wanted to hear their conversation without being seen. Anastasia tried to convince herself that it was necessary to take these measures, but in reality, she didn't trust Kate to be alone with Frost.

The whimsical chime of Kate's doorbell was soon heard, followed by a silence that lasted for several moments. Finally peering over the dashboard, Anastasia found Frost still waiting for someone to answer. He was about to try again when the door suddenly opened to reveal Kate, who was wearing a short red robe and looking beautiful without any make-up on. Kate smiled widely upon seeing Frost, causing Anastasia's disdain for her to increase significantly.

"Hi, Frost," Kate said in a playful tone, before he could speak. "Should I have been expecting you?"

"No, and I'm sorry to come over unannounced," Frost started to say.

"Don't be silly," Kate interrupted, while leaning against the doorway in a somewhat seductive manner. "You're always welcome here, day or night."

Feeling her blood boil, Anastasia had to literally grab onto the edge of her seat to stop herself from running out of the car and slapping Kate. Although Kate must have known that Frost was no longer single, she still obviously wanted to hook up with him – it was so beyond pathetic. Trying hard to calm down, Anastasia remembered why they were there in the first place.

"Um, thanks," Frost replied awkwardly. "Actually, I could really use your help with something."

"Anything," Kate offered quickly. "You don't have to be shy around me."

"It's about a woman named Julia. I believe you two are related, and since I need to talk to her, I was hoping you'd tell me where she..."

"Why would you want to speak with her?" Kate interrupted for the second time, appearing disappointed by

Frost's request.

"It's kind of personal," he admitted slowly, "but it's very important that I find her."

"I can't help you," Kate snapped, her whole disposition changing as she realized that he wasn't interested in her.

"You can't or won't?" Frost asked, preventing her from closing the door.

"I know when I'm being used," Kate said, her tone harsh even though she was visibly upset. "Go back to your freak of a girlfriend and leave me alone. We're done here."

Frost stepped back, allowing Kate to slam the door in his face. He likely knew he deserved such a response, but that didn't change the fact that the information they desperately needed was now completely out of their reach. No longer having a reason to hide, Anastasia returned to her seat, while Frost entered the car.

"I overheard," Anastasia confessed. "Don't worry – we're not out of options. We can ask around town. Surely someone knows Julia."

"I'm not so sure about that. There's something really strange going on with that woman. Kate was totally caught off-guard at the mere mention of her name."

"Then we're the perfect people to solve this mystery," Anastasia stated confidently. "Strange isn't exactly a new concept for us."

Despite himself, Frost smirked. "Okay," he agreed, "we'll try it your way."

Frost started the car and began to reverse, only to come to an abrupt stop seconds later. Startled, Anastasia turned around to discover that another car had entered the driveway. She furrowed her brow in confusion as she realized that the vehicle belonged to Marissa. Anastasia had thought that Kate and Marissa's friendship was long over, so what was she doing here?

"We don't have time for this," Frost stated quietly as a reflection of Marissa exiting her car appeared in their rear-view mirror.

"It's not like we can just leave," Anastasia whispered. "I promise this won't take long."

"Hey," Marissa greeted in a pleasantly surprised manner as she leaned toward Anastasia's window, which was still rolled down. "Chloe and I have been trying to reach you for days. Everything's alright, isn't it?"

"Of course," Anastasia answered, touched by her friend's concern. "We were sick," she added quickly, sensing that Marissa expected an explanation for her sudden disappearance.

"Yeah, you guys don't look the best," Marissa admitted, probably noting their pale complexions and dark bags under their eyes. "Well, at least you're alive. I was starting to think the werewolf got you or something."

Suppressing the urge to cringe, Anastasia asked hurriedly, "What are you doing here, Marissa?"

"I'm dropping off every piece of clothing and jewelry that Kate has ever lent me. Sure, it's worth more than my entire wardrobe, but I'll be glad to see it gone – just like her." She paused slightly before inquiring, "What are you two doing here?"

"We're looking for Julia," Anastasia began to reply.

"Kate's grandmother?" Marissa interrupted in shock. "What in the world do you want with her?"

"You know her?" Frost inquired with wide eyes, ignoring Marissa's question in the process.

"I've heard about her," Marissa corrected him. "I think she's like a family secret because Kate would never mention her. Once, when I was at her house, I overheard Kate's mom and dad talking about Julia. They were discussing the possibility of sending her to a better nursing home. It was obviously a *very* private conversation, and Kate was so embarrassed by what I'd heard that she acted strange around me for a whole month."

Anastasia felt a flutter of hope within her chest. Combined, there were probably only a few nursing homes in Cedar Falls and the surrounding areas. This was exactly the type of lead for which she and Frost had been praying.

"We really appreciate everything you've told us," Frost thanked Marissa as he restarted the car.

"I don't want to discourage you guys from seeing Julia, but I'm pretty sure she's crazy. Why else would Kate's family be so hush-hush about her?" With that said, Marissa gave Anastasia a small wave goodbye and then stepped backwards, allowing them to drive away.

"Slow down," Anastasia cautioned as Frost sped along Kate's street. "You'll get a ticket – or worse."

"I know what I'm doing," Frost reassured her, decreasing his speed nonetheless. "I remember seeing a sign for Mourning Dove Care Residence. That will be the closest senior's home, and it's still on the other side of Cedar Falls, practically on the border of another town. We need to get there now."

Studying Frost's intense gaze upon the road and the way he clutched the steering wheel, turning his knuckles white, Anastasia knew that he was barely holding it together under all the pressure. If they didn't stop the hunters from transforming into werewolves, she worried that he wouldn't be able to live with himself. These thoughts troubled her until they finally found their destination forty-five minutes later. At this moment, she had new fears to deal with, such as if Julia was even here, and if she was, would she agree to see two complete strangers?

Although Mourning Dove was settled amongst the beautiful scenery that Anastasia had come to expect from Cedar Falls, it was a stark contrast to the building, which looked old, gray and in need of some basic maintenance. Shivering, she rushed alongside Frost and toward the entrance. For some reason, Anastasia felt as if she was being watched through those small, frosted windows, even though no one appeared to be there.

Passing through a set of automatic sliding doors, Anastasia and Frost came to a reception desk that was situated in front of a large, open concept room. This room, which seemed to double as the living and dining space, was brighter than the exterior, but it still lacked comfort and appeal – two essential features since the residents likely spent a great deal of time there. Awkwardly, Anastasia realized that almost all the elders were looking longingly at her and Frost, probably wondering whose grandchildren were here to visit. This depressed Anastasia and caused her to vow that she'd never end up in a place like this.

"May I help you?" inquired a straight-faced receptionist, who wore a nametag which read, *Martha*.

"We're here to see Julia McKinley," Frost said confidently, as if he was a regular visitor.

"Are you a relative of hers?"

"More like close friends," Frost lied. "I know she'll be pleased to see us."

"It's our policy that non-family members call in advance," Martha informed them. "I'm afraid we'd need to get permission from Mrs. McKinley's family before you could…"

"I speak for myself," a woman interrupted Martha in a strong, steady tone, "and I say these two are visiting me today."

Unaware that anyone was there, Anastasia and Frost spun around to see an old woman who could easily be in her late eighties. She had unusually pale skin which was deeply wrinkled and a slender, frail-looking body frame. Her appearance contradicted the strength in her voice; although one glance at the sparkle and fire in her dark brown eyes was evidence enough that this woman was very much alive.

"Alright, Mrs. McKinley," Martha said. "Please keep your guests within our sight."

Slowly, Anastasia and Frost followed Julia as she led them toward a blanket-covered couch and a worn chair. Even though these seats were already occupied by three men, they hurried to leave upon seeing Julia approach them. With a small, satisfied smile, she sat down and then gestured for Anastasia and Frost to do the same.

"I'm Frost, and this is my girlfriend, Anastasia," he said politely, once they were seated on the sagging couch.

"It's nice to meet you, Julia," Anastasia said with a flicker of excitement, almost unable to believe that they'd found her so easily.

Julia offered no response. Instead, she stared at Frost, as if studying his every feature. Then, she turned to Anastasia and began visually examining her as well, paying particular attention to her eyes. Although it was extremely uncomfortable to be looked upon so closely, especially by a stranger, Anastasia sensed that she meant them no harm.

Suddenly, Julia sucked in her breath like something delightful and unexpected had just occurred. "I know what you are," she said in a quick, quiet tone, while shifting her attention between Anastasia and Frost. "I know what you *both* are."

Wrinkling her forehead, Anastasia asked carefully, "What do you mean?"

"Don't worry, child, your secret's safe with me," Julia replied, with an extra twinkle in her eye. "However, the truth *will* come out – it always does." Focusing her gaze on Frost once again, she said softly, "You resemble your father when he was your age."

"You know who I am?" Frost was clearly surprised.

"I already told you that. For someone who has such large ears, I'd expect you to listen better."

Anastasia felt her blood run cold as she looked at a stunned Frost. They both knew that he was perfectly proportioned; therefore, Julia couldn't possibly be referring to his human ears. If she really did know that Frost was a werewolf, then it didn't faze her in the least; she just sat there, while stroking her waist-length silver hair which hung over her shoulders.

"Tell me, how is Symon?" Julia inquired. "It's been far too long since I've last seen him."

"He's, um, dead," Frost was hardly able to choke out.

From the pained expression upon Frost's face, it was clear that he was reliving that fatal moment in the woods. In an attempt to console him, Anastasia reached for his hand. When he held onto her tightly, she realized how much he needed her.

"Oh my!" Julia gasped, her eyes filling with tears as she processed the significance of his words. "It...it surely can't be true."

"My father kept a journal and he wrote about you," Frost said boldly, seemingly driven by his grief. "You *and* werewolves."

Julia was silent as she reached for a box of tissues that sat upon a nearby table. She then dabbed her eyes and took a deep, shaky breath before speaking. "I can sense that you have a pure spirit, Frost, and I feel the love that Anastasia has for you. Both of you can be trusted with what I have to say."

Leaning forward and lowering her voice, Julia continued. "Cedar Falls used to be a haven for a special kind of wolf. When my ancestors first arrived over two hundred years ago, we found a way to co-exist peacefully with these most magnificent creatures. Unfortunately, as the town grew larger, so did the fear and paranoia. Humans started to believe that wolves couldn't be trusted, so they slaughtered them, almost down to the last one. The few wolves who did survive fled to the darkest parts of Cedar Falls Woods, where they remain to this day – or so I'd thought."

"Who else knows about this?" Frost pressed anxiously.

"Hardly anyone nowadays. When I tried to pass on the stories of our heritage, my family declared me crazy. That's how I ended up in this dreadful place."

And that's why we never knew who you were, Anastasia thought, disgusted that the McKinleys had treated Julia like she was a shameful secret.

"Perhaps I should make a new family for myself," Julia said, smiling widely at Anastasia and Frost. Ever so carefully, she reached around the back of her neck and released a long, black heart pendant necklace. "I want you to have this," she said, handing it to Anastasia.

Taken aback, Anastasia stared at the necklace. It was a stunning piece of jewelry, and one she hadn't noticed Julia wearing since it'd been hidden behind her hair. "I couldn't take it," she began to object.

"I insist that you do," Julia replied. "You may one day find it useful."

"Well, thank you," Anastasia said graciously, even though she was still confused by the act of charity. "I'll take excellent care of it."

"I'm afraid we need your help, not your jewelry," Frost

stated bluntly, ignoring the warning glare that Anastasia was now giving him. "Cedar Falls is at risk of getting a lot of new werewolves, and we need to know how to stop it."

Julia shook her head in disappointment. "Mistakes like these put everyone in danger. Fortunately, you already have the tools, but you must act fast."

"How?" Frost pleaded.

"Mrs. McKinley, it's time for your treatment," someone suddenly said in a deep voice.

Jumping slightly at the unexpected interruption, Anastasia looked over her shoulder to see a tall, middle-aged doctor with a muscular build. As he stood there, with his arms folded across his bleached white uniform, she knew that he was as stern as he sounded. There would be no use in begging for extra time.

Anastasia's assumption about the doctor must have been correct because Julia obediently stood up and began walking beside him. Not saying goodbye, she instead sang in an enchanting tone as she went. "Queen of poisons' meant to burn. Heal, forget, then all is done." With increasing passion, she repeated the lyrics, treating them like they were some sort of chant.

Julia's singing caused the doctor to hurry her down the gray carpeted hallway and around a bend until she could no longer be seen. Then, he cast Anastasia and Frost an odd, somewhat cautionary glance before disappearing himself. The doctor had seemed so strict and somber, and there was something about him which Anastasia didn't trust. It was like he couldn't wait to put distance between them and Julia.

"We should leave," Frost advised, causing Anastasia to notice how eerily quiet the room had become as everyone, including the staff, gawked at them.

"Good idea," she muttered, feeling awkward as they

passed the reception desk and then exited through the double doors. It was all too evident that they hadn't been welcomed there, even upon their arrival.

Once they'd entered the car, Anastasia let out a frustrated sigh as she thought about what had just happened. Not only had they received no information that would be useful in stopping the transformations, they'd also allowed Julia to assume that Frost was a werewolf. Anastasia wasn't sure if she needed to worry about that, though; Julia had been a friend of Symon's, so it was likely that they could trust her. Besides, it'd already been proven that no one believed her tales about extra special wolves.

The sound of the car's engine snapped Anastasia out of her thoughts. She expected Frost to immediately speed away to their next destination – wherever that may be. Yet, she was surprised to find him remaining idle behind the wheel, even after several moments had passed. As Frost stared out the windshield, without really looking at anything, it was clear that he was greatly conflicted.

"Julia was our only lead, and she could hardly give us a straight answer," Frost spoke gravely, before Anastasia had the chance to inquire if he was alright. "The doctor mentioned that she was receiving treatment – maybe she really is crazy. Besides, I doubt werewolves and humans were ever friends. She probably didn't know what she was saying."

"You don't have the right to be skeptical," Anastasia argued, feeling a little hurt by Frost's disbelief in human-werewolf relationships. "It's not like anyone would readily believe our story, despite it being true."

"Let's just grab some lunch and then return to downtown," Frost suggested with a heavy sigh. "We need to think of a new plan and can't waste any more time here." Without waiting for Anastasia to respond, he pulled out of the parking lot and then drove away, causing a heavy silence to fall over them.

Anastasia had always thought that hope was one of the most precious of sentiments because with it anything was possible, but without it everything would seem bleak. Unfortunately, she was now part of the latter category, and who could blame her? After returning to the downtown core, they'd parked behind a building that saw little to no human activity. Then, for almost two hours they'd sat there, wrapped in blankets which she'd found in the car. They had talked – or rather argued – about what actions they should take next. These proposed plans had ranged from highly impractical to just plain stupid, and in the end they both agreed that none of them would ever work.

Despite the unspoken realization that they would have to go back to the cabin and tell her grandfather that they'd failed, something kept nagging at Anastasia. It was Julia, and although Frost had already written her off as crazy, she couldn't bring herself to do the same. Julia said they had the tools to stop the transformation, yet what did that even mean? Since Anastasia hadn't figured it out by now, she doubted that she ever would.

"I'm sorry for putting you through this, Anastasia," Frost said, gently reaching for her hand as if to show her how much he cared. "Even if coming back here was a mistake, at least I've realized what I have to do – I can't allow your grandfather to kill those men. When they become werewolves, I'll be there to help them."

And how the hell do you plan to do that? Anastasia resisted the urge to ask, believing that the idea was more foolish than noble. Instead, she pointed to the clock which read 3:17 p.m. "Dusk falls in less than three hours, and if I know my grandpa, he won't be waiting until after they've transformed to shoot."

As they hastily started for Hartfield, Anastasia's mind unwillingly returned to thoughts of Julia. Instinctively, she reached into her pocket for the heart pendant. It was a heavy, unique piece made all the more unusual due to the ornate leaves which were etched onto the rounded black heart. Wondering if the back was engraved as well, Anastasia turned it over to discover a slit running along the side. At first she thought it was an imperfection, but upon closer examination, she realized that the pendant was actually a locket. With growing interest, she used her fingernails to carefully pry it open. Inside the hollow heart she found a strange-looking dried flower which had a hint of color still left in it.

"Why would she give you that?" Frost asked, glancing at the flower.

Anastasia shook her head in bewilderment. It was such an odd object to keep in a locket that her curiosity was immediately peaked. Beginning to rifle through her grandfather's belongings, she searched for his copy of *The Encyclopedia of Plant Species*. Although Anastasia distinctly remembered making fun of him for keeping such a large book in the car, she'd never been so grateful to see it lying underneath the backseat. Grabbing for the book, she ignored Frost's warning for her to sit back down and put her seatbelt on.

Opening the encyclopedia, Anastasia flipped through the yellowing pages, searching for a plant which had a delicate thin stem and a long, purplish-blue flower that sort of resembled a hood. Since the flower was so peculiar, she was certain that she would recognize it. The problem was the length of the book; no matter how many pages Anastasia turned, it felt like she was getting nowhere. Then, just when her hand had begun to cramp, she saw a flower identical to the one in the locket. Beneath the picture was the word, *Wolfsbane*.

With a racing heart, Anastasia realized that this was no coincidence. Julia had given her the flower for a reason, and she was going to find out why. Unrelentingly, Anastasia hastened to read the description, learning that wolfsbane grew mostly in mountainous areas of the northern hemisphere and, despite being poisonous, it had long been used for medicinal purposes. There were several other interesting facts about this intricate plant, but nothing else mattered when Anastasia's eyes fell upon the words, *Queen of poisons*; it was an alternative name for Wolfsbane and something which Julia had sung about when she was led away by the doctor.

"Queen of poisons' meant to..." Anastasia muttered, trying desperately to remember the rest of Julia's chant.

"Are you okay?" Frost asked, looking at her in concern.

"Queen of poisons' meant to burn!" Anastasia continued, excited that she'd recalled the first line. "Heal, forget, then..." Creasing her forehead, she frowned, frustrated because she knew that there were merely a few words remaining.

"Seriously, Anastasia, you're freaking me out."

"Then all is done!" she cried, finishing the verse. She repeated the words, contemplating what they could mean until finally, it dawned on her. "Oh my gosh, Frost!" she exclaimed, feeling a renewed sense of hope. "I think I know how to stop the transformation!"

Racing against the setting of the sun, Anastasia and Frost made their way through Cedar Falls Woods on the snowmobile they'd left at the edge of Hartfield. Increasing the difficulty of their ride was the presence of a strong, howling wind which was quickly growing in strength. This prevailing wind seemed to be mocking them, as if morbidly foreshadowing the arrival of four new werewolves.

Not if I have anything to do about it, Anastasia thought, her heart beating a little faster as the cabin came into view.

Bringing the snowmobile to a stop, Anastasia and Frost quickly dismounted, but before they could enter the cabin, something caught their eyes. There, off to the side, was a black tarp covering a large object. Anastasia had only taken one step forward when Frost pulled her back. Noticing that Symon's paw was sticking out slightly from under the tarp, she felt her stomach churn. She didn't want to think about the reason why her grandfather had relocated him outside.

"Come on," Frost said, obviously trying hard to ignore his emotions in order to stay level-headed.

Together, Anastasia and Frost rushed to the cabin's door. Upon entering they found her grandfather standing in the middle of the room, his face stained with tears as he pointed a rifle straight at Leo's chest. Immediately, he looked up at Anastasia and Frost, the desperation in his eyes clearly visible.

"Did you find a cure?" Mr. Lockhart asked, his hand shaking as he continued to hold the rifle in a shooting position.

"Yes," Anastasia heard herself say confidently, despite having no way of knowing if her plan would work. "I'm going to need a bowl and matches."

Finally lowering his rifle, Anastasia's grandfather used his free hand to open his hunting pack which sat upon the table. He retrieved a box of matches, and after tossing them into a nearby bowl, he offered the items to Anastasia.

"What are these things for?" Frost questioned, sounding equally confused and anxious.

"When you asked Julia how to stop the transformation,

she gave us the answer in her song," Anastasia explained, while opening the locket and allowing the wolfsbane to fall into the bowl without her ever touching it. "This plant is wolfsbane, and according to Julia, it must be burned if the victims are to heal and forget. You'll want to cover your nose before we begin – this stuff is toxic."

One by one, Anastasia, Frost and Mr. Lockhart pulled up their coat collars, leaving their eyes exposed. Then, Anastasia struck a match and threw it into the bowl. The wolfsbane instantly burst into an unnaturally bright flame, creating clouds of black smoke which swirled wildly despite the lack of wind. Slowly walking amongst the fallen hunters, Anastasia carefully wafted her hand through the smoke, making sure their faces were well-exposed to the fumes. As the flame began to diminish, Anastasia kept smudging the hunters, until eventually, nothing more than black ash remained.

Standing back, Anastasia placed the sooty bowl on the table and then stared at the hunters, waiting for something to happen. The minutes passed by painfully slow, causing her to fear that the wolfsbane hadn't worked or, worse, she'd killed them with the plant's poison. Concerned, Anastasia peered closely at them, relieved to discover that they were at least still breathing.

"Please wake up," Anastasia muttered softly, her eyes especially falling upon Mr. Fairbanks, "preferably as humans."

In response, Anastasia heard a low moan. Although it had hardly been audible, she leaned further toward Mr. Fairbanks, expecting him to awaken at any moment. Yet, he stayed in the same state, looking as if he was neither alive nor dead. The moan came again, this time louder and more distinct. She now realized that it was Leo who'd made the noise.

Anastasia, Frost and Mr. Lockhart hurried to Leo's side,

watching anxiously as his eyes fluttered open. Appearing confused, Leo scanned his surroundings before attempting to sit up with some difficulty. Mr. Lockhart and Frost steadied him, but Anastasia was too preoccupied with the moans coming from Pete and Mike as they, too, began to rise.

"Why am I here?" Leo asked, his voice hoarse.

"Don't you remember?" Frost pried gently, clearly trying to hide the significance of his question.

Tension filled the room as they waited for Leo's answer. His brow was deeply furrowed, and he was quiet for what seemed like far too long. Then slowly, he shook his head, while still looking very confused.

"What happened to us?" Mike demanded, while standing up somewhat unsteadily and then helping Pete to do the same.

"The four of you were hurt during the hunt," Mr. Lockhart explained. "We had the wolf surrounded, and he wouldn't go down without a fight. You were all so courageous, and without you, I would've never been able to kill it."

"The wolf is dead?" Pete pressed nervously.

Mr. Lockhart nodded. "What's important now is that we return home. It was fortunate that I found Frost and Anastasia's hunting cabin, but our families don't know where we've been, and they'll be starting to worry. Our snowmobiles are outside. Will you men be able to ride back to Hartfield?"

"Of course," Mike spoke for all of them, "but first we want to see the wolf."

"I can assure you that you won't miss it," Mr. Lockhart said to Mike, before turning to the other hunters. "Grab your packs, men. There's still plenty of food and water inside of them."

"I'm not leaving without Fairbanks," Leo stated, looking at him with great unease. "What the hell kind of injuries has he sustained?"

"You have your own wounds to be concerned with," Mr. Lockhart advised, gesturing toward Leo's bloody shoulder.

"I said I'm not leaving."

"Anastasia and Frost are taking him to Hartfield Hospital," Mr. Lockhart told Leo, obviously thinking fast, "and you're holding them back."

Not looking entirely convinced, Leo picked up his pack and followed Mike and Pete out of the cabin. Now that they were alone, Anastasia's grandfather turned to her, offering his rifle to her. Taken aback, she made no attempt to reach for it.

"If Mr. Fairbanks doesn't wake up, I need you to promise me that you'll kill him."

"What?" Anastasia gasped, shocked that her grandfather would ask her to do such a horrible thing. "I...I can't."

"I've seen what these things can do, and it would only take one unruly werewolf to destroy this town. Please, Anastasia, promise me."

Reluctantly, Anastasia took the rifle, but she refused to promise anything. Instead, she said firmly, "I'm going to give him more time."

"Not too much," Mr. Lockhart warned, before kissing Anastasia's forehead and then closing the cabin door behind him.

Anastasia immediately placed the rifle on the table, hating the way it felt in her hands. When she turned around, she saw Frost standing over Mr. Fairbanks, his body language tell-tale signs of his disappointment and distress.

"Why didn't he awaken like the others?" Anastasia wondered aloud.

With a heavy sigh, Frost shrugged. "All I know is that it's

going to be a very long night."

***

When dawn broke the following day, Anastasia awoke to find herself only somewhat rested. She'd spent last night falling in and out of terrifying, abstract dreams which made absolutely no sense to her. All she remembered was being cold, lost and scared. That feeling of fear suddenly shifted from Anastasia's dreams and into reality as she saw Frost placing a blanket over Mr. Fairbanks.

"Is he...?" Anastasia couldn't finish her words.

"He's alive," Frost reassured her. "I'm worried about his temperature, though. One minute he's almost too hot to touch, then the next, he's cold. I've never seen anything like this."

Anastasia felt her heart sink upon hearing Frost's unusual description of Mr. Fairbanks. Although her recent encounter with him had been horrible, in his own obscured way he'd thought that his actions were in her best interest. She also couldn't forget the fact that he was her best friend's father. Straightaway, Anastasia knew what she had to do.

"I need you to pick up Chloe and bring her here," Anastasia instructed, while searching through the pack her grandfather had left for her. Finding a mini notebook and pen, she scribbled a letter to Chloe, urging her to come to the cabin. "Give her this," she said, handing him the note.

"Why?" Frost asked bluntly.

"Well, I don't know how to drive a snowmobile, and even if I did, I can't remember the way through the woods."

"That's not what I meant, Anastasia. What would be the point of bringing Chloe here? She wouldn't want to see her dad in this state."

"She deserves the truth, and in case Mr. Fairbanks doesn't wake up, she's the one who should make a final decision."

"You're right," Frost admitted after a moment of silent deliberation. "It's just, I can't imagine leaving you. This last week we've been together almost constantly, and I don't want it any other way."

Unexpectedly, Anastasia blinked back tears. Those words were the sweetest she'd ever heard, but right now she had to be sensible. "If we can't manage a few hours apart, how will we cope when we return to our separate homes?" She turned her head away from him, not really wanting to hear his answer.

Upset, Frost gently kissed her lips. "Stay safe while I'm gone," he muttered, before taking leave of the cabin.

With nothing else to do but wait, Anastasia filled those long, lonely hours fretting endlessly. She worried about Mr. Fairbanks waking up and what subsequent actions she'd be forced to take. On the other hand, she was more afraid that he would never awaken, leaving him in that petrified state forever. Worst of all was Chloe's impending arrival. She would soon be seeing her father like this, and unfortunately, Anastasia still hadn't figured out the best way to tell her the whole unbelievable truth.

As Anastasia heard an approaching snowmobile, she knew that there would be no more time for thinking. Taking a deep breath and mustering all her courage, she stood up from the rocking chair and opened the door. That's when she saw Chloe, who looked absolutely frantic as she hurried forward.

"Where is my dad?" Chloe demanded, her face red from crying. "Leo told me you and Frost were taking him to Hartfield Hospital, but when I went there, the staff said he'd never been admitted. What the hell is going on, Anastasia?"

At a loss for words, Anastasia stepped aside, revealing Mr.

Fairbanks lying lifelessly on the floor with the blanket still on top of him. As Chloe let out a shriek and fell to her father's side, Anastasia had to look away; she couldn't bear to see her friend in so much pain.

"Call an ambulance!" Chloe screamed. "Quick!"

"You have to calm down," Frost told her.

Reluctantly, Anastasia faced Chloe once again, knowing that she would have to intervene. "There's no point in calling for help," she said softly.

"What is wrong with you two?" Chloe cried, standing up and pulling her cell phone from her coat pocket so she could dial 9-1-1. Immediately, the call failed since there was no reception.

"Chloe, you have to listen to me," Anastasia begged. "What I'm about to say is hard to believe, but I promise you it's true. The Cedar Falls werewolf isn't some myth – it's real, and your father was part of a group that was hunting it. During a fight, he and some other men were bitten. Frost and I found a cure to stop them from becoming werewolves, and it worked, with the exception of your father."

Looking at Anastasia as if she was crazy, Chloe suddenly slapped her across the face. "My dad could be dying, and you're making jokes?" she seethed in disbelief. "You disgust me!"

Tears stung in Anastasia's eyes as she placed her hand lightly against her burning cheek. She winced at the pain of Chloe's words and actions, unable to believe that her friend could be so spiteful, especially toward her. Unfortunately, Anastasia had realized too late that bringing Chloe here wasn't her smartest idea.

"She doesn't deserve that," Frost warned, blocking Chloe from getting any closer to Anastasia.

"It's okay, Frost," Anastasia lied, unwilling to give up that quickly.

"None of this is okay!" Chloe yelled, trying unsuccessfully to shove Frost aside so she could get to Anastasia. "My dad needs help, and you're doing nothing!"

"First, I need you to trust me, Chloe. We can't do this any other way."

As impossible as it seemed, Anastasia's words made Chloe angrier. Her eyes narrowed, and she opened her mouth to respond, likely with something harsh. However, before she could speak, a groan echoed throughout the cabin.

"Chloe, is that you?" someone asked in a dry, raspy tone.

Turning to face Mr. Fairbanks, they watched in amazement as he slowly sat up. Like the other hunters, he appeared unsteady and disoriented, but Anastasia understood that as a normal sign of his recovery. After all, what really mattered was that he was alive and *not* a werewolf. Anastasia let out a sigh of relief, one which she'd been holding in for what seemed like a very long time.

"Thank God you're alright," Chloe sobbed, after reaching her father's side and then throwing her arms around him.

"Yes, I...I'm fine," Mr. Fairbanks replied, casting a curious glance at his surroundings. "I don't know why I'm here, though."

"We can figure that out later," Chloe promised him. "Right now, I need to take you to a doctor." Looking up at Anastasia and Frost, she spoke coolly, "You're going to help me get him out of here, but that's the last thing we'll ever do together."

In an attempt to suppress her hurt feelings, Anastasia concentrated on getting ready to leave. As she retrieved Mr. Fairbanks' pack, she began to ponder why he'd awakened at that moment. Perhaps it was somehow due to Chloe's presence, or it could've been purely coincidental. Even if

Anastasia never knew why, she was just grateful that the hunters had survived; although, more than anything, she wished the same could be said for Symon.

After taking Mr. Fairbanks to Hartfield Hospital and, upon Chloe's insistence, leaving immediately, Anastasia and Frost started for Cedar Falls. This was one homecoming that she wasn't looking forward to, and the closer they came to the town lines, the more anxious she felt. Anastasia still hadn't thought of a probable excuse for where she'd been, and once her mother knew that she was fine, her worry would certainly turn into anger.

All too soon, Anastasia and Frost pulled into the Lockhart's driveway. Strangely, the first thing she noticed was her grandfather looking out the living room window, where he'd probably been waiting for quite a while. Before she'd even unbuckled her seatbelt, he was hurrying from the house and straight toward them.

"I guess some things never change," Anastasia commented, recalling the first time Frost had taken her home.

"Everything's changed," Frost responded with sadness in his eyes.

Giving him a soothing hug, Anastasia whispered, "Not us." However, she worried that Frost didn't feel the same. Was it possible that when he saw her, he was reminded of the horrible events in the woods and, worse, his father's death?

A sudden tapping sounded upon the window, causing Anastasia and Frost to break from their embrace. Slightly embarrassed, they got out of the car, where they were met with her concerned-looking grandfather.

"What happened with Fairbanks?" Mr. Lockhart pressed, not allowing them to speak first.

"He awakened as a human this morning," Anastasia explained, unwilling to divulge all the details. "He's fine now and so are we."

"Then *everything's* been taken care of," Mr. Lockhart said with relief, implying that he'd already given Symon's body to the authorities. In an obvious attempt to make peace, he turned to Frost and added in a good-natured tone, "You know, I'll need my car back at some point. Can I give you a ride home?"

"My SUV is at the edge of the woods, and I'm sure it'll need a boost," Frost accepted graciously, even though none of this could be easy for him. As he entered the passenger side of the car, he gave Anastasia a small smile and mouthed the words, *I love you.*

She smiled back, but that feeling of happiness didn't last long as her grandfather stepped in front of her, appearing very grave.

"Your mother's inside," Mr. Lockhart warned her. "You'll have privacy to talk since Rose is at work. Just choose your words carefully – the less said, the better."

Anastasia shivered as she watched her grandfather get into the car and then drive away. Although she should've been glad that he was starting to treat Frost with respect, she was more preoccupied with what he'd said, or rather, how he'd said it. She felt like he was almost threatening her to keep quiet.

Taking a deep breath and trying to focus on what she would say to her mother, Anastasia headed toward her house. Her grandfather had left the door unlocked, and as she entered, she instantly noticed how silent it was. Nevertheless, Anastasia experienced a sense of comfort, like she'd finally returned home.

"Mom?" Anastasia called, her voice echoing throughout

the house. "Mom, are you here?"

There was a long, tense moment of silence which was broken by the sound of hurried footsteps. Seconds later, Anastasia's mother appeared in the foyer, an expression of disbelief upon her face as she stared at her daughter. Anastasia wasn't sure if that was a good sign or not since she'd never seen her mother speechless before.

"Anastasia," Kendall said breathlessly as she ran toward her and wrapped her in a tight hug. "I thought I'd lost you for good."

"Oh, of course not," Anastasia replied, feeling awkward in her mother's arms. Try as she might, she couldn't remember the last time she'd held her with so much affection.

Kendall pulled away to gaze at Anastasia with tear-brimmed eyes. "No one knew where you were, only that you'd run away with a boy. Goodness knows what could've happened." Suddenly, a look of realization washed over her. "You...you're pregnant – that's why you left." In a shaky tone she added quickly, "It's going to be okay, Anastasia. I'll be there to help you."

"Mom, I'm not pregnant," Anastasia remarked, a little offended that she'd jumped to such a conclusion. Nonetheless, she couldn't deny that she was touched by her offer of support.

"What was it then?" Kendall inquired, after discreetly letting out a sigh of relief.

"It was my last mistake, I promise."

Kendall opened her mouth to respond, possibly to press for more information, but then she hesitated, as if afraid of pushing Anastasia away. Instead, she said calmly, "I doubt it'll be your last mistake. I know because we all make them – especially me." She paused, appearing as uncomfortable as Anastasia. "In hindsight, I could've handled things a little better at home. Our fighting has to stop, and we need to communicate like adults."

"Kind of like what we're doing now?" Anastasia asked with a half-smile.

"It's a start," she said, taking her daughter's hand and giving it a gentle squeeze. "I'm going to call your grandparents to tell them that you're safe. In the meantime, you should take a shower and then pack. I'm sure we can get a train for tomorrow morning."

"No," Anastasia blurted out, quickly turning angry as she realized that her mother was still attempting to control her decisions. "I'm not leaving Cedar Falls."

"Anastasia, you knew that coming here wasn't a permanent solution. Your home is in Toronto."

"What about school?" Anastasia hurried to point out, willing to use any excuse to stay in Cedar Falls. "The teachers are pretty great here, and my grades are actually improving. At least let me stay until the summer break."

Kendall was slow to respond, causing Anastasia to be filled with dread. The mere thought of being without Frost almost made her cry, and after everything they'd been through together, she knew that she couldn't lose him now.

"I suppose that would be okay," she said, somewhat reluctantly. "I can stay for a few more days while you settle back in."

"I'd really like that," Anastasia replied, secretly elated that she'd convinced her mother to change her mind, "and I know Grandma and Grandpa would, too."

As her mother gave her another hug, Anastasia sensed that their relationship would continue to mend and, perhaps, one day be stronger than ever before. Yet, as was usually the case with Anastasia, she couldn't be completely happy because she suspected that something wasn't quite right; not with her mother, but rather, her grandfather. He obviously hadn't told anyone that he'd seen Anastasia and Frost, and although she understood why the whole truth couldn't be revealed, he'd deliberately allowed his wife and daughter to worry. It was so out-of-character for her grandfather that she wondered if he was hiding something else – something worse than the secret they already shared.

❊ ❊ ❊

There was no way that Anastasia could truly return to a normal life, but she knew that she must try. When that failed, she decided to fake it. Attending all her classes, catching up on missed assignments and coming home right after school was Anastasia's new routine, and she played the part perfectly. Not everything could be hidden behind a smile, though, and the aftermath of her experiences in the woods manifested themselves in strange, chilling dreams every single night. Nevertheless, Anastasia understood that under the circumstances, she was coping very well.

Now that she was grounded indefinitely, Anastasia spent a lot more time with her mother and grandmother. At this moment, they were in the living room, chatting quietly while she worked on an essay for English class. Although this would've looked like a typical evening to most people, for the Lockharts it was a rarity. As ironic as it seemed, Anastasia's disappearance had actually brought them closer together.

Anastasia's attention was diverted from the familial scene as her cell phone vibrated, alerting her of an incoming call. Hoping that it was Chloe, who'd been avoiding her since that awful morning almost a week ago, she anxiously grabbed her phone, only to discover that it was a telemarketer. Even though Anastasia felt foolish for believing that Chloe would ever speak to her again, she knew it was odd that she hadn't heard from Frost. They always talked daily and he usually sent her several text messages. Concerned, she started to text him when her grandfather walked into the room.

"Anastasia, you're needed at the library," Mr. Lockhart said abruptly, forgoing any social pleasantries.

"I don't have a shift until tomorrow," Anastasia pointed out, confused by her grandfather's statement, especially since he had no affiliation with the library.

"You have to learn how to be more flexible," he scolded. "Now hurry up. I can drive you there."

Casting a sideways glance at her grandmother, who looked equally bewildered, Anastasia realized that her grandfather was still keeping secrets. Just as peculiar was the fact that he'd been away all day, without even a mention of where he'd gone. Regardless, his serious disposition prompted Anastasia to obediently stand up and get ready to leave. Within minutes, she was in her grandfather's car, driving speedily down the road.

"This isn't the way to the library," Anastasia objected as her grandfather took a left turn onto a darkening road that lacked signs far less any streetlamps.

"I'm so sorry, Anastasia," Mr. Lockhart said in a heavy tone, while looking distraught.

"For...for what?" Anastasia stuttered, greatly unsettled by her grandfather's words and also his unpredictable behavior as of late. A sudden fear struck her – he wasn't capable of putting her in any sort of danger, was he?

"Our relationship should've never come to this," Mr. Lockhart continued ambiguously, causing Anastasia's anxiety to increase. "I will always cherish the memories of those summers we spent together when you were a child, but as difficult as this is, I have to accept that you've grown-up. I refuse to let that come in between us, though. Whether you like it or not, I'm your grandfather and that will never change."

Feeling like a complete idiot for thinking that her grandfather could ever hurt her, Anastasia smiled meekly at him. "That's what I've always wanted," she confessed.

"Good," he replied, obviously trying hard to keep his emotions under control, "because I'm very proud of the young woman you've become."

Before Anastasia could tell her grandfather how much his approval meant to her, he brought the car to a stop alongside an isolated part of Cedar Falls Woods. It was the last place she wanted to be, and she couldn't fathom why he'd taken her there.

"Get out of the car," Mr. Lockhart ordered in a serious tone, despite the smile which played at the corners of his mouth.

"You want me to get out *here*?" Anastasia asked skeptically.

"Yes, and have a good time," he added, no longer able to hide his signature toothy grin.

Trusting that there was a reason behind her grandfather's ludicrous instructions, Anastasia exited from the car. As she stood seemingly on the edge of nowhere, illuminated by the car's headlights, she listened, only to hear the gentle pitter-patter of the slowly melting snow. The last couple days of mild temperatures had brought the first thaw, but Anastasia still shivered in response to her surroundings.

Suddenly, someone emerged from the outskirts of the light, approaching her at a steady pace. Frightened, Anastasia began stepping backwards until she realized who the tall, muscular silhouette belonged to – it was Frost, and as he drew closer, she saw that he was holding a bunch of roses.

Frost greeted Anastasia with a soft kiss and then handed

her the black roses which were dusted with tiny silver sparkles. "You're just in time," he said with a mischievous grin.

"They're gorgeous – thank you," Anastasia said, admiring the unique and unexpected gift, "but do you mind telling me what's going on?"

"Trust me," Frost whispered, while leading her into the woods.

Anastasia had been doing a lot of trusting lately, and she didn't feel the need to stop now, especially as her grandfather drove away, leaving Frost and the pale moonlight as her only guides. They were walking in a straight, slightly upward direction, and since the trek was fairly easy, Anastasia guessed that they were on some sort of path. Soon, she spotted a tower of small golden lights twinkling through the trees, accompanied by the sound of a humming generator.

"What is this place?" Anastasia asked breathlessly, arriving at the base of the beautifully decorated tower.

"Welcome to the lookout," Frost responded, taking her hand as they ascended the stairs which were also lined by lights. "It's one of my favorite places in Cedar Falls."

When Anastasia and Frost reached the top, she let out a gasp. The platform, which featured a pointed roof and an open, unparalleled view of Cedar Falls, had been transformed into a romantic picnic area for two. A wicker basket, filled with sparkling cider and delectable treats, sat in the middle of a white Sherpa blanket that was spread over the floor. It was clear that Frost had planned this thoroughly because in the corner, Anastasia saw a portable heater that provided just the right temperature.

"I thought we should finally have our first date," Frost said, looking intently upon Anastasia with those swoon-worthy eyes. "I can't take all the credit, though. Your grandfather helped to bring everything together – including us."

"It's perfect," Anastasia replied, deeply touched by the extravagant gesture, even if she did find her grandfather's involvement a tad unusual.

"Shall we?" Frost asked, while motioning toward the picnic.

After sitting down on the warm blanket and placing the roses beside her, Anastasia watched as Frost retrieved the bottle of cider. He poured her a glass, before getting one for himself and then settling next to her. She'd almost taken a sip of her drink when he gently stopped her.

"There's something I want to say first," Frost spoke softly, appearing almost shy. "You've always stood by me no matter how difficult the situation – or I – became, and I could never thank you enough for that. For all the unconditional love and support you've given me, I promise to return it to you a million times over. I love you, Anastasia, more than I ever thought possible."

Blinking back tears, Anastasia raised her glass to meet his. "I can definitely drink to that," she said bashfully, before tasting the sweet cider.

As Anastasia and Frost cuddled together, enjoying the drink and treats, she thought about how lucky she was to have found someone like him. He truly was everything that she'd ever wanted – and more. If she had one wish, Anastasia would ask that this moment last forever.

"Why so quiet?" Frost asked, his hot breath tickling her ear. "Have I done something wrong?"

"Never," Anastasia reassured him. "It's just..." She paused, not wanting to ruin the mood.

"You can tell me anything. Surely you know that."

"I can't stop thinking about what Julia said," Anastasia

admitted hastily. *"I know what you* both *are* – what could that mean? She doesn't think I'm a werewolf, too, does she?"

"Shhh..." Frost whispered, while stroking her hair. "I'm sure it's nothing, and to stop you from worrying needlessly, maybe I can take your mind somewhere else." Appearing nervous, Frost leaned forward and kissed Anastasia.

This wasn't the kind of kiss that she'd come to expect from Frost. With increasing passion, his lips pressed hard against hers, gliding effortlessly over her cherry flavored lip gloss. At first, Anastasia thought he was crazy, fearing that he'd turn into a werewolf at any second. Then, as he strengthened his grasp on her body, she slowly gave in to her desires, stopping only when she felt the need to catch her breath.

"You didn't shape-shift," Anastasia murmured, overcome with happiness as she placed her head against Frost's chest and listened to his rapid heartbeat. She'd never felt as close to him as she did right now, and that made her smile uncontrollably.

"I guess I needed an incentive to try harder," Frost murmured back, "and I found that in you."

Moved by his words, Anastasia was about to tell Frost how much she loved him when suddenly, the sky brightened with a greenish glow, startling her in the process. "What the..." she began to mutter.

"It's starting," Frost interrupted, urging the somewhat reluctant Anastasia to stand up and look out into the northern night sky. "We'll have the best view in all of Cedar Falls."

Silently, Anastasia and Frost watched as a display of green rays grew large and vibrant, seemingly coming from the Heavens themselves. They appeared like curtains of light swirling in the wind, one second strong and radiant, the next, retreating and reappearing in another part of the sky. The hues pulsated with life as they curved and rippled, casting their glow upon the woods. Utterly mesmerized, Anastasia realized that this was the aurora borealis – a natural wonder she'd often heard about but had never seen, and it was far more beautiful than anyone could have ever described.

We made it, Anastasia thought, her chest swelling with pride as she looked at Frost. *No matter how impossible the odds, how tough the hardships, or how painful the tragedy, we weren't broken or torn apart, and in the end, I finally found my happiness.*

Returning Anastasia's gaze, Frost smiled and pulled her closer. He then carefully lifted her chin upward, their lips about to meet when her cell phone began to ring. Grudgingly, Anastasia answered it, cursing the timing of whoever was on the line.

"I...I need your help," someone said frantically, not giving Anastasia a chance to say hello first. "I thought you were lying – crazy even – then I saw it with my own eyes. My...my dad turned into a monster right in front of me. He fled from our home and straight into the woods. Please, Anastasia, I know he's out there somewhere, and we need to find him before anyone else does."

Anastasia's blood ran cold as she processed what she'd just been told. "Chloe, you need to stay in your house. We'll be there as fast as we can, but in the meantime, don't do anything or tell anyone."

Quickly ending the call, Anastasia dialed her grandfather's number and waited anxiously as it rang. When he eventually answered, she spoke shakily, "Find Mike, Leo and Pete, and see if they're okay."

"What are you talking about, Anastasia?" Mr. Lockhart asked in a confused tone. "We're all at Pete's house watching the hockey game. Everyone's fine, but you don't sound too good. Do you want me to come and get you?"

"No, I have to go," Anastasia replied, hanging up before her grandfather could say anything else.

Slowly, Anastasia turned to Frost, and one look at his shocked expression made it clear that he'd heard everything. "How...how could this have happened?" she stammered. "Why would Mr. Fairbanks transform into a werewolf, while the others remain human?"

"There's one difference between Mr. Fairbanks and the other men," Frost said gravely, his eyes narrowed as if he was experiencing a frightening revelation. "*I* bit him, and because I'm a younger werewolf than my father, my venom must have been too strong and powerful – even for wolfsbane. I don't think Mr. Fairbanks had a chance regardless of what we did."

A loud wolf howl suddenly ripped through the night, causing ravens to caw wildly as they flew away in fear. There was nothing ordinary about that howl, and it could've only belonged to a certain new werewolf. Reaching for Frost's hand and holding on tightly, Anastasia stood tall and ready to fight. However, she couldn't stop herself from gulping nervously as she realized that while all nightmares come to an end, sometimes that end is merely the beginning.

❋ ❋ ❋

About the Author

Heather Beck is a Canadian Author and Screenwriter who began writing professionally at the age of sixteen. Since then she has written eleven well-reviewed books, including the bestselling series, *The Horror Diaries*, which has sold in six continents.

Heather received an Honors Bachelor of Arts degree from university where she specialized in English and studied an array of disciplines. Currently, she is working on the *Frostbitten* series and has two anthologies slated for publication. As a screenwriter, Heather has multiple television shows and movies in development. Her short films include: *Young Eyes*, *The Rarity*, *Too Sensible For Love*, *Circular*, and the forthcoming *Witch's Brew*.

Besides writing, Heather's greatest passion is the outdoors. She is an award-winning fisherwoman and a regular hiker. Her hobbies include swimming, playing badminton and volunteering with non-profit organizations.

http://heatherashbeck.wix.com/writer